Reputation at Risk

A CHRONICLE OF MISADVENTURES

Reputation at Risk

A REGENCY ROMANCE

PARADIGM
PRESS

MARTHA KEYES

For Grandma Janet

1

CHARLOTTE

To live near the most frequented inn outside of London was to be an observer—whether willing or unwilling—of both pomp and prestige. On a day when many of the country's most wealthy and powerful were making their way to Town for the opening of Parliament, the spectacle was something indeed to behold.

Charlotte Mandeville walked side by side with her two sisters and Mama toward the village of Stoneleigh, pink magnolia blossoms fluttering around them in the breeze. The flowers lent their sweet scent to the air, marred only by the dirt kicked up by passing carriages and carts, most of them familiar to Charlotte.

She glanced at the chaise drawing near, and her eyes fixed on it curiously. It had no crest, but it boasted a fine, glossy black body, gilt detailing, and a pair of matched bays. The man within stared ahead, dark brow furrowed, the frown on his face just visible in the shadow of his top hat's brim. He was as handsome as his carriage—and every bit as intimidating.

He turned his head, catching eyes with Charlotte for a moment before the equipage's progress took him out of view.

"Is that Lord Scarsdale?" Charlotte's younger sister Tabitha asked as the four of them passed into the village.

"No," Charlotte answered immediately.

Her mother and both sisters looked at her, all six brows raised in surprise at her firm answer. The three of them were a great deal alike, with hair of varying colors but fair complexions and soft features. If the months since Papa's death had not added so many wrinkles and a sprinkling of gray hair to Mama's golden head, she might have been thought a fourth sister.

Charlotte's fingers tightened on her reticule—a guilty gesture if ever there was one. Thankfully, none of her family seemed to notice. "Did you not see the young man who glanced through the window?" she asked, hoping to cover her overconfident response; the breadth and depth of her knowledge of the *haut-ton* was not something she wished her family to know of. But everyone knew that Lord Scarsdale was an old man, and the surly gentleman she had seen within the carriage could never be described in such a way. On the contrary—he was in his prime. And unhappily so, it seemed.

"His son, perhaps?" Lillian, the eldest and fairest of the three Mandeville daughters suggested.

Certainly not, Charlotte thought, for the earl had only daughters, not to mention the fact that his chaise had a large, scarlet crest on both doors. Rather than betray such knowledge, though, she said, "Perhaps."

"Do you think the post has come?" Mama asked, looking toward the inn with a crease in her brow.

Charlotte and Lillian shared glances. Mama was becoming almost obsessive about the post. All of them were nervous for the time when *the letter* would arrive, but none more than she.

Little wonder, for though its contents would affect them all, they would affect Mama most nearly. She alone was responsible for her three daughters now, and once the estate's heir was located, they would be obliged to leave their beloved Bellevue House. It often felt as though they were living on borrowed time there now.

"I have a letter to post," Charlotte said. "I shall go find out if anything has been received for us."

"You shan't discover anything at all if those people have aught to say on the matter," Tabitha said, nodding toward the inn.

Apart from the ostlers and carriages in the bustling inn yard, a host of people stood before the windows, blocking the entrance as they vied for their turn to look at whatever was holding everyone's interest in the glass panes.

"There must be a new caricature," Tabitha said, going on her tiptoes as though, from such a distance and with such a small frame, that would be sufficient to enable her to see.

Charlotte tried to strike an expression of mild interest, while her hand clutched the strings of her reticule more tightly. She hated deceiving her family, but she hated the alternative even more. She would not see them reduced to penury while she had the ability to ensure otherwise, whatever the risk to her reputation. Papa had always encouraged them to be enterprising, had he not?

"Do you think it is Rowlandson doing the caricatures?" Tabitha asked.

Charlotte hid a smile, unable to be anything but flattered at being compared to one of the country's finest caricature artists.

"No," Lillian said definitively. "They say the art is original, not produced *en masse*, as Rowlandson's is."

"Then why send them to Stoneleigh, of all places?" Mama asked. "Would they not be better suited to London?"

Charlotte's jaw ached from clenching her teeth, and she forced herself to relax. She should be accustomed to these discussions by now. It was different, though, to hear her own family speculate on the identity of the artist while remaining silent.

"If the rumors are true," Lillian said as they stopped on the corner across from the inn, "it may be someone local."

Tabitha turned to stare at her. "Surely, we would know if that were the case."

"Whoever it is," Lillian said in her reasonable voice, "he is bound to bring himself trouble. It seems spectacularly unwise to cross such an array of powerful people."

Charlotte's heart fluttered nervously. Why did it feel as though everyone's eyes were upon her when they were not? She could not defend the art without the risk of betraying her secret, though, so she chose the alternative. "I, for one, cannot understand what the fuss is. They aren't particularly skillful drawings, are they?"

"Not particularly, no," Lillian agreed, making Charlotte's brows draw together in offense.

"*I* quite admire them," Tabitha said. "They are witty and diverting. Did you see the one about Prinny last week?"

Charlotte turned her head to hide the smile of satisfaction that stole across her lips. She was not immune to praise, after all. "I think I shall try my luck with the crowd. You go on ahead without me. I need no ribbons."

Mama nodded, and Charlotte parted ways with her family, crossing the street after a cart while the others made their way toward the haberdasher. She was obliged to excuse herself multiple times as she gently shouldered her way to the door of the inn, keeping her gaze away from the caricature. It was not as though its contents were a mystery to her. The mystery, rather, was why it was drawing such attention.

This particular piece had been a grasp at straws, for there had been no substantial gossip garnered all week. Charlotte had been obliged to settle for a drawing of Sir Charles Perrington in his conservatory, hands covered in dirt, exotic vegetables popping out of the ground like fireworks while he smiled maniacally.

She had nearly groaned when she had handed the drawing to Mr. Digby, the innkeeper, and the pinching of his lips told her he knew it was unlikely to cause the type of stir he sought.

Apparently, they had both been wrong. Plenty of people were finding it interesting enough to stare at for a great while. What would they do if they knew Charlotte held in her reticule the caricature that would appear in the window in a week's time?

It was the irony of Charlotte's secret that it not only attracted more and more of the people she so disliked, but it also made her reliant upon everything she most despised about their world—corruption, greed, and invincibility. Without it, she had no material, and without material, she had no money to save against her family's uncertain future.

Charlotte pulled open the inn door, and the buzz of conversation within joined that of the people without until she tugged the wooden door closed.

A maid named Mary appeared, holding a tray with three tankards and a plate of bread and butter. A few loose blonde hairs escaped from her cap, complementing the harried look on her face. She glanced at Charlotte, then back again.

Charlotte held up her reticule, and Mary nodded, putting up a finger to signify she would return shortly. Charlotte nodded and took a seat at the nearest empty table in the corner, setting her reticule beside her. She might be the artist behind the caricatures, but without Mary listening for gossip at The Crown and Castle, she would have very little material at all.

Charlotte gazed around the room, identifying a few familiar faces. Familiar, that was, to *her*. Lord Marchwood and Mr. Jameson wouldn't know her from Eve.

"Miss Mandeville."

Charlotte knew to whom the voice belonged without having to look the innkeeper in the eye, but she did so despite that out of politeness. With his ruddy complexion and dark though receding hair, Mr. Digby smiled at her.

"I hoped we would see you today," he said. "Have you brought...?"

She nodded, glancing around to ensure no one was listening.

"May I see it?"

After a moment's hesitation, Charlotte opened her reticule and pulled out a folded paper, trying not to betray her nerves as she handed it to him. If he disliked the last drawing, he would loathe this one: Mrs. Gattenby surrounded by a crowd of both dogs and husbands. The woman seemed to collect and lose both things at an alarming rate.

Mr. Digby took it and unfolded it. He seemed far less concerned than she with the chance someone might be watching them, but at least with the way he angled his body, no one could see the paper over his shoulder.

His brow furrowed, and his gaze flicked to Charlotte for a moment before he refolded the artwork. "Hardly thrilling, is it?"

She lifted her chin at the insult to her work. How dared he agree with her? "I rather think today's specimen goes to show

how hungry people are for *ton* gossip, however inconsequential it might seem."

Mr. Digby's gaze rested on her until the hairs on her arms began to tingle. "They will tire of such mundane things quickly, Miss Mandeville. We need more."

Her jaw clenched. What, precisely, did he expect of her? To magic scandal out of thin air? "No doubt there will be more material as the Season gets underway."

His eyes never left hers. "Let us hope so. I am not paying you for news on gardening or pets. I would hate to be obliged to end our arrangement—and equally disappointed if word got out who is behind the drawings."

Charlotte's eyes widened. Was he threatening her?

One of the ostlers' heads appeared around the corner, searching the room until his gaze landed upon Mr. Digby. "Ye're needed outside, sir. Right away."

Mr. Digby handed the paper back to Charlotte. "Give this to Mary. But I expect better next week, Miss Mandeville." He fixed her with one last severe gaze, then he walked away.

Charlotte watched his back until he disappeared around a corner. She drew a long, steady breath through her nose, willing it to calm her heart. Would he truly betray her identity if she didn't manage to produce something more titillating? To be certain, finding material more exciting than Mrs. Gattenby shouldn't be too terribly difficult. But if the people who frequented the inn were not confiding gossip to one another within earshot of Mary, there was little Charlotte could do. Perhaps they were beginning to distrust the inn.

When Charlotte had first struck up an arrangement with Mr. Digby, she would never have believed him capable of betraying her identity. He had been genial and enthusiastic about the prospect of working together: Charlotte would utilize the gossip passed within the walls of the inn to create caricatures that would, in turn, bring *more* business to The Crown and Castle.

But over time, he had become decidedly less amiable and far more demanding.

If he felt she was not bringing him the business he wished for, he might well betray her. Then, not only would the money stop, but Charlotte's reputation and that of her family would be injured past reparation. They needed those reputations intact if they were to make smart matches and take care of Mama.

Charlotte *needed* more gossip.

She fumbled to put the caricature back in the reticule, but the bag slipped to the floorboards beneath the table. She leaned down, ducking her head and reaching for it. Her fingers found purchase on the strings, and she came up, hitting the crown of her head soundly on the table's underside.

Wincing, she rubbed at the spot, her head still beneath the table. It took a few moments for the pain to begin to subside, and she opened her watering eyes slowly, her free hand still cradling the careless injury.

As she moved to withdraw her head—carefully this time— her gaze fixed on the underside of the table, and her brow knit.

Something seemed to be lodged in a gap in the table's wooden under-planks. What *was* it? She reached a hand toward the object, squinting in the little light beneath the table to try to make out what it was. It looked like a small book, but what would a book be doing in such a place?

She grasped the object, her fingers brushing the pages briefly. It *was* a book. She gave a tug, and it slid out more easily than anticipated.

"Miss Mandeville?"

Charlotte's head came up with a snap, hitting the precise spot on her crown as before. Grasping it, she emerged from beneath the table to face Mary, who sucked in a breath through clenched teeth at the sight of Charlotte holding her now-throbbing head.

"Oh dear," Mary said. "I'm ever so sorry, miss!"

"It is nothing," Charlotte lied through clenched teeth. "Is there any post?"

"No, miss," the maid said. "And I only have a moment. We are terribly busy today, and Mr. Digby says Mr. Anthony Yorke has just arrived and must be attended to without delay." She shivered.

"Anthony Yorke?" Charlotte had heard the name a number of times but never yet seen the man. The Yorke family had powerful connections—ducal ones, if she remembered correctly—so his presence immediately made her tingle with anticipation. Perhaps his presence would provide her with the sort of material Mr. Digby demanded. She had some small fear that, if she did *not* manage to produce something significant next week, he would withhold the money he owed her, for she was paid every other week. "Does Mr. Yorke intend to take refreshment?"

Mary nodded, glancing over her shoulder toward the door as though she feared he might be standing there already, waiting for her to serve him.

"Excellent," Charlotte said. "Let us hope a few tankards of ale will loosen his tongue. And if they do . . ."

Mary nodded her understanding. "I shall serve him diligently and keep my ears open. Even though he frightens the daylights out of me." She shuddered again.

"Why?" Charlotte's curiosity was successfully roused. Where a person elicited such strong reactions, there was undoubtedly fodder for gossip to be found.

"He is so very forbidding." The front door opened, and

Mary whipped around. "He is here," she hissed as though the devil himself had arrived. "If you wait for me—"

"No." Charlotte shook her head. If she lingered too long, it would elicit questions from her family. "I must go. We will speak later."

"What of the . . .?" Her gaze darted to Charlotte's reticule as she took backward steps toward the door.

Charlotte hesitated. She couldn't give the caricature to Mary when the maid was going directly to Mr. Yorke. It was far too dangerous. Her gaze lighted upon the book in her hand, and an idea struck her. "There is a little nook beneath this table. I shall leave it there."

Mary nodded swiftly and went to attend to Mr. Yorke.

With a quick glance to ensure no one was watching, Charlotte slipped the book inside her reticule and pulled the folded caricature out. As inconspicuously as possible, she slid the caricature under the table, feeling around for the small space where she had found the book. She kept her hand there until she was satisfied the paper would not fall. Heaven only knew how long the book had been there. Or *why* someone had thought to put it in that particular spot. But Charlotte intended to find out. She was simply that desperate for any tidbit she might use for the next caricature.

Slipping the strings of her now-heavy reticule over her wrist, she slid out from the table and hurried toward the front door, colliding with something solid as she turned the corner.

Two firm hands grasped her above the elbows, and Charlotte stepped back, blinking. "Pardon m—"

The last of the word hung on her lips as she looked into two dark brown eyes under heavy, furrowed brows and dark hair, brushed away from his face—the same one she had caught a glimpse of in the chaise just a quarter of an hour ago.

His gaze fixed upon her, hard as steel, sapping the breath from her lungs with its intensity.

Her eyes darted to Mary just beside the man, then back to the foreboding face looking down at her.

This must be Anthony Yorke.

2

ANTHONY

Wide, brown eyes stared up at Anthony with a mixture of curiosity and wariness. These were the same eyes he had caught for the briefest of moments on his way into the village. The young woman's brows were now arched, her soft, pink lips parted in surprise.

Upon entering the inn, he had noticed her fiddling with something beneath the table. What *had* she been doing with her hands under the table? Anthony's jaw tightened at the unwelcome possibility that presented itself to him, and his gaze flitted to the reticule hanging over her wrist. A sagging, heavy reticule.

His gaze darted back to her, and the wary look in her eyes gave way to something more mulish.

"If you please, sir," she said roughly, tugging her arms back and bringing to his awareness just how tightly he was holding them.

He released her, and his gaze slipped back to the reticule. Of course, it was possible it was nothing but a fan and a mirror weighing it down. A particularly heavy mirror. He could hardly ask her what it contained, though.

"Excuse me," he said brusquely, pushing past her and to the table. The maid bid the young woman a hasty goodbye and followed him.

"I have a table near the window, sir," she said. "The bench is more comfortable, and there is more—"

"I want this one," he said, taking a seat. When the maid lingered, he looked up at her. "Refreshment, if you please."

She nodded, then, after a brief hesitation, disappeared.

When he was satisfied no one was watching, he slid his hands under the table, feeling for the spot where Harris had told him he would conceal the diary. His fingers made contact with something, and he breathed out his relief.

It was short-lived.

He pulled what was decidedly a paper rather than a diary toward him and onto his lap, his chest tightening with misgiving.

He unfolded the paper and found himself looking at a painting. No, a drawing.

It was both, really. It reminded him of the caricatures that often appeared in the windows of London print shops, but this one was a bit less refined and more vibrant in color. It portrayed a woman surrounded by dogs and men. Mrs. Gattenby, if he was not mistaken.

He lowered his head until he could see under the table, then reached a hand toward the place he had expected to see the diary. But both his eyes and his hands told him precisely what he had been afraid of: there was nothing more there.

He swore under his breath and hurried up from his seat, going over to the window. His eyes searched for the young woman who had been here just before him. What had she been doing with her hands under the table? And what had been in that overly burdened reticule?

It was no use, though. The window was crowded with people staring at the sole piece of paper hanging from it—one very similar to the one Anthony held in his hand.

He slammed a fist against the wall in frustration, and a few people nearby startled. He stalked back toward the table, stopping the maid with his hand on her arm as she appeared in the large doorway with his refreshment on a tray.

"Who was the young woman sitting at that table before me?" he asked.

The maid hesitated, her gaze shifting to the paper in his hand. She swallowed and said nothing.

Anthony's grip tightened as a sort of panic began to take hold. Without that diary, how could he save his brother? Fate couldn't serve him such a trick—it wouldn't, surely.

"Her name," he said. "What is her name?"

"Is there a problem, Mr. Yorke?" Mr. Digby came up behind the maid, his mouth arranged in a smile and his tone attempting a lightness belied by the intent curiosity in his gaze.

Anthony's jaw clenched. He despised Digby, and he would never have chosen to come to The Crown and Castle of his own volition. It had once been his custom to break his journey here when he came to London, but the inn had recently garnered a reputation for attracting Society's biggest gossips. It was Harris who had chosen the inn, though, not Anthony. Confound the man's insistence on doing things in the most inconvenient and secretive way.

Digby's eyes roamed, and Anthony shifted the folded paper out of sight. Why was everyone at this inn so blasted inquisitive? "I wish to know the name of the young woman sitting at that table when I arrived."

"Ah, that would be Miss Mandeville, sir," Digby replied, happy to be of help.

Mandeville. Anthony committed the name to memory.

"A frequent guest of yours?" Anthony needed more than just a name if he was to follow the path of his suspicions. If she had merely been passing through, he needed to know her destination.

Digby chuckled. "Not quite, sir. Her family lives just down the lane"—he gestured with a thrust of his chin, making the skin beneath it jiggle like a turkey's neck—"at Bellevue House."

The maid clenched her eyes shut and turned her head away. Why the chagrin? What did it matter to her if Anthony knew the young lady's name or where she lived?

The whole thing smelled highly suspicious. What he wished to do was to stalk straight to the Mandeville house, but it would be terribly awkward if his suspicions were incorrect.

Perhaps Harris—the man Anthony had hired to help him clear his brother Silas's name—had misinformed him of where to look, or even run out of time to place the diary where he had said he would. Or perhaps Harris had put the caricature there instead of the diary by mistake. Anthony would have no trouble believing something of the strange man.

He would need to verify things with Harris before taking any action against Miss Mandeville.

"Thank you, Digby," Anthony said, walking around both the innkeeper and the maid.

"Will you not stay, sir?" Digby asked, scurrying after him.

"Not today," Anthony said. Or ever, if he could help it. The last thing he needed was to catch the attention of those fueling the talk of the *ton*.

His errand required the utmost secrecy—his brother's future depended upon it. And that diary was the key to it all.

Anthony brushed a petal from the shoulder of his tailcoat and glanced up at the magnolia tree currently offering him shade. The grass below was littered with its pink petals, and this was the third that had fallen on his person.

He pulled out his pocket watch and gritted his teeth at the sight of the time. He had intentionally set the meeting for the hour *before* Hyde Park was inundated with every member of the *ton*, all wishing to be seen now that London was filling with the *beau-monde*.

A rustling brought him whirling around in time to see Harris's head emerging from the bushes.

"What the devil?" Anthony said as Harris motioned for him to approach.

The man wore a serviceable if somewhat threadbare brown coat and an equally well-used gray top hat. His gaze shifted warily around the surrounding area.

"For heaven's sake," Anthony said. "Come out of those plants, Harris."

He shook his head, still eyeing the environs with mistrust. "Don't like meeting in public. Told you that. Too many roving eyes."

"And no wonder if you insist on acting like a dashed loose screw." Anthony took hold of the man's arm and pulled him from the bushes. He relied on Harris, but heaven help him, the man had a head full of as much conspiracy as common sense. "Where is it?"

"Where is what?"

"The diary, man," Anthony said impatiently. "It was not at The Crown and Castle."

Harris drew back, affronted. "It was. I saw it with my own

eyes. Put it there with my own hands—under the round table in the corner. Perhaps you went to the wrong one."

Anthony's jaw clenched. "I assure you, I did nothing so dunderheaded." He pulled something from the inner pocket of his coat. "Perhaps *you* put the wrong thing there, as this was the only thing under that table."

Harris frowned and took the paper, unfolding it. He tilted his head as he surveyed the drawing until his eyes lit with recognition. His wide gaze shifted to Anthony's. "How'd you get your hands on this?"

Anthony pulled it out of his grasp, his patience wearing thin. "I just told you that. It was under the table."

Harris's gaze fixed on the paper again. "That's one of those caricatures, that is."

"Your powers of deduction are astounding."

Harris's fingers reached slowly for the paper, his eyes suddenly hungry. "Could I have it, sir?"

Anthony shifted the paper out of reach. "You may not. I need it to track down that blasted diary. If you had simply handed it over in person as I asked you to do, we wouldn't be in this predicament. Instead, you insisted on a ridiculous and unnecessary game of hide and seek, all while my brother is forced to bide his time in France for a murder he did not commit."

Harris's lips turned down at the sides. "I've used that hiding place a dozen times, sir. No one knows it but me."

"You and the eleven other people you've left things for, I surmise, not to mention the person who left the caricature," Anthony said dryly. "You could hardly have chosen a more well-frequented inn."

"Sometimes the best hiding place"—he tapped his temple and smiled—"is right under people's noses."

"Evidently not in this case," Anthony said. But there was

little use dwelling on the mistake. The only thing it accomplished was to waste precious time. It had been nearly five months since the fateful night Silas had been obliged to flee England, and the diary was the nearest Anthony had come to finding a way to exonerate his brother of blame—something that would not have been necessary if only Anthony had accompanied Silas to the meeting as he had promised to do.

"Do you know who is responsible for these caricatures?" Anthony asked.

If anyone knew, Harris would. He made it his business to snivel out every bit of useful—and useless—information that might put a shilling in his pocket.

Harris shook his head. "No one does."

"*Someone* does," Anthony muttered as he looked at the drawing again. The face of the young woman at the inn flashed across his mind again. He couldn't help but believe she was the key to this particular question, though what a young woman like that had to do with the diary or the caricature, he had no idea, for she was obviously well-bred.

Whether Miss Mandeville had taken the diary for herself or handed it off to someone, she was the one Anthony needed to speak with. "Do you know the Mandevilles, Harris?"

"Mandevilles . . ." Harris's eyes narrowed. "Stoneleigh folk?"

"Yes. Bellevue House."

He nodded. "Family of daughters—pretty ones too. None too plump in the pocket, though."

"Oh?" Anthony said with interest. If that was the case, Miss Mandeville's tongue might be loosened with a bit of money. And a bit was all Anthony currently had, for he had not only lost his brother Silas that dreadful night—he had lost the money he had invested in Lord Drayton's business. His jaw clenched at the mere thought of Drayton.

Anthony folded the caricature and put it in his pocket
again, ignoring the way Harris's hungry gaze followed his
every move. "Given that it is your fault that I find myself
without the pivotal piece of evidence I require, I must insist
you work to discover more information about the Mandevilles
as well as seeking other possible avenues to exonerate my
brother."

Harris's gaze widened. "But, Mr. Yorke, sir. You haven't yet
paid me for the diary."

"Neither shall I until it is in my hands. What good is it to
me otherwise? Perhaps next time you will listen when I request
you to hand it to me directly."

He was coming to accept that Silas's exoneration would
cost a small fortune. Of course, he couldn't complain. Not
when it was his fault Silas required exonerating in the first
place. He had let Silas and their business partner Langdon go
without him to the meeting with Drayton—and all so Anthony
could pursue a pretty face. It made him sick every time he
thought on it.

"I shall do my best, sir," Mr. Harris said, "but . . ."

"But what?" Anthony asked when the thought remained
unfinished.

"I was only thinking, sir, that Drayton is a powerful man,
and we would stand a better chance against him if we had your
brothers to—"

"No." Silas had begged Anthony not to confront Drayton,
nor to involve anyone else, least of all his family. As one of the
wealthiest peers in the country, Drayton was simply too
powerful and too dangerous a man to confront. He had killed
Langdon in cold blood, then framed Silas for it without a
second thought, knowing well that the public was aware of
Silas and Langdon's disagreements.

Even when Anthony had tried to broach the subject of

Silas's innocence with William and Frederick, it had quickly become clear they believed him guilty. Silas's strained relationship with and suspicions of Langdon, Drayton's assertions of what had happened that night, and Silas's escape to France had been enough to convince them. Anthony's defense of the brother he had always indulged meant little, particularly when he had not been there to witness the night's events.

"As you wish," Harris said, his wide eyes on something behind Anthony. "I shall send word when I have anything."

Before Anthony could follow the direction of his gaze or respond, the man disappeared into the bushes again, leaving Anthony blinking.

"Is that my dear nevvy?" a woman's voice called.

Anthony clenched his eyes shut and swore before turning to face his Aunt Eugenia. She wore a smart riding habit of jonquil hue, with a matching hat set at a jaunty angle on a head of graying hair. She sat alone in an enormous barouche Anthony had never before seen—undoubtedly a new purchase, as he had seen her just a month ago. She was as close to a mother as he or his brothers had possessed, as their mother had died shortly after Frederick's birth, and their father two years ago.

"Aunt Eugenia," he said, walking over. "What a pleasant surprise."

"None of your fiddle-faddle now, Anthony. You never could manage to school your expressions." She leaned forward and patted the seat in front of her. "Come. Sit up beside me as though you *were* pleased to see me."

Anthony obeyed, motioning the coachman away from helping him in. Normally, he wouldn't mind seeing his aunt. He simply couldn't find it in himself to be glad she had seen him when he was in company with Harris.

"Who was that you were talking to?" Aunt Eugenia asked

as she placed an extra fur rug over Anthony's legs as if it were December rather than April, and he a quivering invalid. "He looked to be a seedy sort of fellow. Not in a scrape, are you?"

"No, Aunt."

The carriage lurched forward as the horses began their forced stroll around the park. Meanwhile, the woman's gaze surveyed him intently. "Good. We've had enough scandal in this family."

Anthony forced his muscles to unclench, just as he had to do anytime someone referenced Silas's plight. One of these days, he would inevitably snap when someone spoke of him as ignorantly as they all did. They all thought him a bad apple, and it grated Anthony to no end that it had to remain that way for the time being.

If only he could get his hands on that diary, then the end of his silence—and Silas's unmerited ignominy—would be within sight. He would be able to *prove* what no one seemed willing to believe. Heaven knew Silas's suffering had lasted long enough. The few letters Anthony had received from France had contained an air of forced nonchalance and resignation. But the last one had nearly broken Anthony.

"*Do you think it is safe for me to return to England? Not home, of course, but perhaps somewhere up north. Scotland, even.*"

Aunt Eugenia cleared her throat, and Anthony's gaze flew to hers.

One of her brows was cocked. "What a very dark brow you have. It did not use to be so. Unhappy thoughts?"

Anthony relaxed his expression. "I have a tendency to look forbidding without wishing to do so."

Her gaze rested on him searchingly. "Better than a face hiding unsavory thoughts behind simpering smiles. I like you, Anthony. But I wish you would settle down."

"I assure you, Aunt, I am very much settled."

"Enough of your impudence, boy. You know what I mean. Find a wife, for heaven's sake. Or does every last one of my nephews intend to die a bachelor?"

"I think it unlikely in the extreme." Though, for Anthony's part, he couldn't imagine marrying. Women had only ever brought him trouble. Not just to him, either. Silas's hopeless situation was a direct result of the problems women had brought Anthony.

"Well," Aunt Eugenia said, rearranging her skirts more prettily upon her carriage bench, "I surely hope not. I refuse to settle my fortune on any of my nephews if *they* refuse to show the smallest bit of initiative."

"On the contrary, there is a great deal of initiative amongst us. William is shaping up to be the most unimpeachable and boring eldest son in all of England. Frederick's political aspirations grow stronger by the day and are on track to rival Napoleon's by Michaelmas."

Silas, too, had plenty of ambition before he was forced to flee England—investments in various businesses that would have stood him in good stead if everything hadn't gone to shambles so abruptly. But Anthony knew better than to bring up Silas in front of Aunt Eugenia.

She waved an impatient hand. "As eldest, William needs no fortune. As for you and Frederick"—she leaned forward slightly, pegging him with her gaze—"between the two of us, I would rather settle my fortune on *you*." She sat back, cocking a brow. "*But* if you are carrying on with peculiar figures like that man back there and refuse to give any woman the time of day ..."

Anthony frowned. "Are you trying to bribe me to marry, Aunt Eugenia?"

"Of course I am. I want no more scandal in this family,

Anthony." Her brows drew together suspiciously. "What are you smiling about?"

"Nothing."

Her lips pinched together. "Out with it, boy."

Anthony chuckled softly. "It is just that you yourself are not exactly the pattern card of propriety you seem to wish me to be."

Her mouth twitched at the side, but she controlled it. "My reputation was spotless."

"*Was* being the operative word."

She jabbed a finger at him. "I served my time, young man. I kept my reputation unblemished, made a good match, and now I benefit from the freedom it has afforded me. You do the same, and there may be a pretty fortune in it for you."

Anthony clasped his hands in his lap and met her intent gaze. "Forgive my frankness, Aunt, but you are not precisely at death's door."

She threw her head back and let out a cackle of laughter. "Not an imminent enough reward for you, is it?"

Contrary to what his aunt seemed to think, Anthony had no desire for her to meet an early demise. He liked her a great deal. But the prospect of receiving a fortune in thirty years' time was not a powerful enough one to send Anthony to the altar.

"Fair enough," she said. "What if we liven things up a bit, then, hm? Say, five hundred pounds to the first of you to marry?"

Anthony's smile flickered. Five hundred pounds?

His aunt smiled knowingly, and Anthony composed himself. He had no intention of getting tangled up with any woman while Silas's affairs were in such a state. Besides, he had the devil's own luck choosing women.

It was a shame, for he could certainly use Aunt Eugenia's

money to expedite Silas's return to England. How many fists could be greased, how many tongues loosed with such a sum?

"Do you know the Mandevilles, Aunt?" Anthony asked, his mind returning to his most pressing errand. He couldn't allow himself to be distracted by his aunt's games, however lucrative they might be. He owed his full and complete attention to Silas.

Aunt Eugenia's brow furrowed. "The name is vaguely familiar. Why?"

He shook his head. "No reason."

His aunt gave him another one of her knowing looks, which he promptly chose to ignore. Miss Mandeville was hardly a prospect for marriage.

He banged on the side of the barouche, and the coachman slowed the horses just before the Park gate. "I must take my leave of you here, dear aunt." He reached for her gloved hand and kissed the back of it before stepping down to the dirt path.

"See?" she said as he closed the door. "Very pretty manners when you choose to use them. Plenty of women would faint with a kiss like that to their glove."

"My concern precisely," he said dryly as he nodded at the coachman.

"Remember the arrangement, Anthony," she called out. "And don't forget my party next week!"

He watched the carriage pull away, then took long, quick strides toward the Park's exit. If he hurried, he could make it to Stoneleigh with enough time to pay a visit to Miss Mandeville.

3

CHARLOTTE

"What do you mean it is gone?" Charlotte stared intently at Mary, whose expression was pulled into something very near to despair as they stood on the side of The Crown and Castle. Charlotte had received a quick and poorly written note an hour ago, requesting she come to the inn without delay.

"I mean," Mary said, wringing her hands, "that when I went to retrieve the caricature from beneath the table, there was nothing there."

"Impossible," Charlotte said, but of course that was not true. If Mary said the caricature was gone, it must be gone. She fought the creeping panic bubbling within her. What did it matter who had the caricature? There was no way for them to tie it back to her. It was not as though she signed her name on the paper—though, that was not to say she hadn't been tempted a time or two. Anyone would be, surely.

The biggest annoyance was that she would now have to redraw it—or draw something new. Caricatures were posted on Fridays, and everyone knew that now. They expected it. Most importantly, Mr. Digby expected it.

"That is not all, miss," Mary said, looking more than ever as though she was about to confess to murdering Charlotte's entire family. She swallowed. "I believe I know who has it."

Charlotte stared intently at the maid, eagerly waiting for her to expound. If Mary knew who had it, perhaps one of them could retrieve it and save Charlotte the trouble of drawing something again.

Mary looked at her wretchedly. "Mr. Anthony Yorke."

Charlotte went still. Something about her short interaction with that man had stayed with her, like a sliver under skin.

"After you left, he asked for your name," the maid explained, "but I said nothing, for he had insisted upon sitting at the same table as you, and he had a paper in his hand, so I could only assume what it was. Only, Mr. Digby overheard his question and told him not only your name but where you live, as he hadn't any idea why he was asking. I am terribly sorry, miss."

Charlotte's vision blurred in front of her fluttering lids. If Mr. Yorke had been asking her name and he did indeed have the caricature, did that mean he knew she was the artist? And, if so, what would he do with such information? A dreadful image raced across her mind—that of her family being dragged through the streets of Stoneleigh while people pelted them with rotten vegetables.

She took Mary's hands in hers, brushing aside the ominous feelings engulfing her own chest. "Do not fret, Mary. It is not your fault, of course, and likely nothing to worry about." If only Charlotte could believe her own words.

"But it is Mr. *Yorke*," Mary countered.

Charlotte laughed, but it sounded forced even to her own ear. "So what if it is?"

"He is so . . . haunting. And surely you have heard about his brother."

Charlotte shook her head.

"He killed a man, miss," said Mary. "And Mr. Anthony looks every bit as dangerous—as though he could make anyone bend to his will."

The uneasiness that had been spreading in Charlotte's stomach was overtaken by her flaring pride. "And pray, what should he want with *me*? I have never drawn him, nor any Yorke, for that matter."

Mary chewed her lip, looking a bit less harried. "I do not know. Only, I did not like the look in his eye when he asked your name."

Charlotte glanced at the inn as her skin prickled. "Is he staying here?"

Mary shook her head. "He left almost immediately after asking about you."

"Left where?"

"To London, I believe."

"Ha!" She laughed with relief. "You see? All is well."

Mary looked unconvinced. "What will you do? Mr. Digby thinks I have the caricature."

"I shall forget about that dreadful, meddling Mr. Yorke and create a new drawing, of course." Charlotte spoke with nonchalance, but she walked home accompanied with a chest full of unease.

Charlotte's cheek rested on her hand, her elbow supported by her writing desk, which her pencil tapped an impatient beat upon. Her eyes, glazed over for the past few minutes, were fixed upon the view from her upstairs sash window, which stood ajar a few inches, offering a small breeze and a lovely view. A babbling brook passed by the north side of the home, while the ivy crept around the edge of the window panes, and the sea of green leaves in the distance showed trees finally in bloom.

Despite the beauty of the view, however, it could not inspire Charlotte with what she needed. She needed whispers and scandal. What in the world was she to draw? Her mind was a blank. What good was everything she had come to know of the *ton* if it deserted her when she was most in need?

She *could* redraw Mrs. Gattenby and her dogs, of course, but after the interaction with Mr. Digby and his veiled threats, she was determined to find something better.

Her gaze shifted to the drawer of the desk.

She stared at it for a moment, then set down her pencil and pulled it open.

The small, leather book she had found at the inn was the sole occupant of the rickety drawer. She had yet to do anything but glance inside it, for her conscience pricked her whenever she considered doing more. This, she had realized upon seeing the neat script within, was no regular book. It was a diary or record book of some sort—belonging to a Mr. Marlowe, based on the inscription—and it felt wrong to nose about in such a thing, even if her curiosity was piqued.

How, for instance, had it come to be in such an unlikely place? And who had put it there? Mr. Marlowe himself?

Charlotte barely noticed a knock downstairs on the front door as she picked up the diary and ran her finger along the spine. It likely contained nothing but bland notations on the weather or some such thing—nothing that could be useful to her in her predicament.

She set it in the drawer and slammed it shut. She hadn't

time for idle speculation. She needed to produce a drawing by tomorrow for Mr. Digby, and she had no inspiration at all.

"Is Miss Mandeville at home?"

Charlotte's head snapped up. The voice was male, young, and the manner of speaking refined. What man of such a description would be asking to see Lillian?

Not that there was any reason a gentleman *shouldn't* be asking to see Lillian. It was only that, despite Mama's best efforts to help them find eligible suitors, neither Charlotte nor her sisters had any prospects at all.

Overcome with curiosity, Charlotte rose to her feet and rounded the desk just as the Mandevilles' maid asked, "May I inquire the nature of your business with her, sir?"

Charlotte peered through the window, and her heartbeat came to a thudding halt at the sight of Mr. Anthony Yorke standing below.

"I believe she left something at The Crown and Castle the other day," he said. "I wish to return it to her personally."

Charlotte's eyes widened as he pulled from his coat pocket her folded caricature.

Without another thought, Charlotte raced from her bedchamber and down the stairs just as Lillian emerged from the sitting room, her expression one of confused curiosity as she beheld the stranger asking for her at the door.

Mr. Yorke's bafflement at seeing Lillian, on the other hand, would have been comical to Charlotte if it hadn't been for the piece of paper he held.

Charlotte brushed past her sister, grasping Mr. Yorke's hand in hers so that the caricature crumpled in his fingers. "Mr. Yorke," she said with as much joyful surprise as she could muster. "How good of you to come."

Lillian's confused gaze tripped between Charlotte and Mr. Yorke, then to their hands, clasped strangely in the air.

Charlotte daren't let go, though, so she chose the only alternative which occurred to her: she forced their joined hands toward Mr. Yorke's face, presenting him with the back of her hand.

His piercing gaze went to hers for an agonizing moment before he pressed a quick, dispassionate kiss to her ungloved skin.

The place his lips touched tingled at the warmth, and Lillian's eyes widened.

"Mr. Yorke is a friend," Charlotte explained quickly, praying to heaven he would go along with her act. "Mr. Yorke, this is my older sister, Miss Lillian Mandeville. Lillian, this is Mr. Anthony Yorke."

Lillian curtsied, and Mr. Yorke offered a stiff bow.

"Shall we take a little stroll?" Charlotte asked him. She needed to prevent further conversation between Lillian and him. "It is such a fine day."

There was a sustained, uncomfortable moment of silence while Mr. Yorke's gaze held Charlotte's. He was about to disavow her. She could see it in those dark, calculating eyes.

Her fingers tightened instinctively around his, an unconscious plea.

Inconspicuously but firmly, Mr. Yorke began to pry Charlotte's fingers from their grasp on his hand.

Mouth set in a smile full of clenched teeth, Charlotte resisted, her nails digging into his skin. But it was no use. He was too strong, and all-out resistance on her part would only make Lillian wonder all the more.

This was it. Charlotte's secret would be a secret no longer. Mama, Lillian, and Tabitha would all be scandalized by the truth: Charlotte had been peddling art targeting England's most powerful names, and she was doing it for filthy lucre.

By next week, news of her shocking conduct would be all

over Stoneleigh—no, London. England, even. Her family's reputation would be irreparably ruined, and once the dreaded letter arrived stating that the heir of Bellevue had finally been located, they would be cast out of their home, obliged to make their way in the cruel world as best they could.

Resignation making her stomach tight, Charlotte allowed her fingers to be removed from Mr. Yorke's hand.

But he moved them to wrap around the nook of his arm, then tucked the caricature into his coat. "A stroll sounds agreeable." He gave a nod to a thoroughly bewildered Lillian, then guided an equally bewildered Charlotte away from the house.

She looked up at the man beside her. How did one manage to be so simultaneously handsome and formidable? She couldn't at all decipher what he was about, coming to Bellevue in such a way, but she sensed—and she believed Mary would agree—that it was unlikely to be motivated by charitable reasons.

Well, whatever he expected from this visit, Charlotte had no intention of making it easy for him.

"*Not* Miss Mandeville, then," Mr. Yorke said, glancing at her.

"One of the Misses Mandeville, but no, not *the* Miss Mandeville. Lillian is the eldest."

"A misunderstanding on my part which, I gather, almost cost you dearly."

She kept her gaze straight ahead. "I haven't any notion what you mean."

Even in her peripheral vision, she could see one of his thick brows cock. "You make a practice, then, of forcing your hand into men's, obliterating whatever object they are unfortunate enough to be holding at the time, and then compelling them to kiss your hand?"

Charlotte stopped and pulled her hand from his arm, her nostrils flared and her cheeks stained red.

Mr. Yorke turned slowly, regarding her through those penetrating eyes. They reminded her of the nearby pond on a particularly gray day. She hated particularly gray days.

"Have I misunderstood?" he asked, though his amusement made clear it was a merely rhetorical question. "Do you, in fact, have no notion why I have come? I confess I find it difficult to believe given the marks you so generously engraved into my hand with your nails."

His words acted like flint on the steel of Charlotte's pride. "You must make allowances, sir. I was acting out of a desire to protect my sister."

His dark brows drew together. "Protect her?"

"Your reputation precedes you, Mr. Yorke."

There. She had caught him off his guard with that, at least. In point of fact, she had only a vague awareness of what his reputation included, but her imagination was lively enough to supply a number of ideas for a man so attractive and, as Mary had suggested, so ruthless.

"Well," he said, the surprise masked as quickly as it had appeared, "I admire your pluck. It is not every young woman who, fearing a man's evil designs upon her elder sister, would so quickly and tenaciously offer herself in her place."

Charlotte stiffened. When he put it *that* way, it certainly made her seem loose in the shaft—or simply loose.

Who did he think he was, appearing at her home without any prior acquaintance and nearly ruining her chances at saving her family's future?

But she knew the answer: he was just like all of his ilk. The wealthy, well-connected, and influential did as they pleased, and they did it without regard for anyone they deemed below them. It mattered not that Charlotte was a gentleman's daughter. The Mandevilles lacked the pedigree and money that would make them acceptable to the *ton*'s most powerful.

"What do you want, Mr. Yorke?" she asked stonily.

"Only our mutual benefit," he replied with a hint of a smile and a glint in his eye.

Charlotte's lips parted, her gaze becoming intent. *Mutual benefit.* Did he mean what she thought he meant? Could he possibly be suggesting . . .?

He pulled the caricature from inside his coat and held it up. "I assume that, when he gave this to you, the artist did not intend for you to convey it to me."

Charlotte's brows drew together. *He? The artist?*

She stared at Mr. Yorke. Evidently, he did not know she was the artist. Why would he make such an assumption? Did he think a woman incapable of intelligent and stimulating art? Of course, this was hardly the epitome of her best work, but still; it was the principle of the thing.

Her pride in her work warred with the good sense telling her to be grateful for his ignorance rather than trying to correct it.

"No," she said slowly, resignedly allowing sense to overcome pride. "He did not. But neither *did* I convey it to you."

"Not purposely, perhaps. But I am in possession of it despite that. And you have something I want. Nay, need."

Relief that her secret was at least partially intact was instantly supplanted by the reminder that this viciously handsome man meant to hold the caricature over her head—and, from what she could tell, he meant to do so for purposes that made her feel faint and wonder if she had perhaps allowed their stroll to take them too far from the safety of Bellevue. Surely, he wouldn't kiss her or ravish her here and now, in such proximity to her own house, though.

What, then, would he propose?

A little shiver ran through her. Would her choice be between surrendering to his baser instincts or having her secret revealed? Either way, her reputation would be forfeit.

Well, she would rather the latter than the former. There was at least *some* dignity in putting her name to her work. There was none at all in submitting to Mr. Yorke's nefarious designs upon her person.

"Mr. Yorke," Charlotte said icily, "you may hold my reputation cheap, but I assure you I do not."

His brows snapped together. "Your reputation?" His eyes searched hers. "What the devil do you think I mean?"

Charlotte's righteous anger flagged at his confusion. "I thought . . ." The speculation hung lame and unfinished. She couldn't possibly voice that she had assumed he wished to enter into some sort of . . . *intimate arrangement* with her in exchange for the caricature's return.

This was what came of living her life with all the scandal of the *ton* floating around in her head all day.

"Miss Mandeville," Mr. Yorke said firmly, "allow me to be clear. I believe you have a diary in your possession. A diary that belongs to me. I am here to return this caricature in exchange for it."

"Diary," Charlotte repeated in a soft and bewildered voice. The diary in her drawer belonged to *him*?

No. That couldn't be. It said quite plainly that it belonged to Mr. Marlowe.

Mr. Yorke watched her intently. Very intently, in fact. This diary which decidedly did *not* belong to him must be important. Important enough that he had come to the home of a stranger for it. What could he possibly want with another man's personal record?

Charlotte's curiosity was immediately piqued. "It is not your diary."

A muscle in his clenched jaw jumped. "Neither is it yours."

Well, she couldn't argue with that.

"Miss Mandeville," he said, "allow me to impress upon you the gravity of your situation. This caricature"—he patted his chest—"was given into your care by the artist—someone who clearly wishes to keep his identity a secret. Through your actions, it has come into *my* hands. Something tells me he will not be thrilled with this carelessness on your part."

Charlotte met his gaze, unflinching. The diary became increasingly of interest to her with every word Mr. Yorke said.

"If you refuse to give me the diary," he continued, "I will have no choice but to discover the identity of the artist—which, I assure you, I shall—and to make both his identity and your involvement known. Given the number of powerful people targeted by the caricatures, I cannot think that would end happily for either of you."

She let out a breathy scoff through her nose. The arrogance, the assumptions, the thinly veiled threats the man was making were astounding. This was what Mary had guessed at: Mr. Yorke was accustomed to having his way. He and the rest of his kind.

Well, he would not have his way today.

"It would be remiss of me to place the diary in the hands of anyone but the owner, Mr. Yorke."

"You may find that difficult. The owner is dead."

Charlotte's eyes widened as the sense of power shifted away from her. Dead? "How? When?" Her mind was already exploring the possibility that Mr. Yorke was the one responsible—a murderer, just like his brother. Confound Mary for putting such dramatic ideas into her mind! He might be intimidating, but she did not truly believe he was as evil as that.

"I will not only give you the caricature," he said, ignoring her question, "but thirty pounds besides."

Charlotte blinked. Thirty pounds? That was a tidy sum. How she would love to add it to the little box under the floorboards where she was saving what she earned from Mr. Digby.

She shook herself. The offer was unabashed bribery. Mr. Yorke must have a very poor opinion of her character to even suggest such a thing.

That he was willing to pay so much to take the diary from her possession convinced her even more firmly that it contained something important—perhaps many somethings. Enough somethings to sustain her caricatures for the foreseeable future, even, if fortune was on her side.

"I have no interest in bribes, Mr. Yorke," Charlotte said.

He held her gaze for a moment, his own becoming hard and inflexible. "You disappoint me greatly."

"Behold my dismay," Charlotte quipped.

He tucked the caricature back into his coat, eliciting a flutter of nerves from Charlotte. What if Digby betrayed her to him?

"I fear you will regret this decision," Mr. Yorke said.

Charlotte feared the same thing, but she wouldn't allow it to show. "I imagine it is *you* who will regret it."

He looked at her with patent dislike.

"Thank you for the pleasant stroll, Mr. Yorke." Charlotte gave a little nod, then turned and walked back to the house, refusing to indulge the burning curiosity which urged her to look over her shoulder.

When she closed the door behind her, she pressed her back against it and let out a long, slow breath through rounded lips.

"Charlotte." Lillian shut her book and set it on the sofa before hurrying over. "What in heaven's name was that about?"

Charlotte forced a smile, though her heart beat rapidly. "Nothing of note."

Lillian searched Charlotte's face, her own frowning. "You said he was your friend, but I have never seen the man."

"I bumped into him at the inn, Lily. That is all." She left the door and walked toward the stairs.

"He said you left something there?"

"He was mistaken. Now, if you will excuse me . . ." Charlotte needed to take a closer look at that diary.

Before Lillian could stop her, Charlotte took the stairs to her room, shut the door, and latched it. She glanced down at her hands, which were trembling slightly. The encounter with Mr. Yorke had unsettled her, curse him.

With determined strides, she went to her desk and opened the drawer, taking out the small book. She sat down slowly, her eyes on the leather cover while her mind fluttered about.

Given the interest Mr. Yorke had shown, Charlotte doubted he would simply give up. If he was willing to bribe her for this diary, one could only assume his intentions with it were not benevolent. The members of the *ton* could be cold-blooded and callous when it suited their purposes. The Mandevilles knew that better than most.

It was part of why Charlotte's heart still hadn't slowed. She had made an enemy today—there was no mistaking that. No doubt it had been foolish of her. But nothing was apt to make her blood boil like the entitlement of the *ton*. It was that same entitlement which had led to the loss of Papa's hard-earned money and his subsequent death. It was the motive behind her caricatures—a way to bring to light the things the rich and powerful would rather keep in the dark.

She opened the diary and turned to the first page. It was an entry from just over a year ago. Her gaze flew over a few lines, then she flipped the pages to read more. Her gaze grew more intent and her perusal less rapid the more she read.

She lowered the book to her lap after a few minutes and

stared ahead at nothing, her heart beating a quick rhythm against her chest.

This was no ordinary diary.

This was a man's daily account of his knowledge of the *ton*'s dealings. Politics, gossip, dinners, balls, meetings with prominent figures.

This diary was, in fact, a treasure trove.

4

ANTHONY

Anthony had watched Miss Mandeville walk back toward her house with misgiving. She had not been the biddable, money-hungry young woman he had anticipated. In fact, she had been downright unpleasant. And stubborn.

Perhaps he should have offered her more money, but that was the trouble with the situation in which he found himself: the more he offered, the more he alerted her to the value of the diary. He had seen it in her eyes already—the curiosity he had sparked. But there had been no avoiding that.

Now he ran the danger of her taking the diary to whoever was responsible for the caricatures. Its information regarding Silas's predicament needed to keep guarded until Anthony could use it himself. It would not do for it to be plastered on the window of The Crown and Castle.

He needed that diary, and he needed it soon.

He sighed as he walked to his horse, tied up at the side of the Mandevilles' home. It looked as though he would be spending more time at The Crown and Castle after all. If money was not enough to persuade Miss Mandeville to give him the diary, something else would be. Everyone had their weak spot. He just needed to find hers.

He rode back to Stoneleigh in frowning abstraction, pulling the caricature from his pocket just before he entered the village. There was something strange about it all. Why was she involved with the caricature in the first place? Why would someone employ *her*—a genteel if maddeningly stubborn young woman—as his errand girl? If she had not been so genteel, he might have thought her the caricaturist, but she *was* genteel, even if not precisely high society. In fact, if her family had more money, Anthony suspected she would be causing quite a stir in Town. She was an attractive young woman—if one ignored her headstrong, disagreeable temperament.

He snorted softly. As if it was *possible* to ignore those things. She'd had the gall to say she was trying to protect her sister from him.

Light was starting to fade as he handed off his horse to the ostler and made his way inside The Crown and Castle, trying to decide how to best approach finding out more about Miss Mandeville—and who to ask. There was a distinct awkwardness to an unmarried gentleman asking for detailed information about an unmarried young woman. It had the potential to raise eyebrows.

The maid at the inn clearly knew more than she wished to reveal, though. Perhaps *her* tongue could be loosed with an offer of money. Aunt Eugenia's five-hundred pounds was sounding more tempting by the hour.

Mr. Digby looked pleased as punch when he discovered Anthony meant to put up at the inn for at least two nights. Despite Anthony sitting in the taproom all evening, however, the maid he was looking for never came within ten feet of him.

She flitted around the inn like a butterfly, but it was a different servant who brought Anthony the drink he requested. He had no doubt this was intentional, and he retired for the evening annoyed.

In the morning, he lay in the uncomfortable bed for a few minutes after waking, staring up at the ceiling as he tried to come up with a strategy for getting his hands on the information he needed. The maid couldn't avoid him indefinitely.

He dressed for the day and made his way to the stairs, smiling as he caught sight of her sweeping at the bottom. She glanced up at him and froze, then hurried to sweep her way elsewhere.

There it was. Confirmation she knew things she didn't want him to know.

Anthony picked up his pace down the stairs, only to be intercepted by Digby, who emerged with a letter in hand and a smile on his ruddy face. "Mr. Yorke. Good morning. This came for you just an hour ago."

Anthony's gaze flicked to the familiar, rough script on the front. It was from Harris. Of course it was. He was the only one who knew Anthony had come to Stoneleigh.

He took the letter from Digby and glanced at the wafer sealing. One edge was lifted, and Anthony's gaze flicked to the innkeeper. He wouldn't have been surprised to discover the man made a practice of opening and resealing the post he received.

"Thank you," Anthony said, an ironic edge to his voice.

Digby hung about as though he intended to watch him consume the letter's contents. Anthony held his gaze until Digby bethought himself of an unfinished task and made his excuses.

Anthony lifted the wafer and unfurled the letter. It was, as usual, fairly to the point. Harris wasn't one to couch his messages in flowery prose. One paragraph in particular Anthony found of interest.

The M family's fortunes were on the rise until the abrupt loss of Mr. Mandeville nearly a year ago, following a stunning financial blow from an investment gone wrong. All plans—including one for a Season in London—were laid aside, not only due to mourning but to the sudden change in fortunes. The estate is entailed, though the heir has yet to be located. Mrs. Mandeville is desperate to marry her daughters well, for as soon as the heir is found, Bellevue will no longer be theirs.

Anthony felt a glimmer of sympathy for their sudden loss and the way it had transformed their lives. Anthony had lost both parents, but it was the loss of his brother that had upended everything for him. Not that Silas had died, but sometimes it felt that way.

Why, then, had Miss Mandeville been so stubborn about the diary? She didn't seem to be in a position that allowed for such intractability. He had seen the way her eyes had widened at his offer of money. The claim that she would prefer to return the diary to Mr. Marlowe Anthony couldn't bring himself to give credit to. Someone acting as an accomplice in publicizing the *ton*'s secrets could not believably stake her claim on the moral high ground.

Anthony folded up the letter and looked around, but there was no sign of the maid. Thankfully, he had plenty of time on his hands today.

He walked through the taproom to the fireplace and tossed the paper in. Once it was nothing but charred bits and smoke, he took a seat at the table by the window, where the last caricature was still posted. It was Friday, which, according to Digby, was when new caricatures were posted.

As Anthony had the piece he assumed had been intended for that purpose, he was very curious indeed to see what the day brought. Would the artist have created a new one? Would he forgo it entirely?

A tankard in front of him and his tailcoat folded beside him, Anthony bided his time at the table, watching the comings and goings of the people of Stoneleigh through the window as the sun slowly shifted across the sky.

It was just before noon when he caught sight of her. Only the surreptitious glance she cast about allowed him a glimpse of her face, for Miss Mandeville wore a large straw bonnet and kept her head down as she hurried down the street toward The Crown and Castle.

Anthony chuckled softly. The young woman could take a lesson or two in looking less guilty.

He rose from his seat, shrugged into his tailcoat, and set his hat atop his head, making his way toward the entryway of the inn. Miss Mandeville was at the counter, speaking in low tones with Digby.

Miss Mandeville handed Digby a familiarly folded paper, and her gaze darted to Anthony. Her eyes widened slightly in surprise, and her cheeks took on a pink hue.

Whatever smidgeon of sympathy he had felt for her or her family had vanished. Anyone who conspired with Digby deserved no sympathy. Feeling a sense of victory at catching her in a situation in which she did not wish to be caught, Anthony cocked a brow.

To his surprise, Miss Mandeville smiled smugly at him. Clearing her throat, she looked at Digby. "To be posted as soon as possible, of course."

Posted. An interesting choice of word. Did she mean sent by post? Or posted in the window? He could only assume she was being enigmatic on purpose.

"Of course, miss. Right away."

Miss Mandeville nodded, shot another self-satisfied glance at Anthony, then walked to the door and out of the inn.

Anthony followed right behind, ignoring the way Digby watched his every step with interest. Once he had pulled the door closed behind him, he strode after Miss Mandeville, quickening his pace until he was walking abreast with her. "A pleasure to see you again so soon, Miss Mandeville."

She seemed not at all discomposed by his presence. "If only I could say the same."

Anthony couldn't help but smile.

"If you are hoping to speak about the diary," she said, her expression full of pleasant indifference, "you may as well save your breath. I shan't be giving it to you."

"Name your price, Miss Mandeville."

She looked over at him, surveying him for a moment before returning her gaze forward. She certainly kept a clipping pace. "You could not afford my price, Mr. Yorke."

"Try me," he said.

"Ten thousand pounds," she said without hesitation.

Anthony scoffed at the outrageous sum, and Miss Mandeville smiled at him—a pleasant expression on an entirely unpleasant person. "I did warn you, did I not?"

Anthony clenched his jaw. He would have to change his approach if he wanted that diary back. "Miss Mandeville, that diary means nothing to you, but for at least one person, it means the difference between life or death."

Her pace slowed slightly, and she looked at Anthony with intent brown eyes. "Is that one person yourself?"

"No."

"Then I see no reason to give it into *your* hands."

"I beg you will reconsider." Every fiber of Anthony's being fought the use of such plaintive words.

"Oh, I shan't," she said sunnily.

Anthony took hold of her arm, and she faced him, her eyes bright with warning.

"Please, Miss Mandeville," he said softly, his teeth gritting at the humility this required of him.

She held his gaze for a moment, then looked down at his hand on her arm. She wrested it from his grasp, and he let her, for his focus was on a spot on her cheek. A dark gray smudge.

"Goodbye, Mr. Yorke," she said stonily before turning on her heel and leaving him.

Anthony's feet stayed planted, but his eyes followed her, glazed over and unblinking as his mind worked and worked. Only when he was bumped by a young boy carrying a large sack of potatoes did he turn and make his way toward The Crown and Castle, his thoughts still a jumbled mess of questions and speculation.

Surely that smudge on her cheek did not mean what he thought it meant. But then, it would make a great deal more sense, would it not? Her involvement with the caricature, her reaction to his appearance at her home, why she didn't wish to return the diary to him . . .

"Pardon me," he said as his shoulder bumped someone else's. He took in the crowd before him, all staring up at the window of The Crown and Castle and followed the direction of their gazes. His brows rose slowly at the sight of the new caricature.

It depicted a thick-browed man wearing a sneering smile as a pair of high-headed horses pulled him in a carriage. Trampled beneath their hooves and the wheels of the equipage were a half-dozen people, their arms reaching out for help.

Anthony had no trouble at all recognizing himself as the driver of the carriage. Based on the whispers and furtive glances of those around him, neither did anyone else.

That confirmed his suspicions better than anything could have.

Miss Mandeville herself *was* the artist.

"Well-played, Miss Mandeville," he said under his breath. Against his will, a bit of admiration crept up inside him. She certainly had skill. And bravado.

The woman at Anthony's side looked at him, then at the caricature, then at him again.

Anthony held her gaze, raising a brow, and she looked away hurriedly.

He chuckled softly and made his way to the door. There was plenty of reason *not* to laugh, of course. If Miss Mandeville was the caricature artist, the diary she now had would give her ammunition for the foreseeable future. And she would be particularly loath to give it up. Did she realize this?

Perhaps more to the point, what would she think if her secret got out? He doubted she would welcome it. Particularly if her mother was anxious to marry her and her sisters off. A family like theirs, on the fringes of Society, was held to much higher standards than their wealthier and better connected counterparts. Money and influence could cover a multitude of sins.

But Miss Mandeville had neither; she needed her secret to remain a secret, then.

"I have found your weak spot, Miss Mandeville," Anthony murmured.

He was not in the habit of threatening to expose respectable young ladies, but that was hardly a fit description of Miss Charlotte Mandeville. She was using the private business of the *ton* for her own personal gain. There was nothing respectable about it.

At least *his* aims were noble.

He would have to pay her a visit tomorrow and attempt to

. . . make her see the light. Frankly, he had no wish to divulge her secret; he simply wanted the diary. But short of breaking into Bellevue House to take it back, he had few options available to him. The girl was as stubborn as she was beautiful, and his encounters with her had given him plenty of opportunity to admire that beauty—even with that ridiculous pencil smudge on her face.

To his annoyance, it was Miss Charlotte Mandeville's self-satisfied smile that accompanied Anthony to bed that night as he dropped off to sleep at The Crown and Castle.

5

CHARLOTTE

"Will you fetch the post, my dear?" Mama asked from the small escritoire in the sitting room.

Charlotte hesitated. It was the first time since Papa's death that she was tempted to ask the maid to go instead. She suspected Mr. Yorke was still at The Crown and Castle, and she did not wish to see him just now. Upon reflection, the caricature she had done of him had perhaps not been the wisest of decisions.

"Of course," Charlotte answered, not wishing to provide the explanation for her sudden reticence to do the very thing she had insisted upon doing for so long.

She fetched her bonnet, pelisse, and gloves, then made the walk into the village, trying to determine a strategy which would allow her to avoid Mr. Yorke. It was not that she regretted the caricature. He deserved to be put in his place. But now, there would be no doubt in his mind that she was the artist. Not to mention, when she had returned home after seeing him yesterday, Tabitha had informed her that she had a pencil smudge on her cheek. No wonder Mr. Yorke's gaze had fixed there.

She slowed her pace as she approached the inn, her gaze watchful. But she saw no sign of him anywhere outside.

There were a few people standing in front of the inn window, staring at the caricature.

"It is not Silas, I assure you," said a man definitively. "It is Anthony, my dear. Only look at the thick brows."

Charlotte stopped on the pretense of retying the lace of her half-boot, listening with keen ears.

"Ah," said the woman beside the man, as though she finally understood. "Right you are. The eldest."

"No, no, my dear. You are confused. *William* is the eldest. You remember him, surely. Strait-laced fellow. Thinks mighty highly of himself."

"You would, too, if you were in line for a dukedom."

The man snorted. "The Duke of Rockwood and his two sons are in perfect health, and they want nothing to do with the Yorkes. Not to mention, he has started paying his attentions to Harrison's widow. I would not be surprised if he had two or three more sons just to put more distance between the Yorkes and the title."

"That may be, but the Yorkes seem not to suffer for it. They are accepted everywhere."

One could only tie one's shoelaces so many times before attracting attention, and Charlotte rose reluctantly and continued to the door of the inn. She pushed it open slowly, holding her breath as the entry came into view. There was no sign of Anthony Yorke, however, and she closed the door behind her.

No one attended at the desk where Mr. Digby kept the post, and Charlotte hesitated, then peeked her head around the doorway that led to the taproom.

She retreated instantly at the sight of Anthony's head, her heart hammering. Why could he not simply leave the village and let her be? No doubt, he was plotting his revenge for the caricature.

Turning her head so her bonnet obscured her face from view of the taproom, she slipped past the open doorway and stood in front of the desk, tapping her finger upon it impatiently and looking over her shoulder every few seconds.

"Mary," she hissed when the maid finally appeared, a tray in hand.

"Miss Mandeville," Mary said in surprise.

"Is there any post?" Charlotte asked in a whisper.

Mary nodded and set the tray down on the desk. She stepped behind it and crouched until she was hid from Charlotte's view. "How long does Mr. Yorke intend to remain?" Charlotte asked in hushed tones.

Mary stood. "One more night at least, according to Mr. Digby. Here." She handed Charlotte a sole letter.

Charlotte's gaze took in the script and the fact that it was addressed to Mama. Her stomach dropped. It was from the executor. She was certain of it.

All thought of Mr. Yorke fled her mind as she tried to grasp the implications of the letter she now held. They must have finally found the heir, which meant the Mandevilles' days at Bellevue were numbered.

"Thank you, Mary," she said faintly, handing the maid a fistful of coins.

"This is far too much," Mary protested.

"You deserve it," Charlotte said, smiling feebly. "For all the ways you have helped me. I must go now." She hurried back to the door, shooting a quick glance at Anthony in the taproom just as he looked at her.

He rose from his seat, but Charlotte raced outside, charging down the street at a pace no genteel woman would take, then slipping between the baker's and the mill. Breath coming quickly, she hid behind the baker's, staring at the letter until she felt confident Anthony would have given up looking for her.

She adopted a rushed pace between a walk and a run for the rest of the way, slowing only when she came within thirty feet of home. Trying to slow her rapid breathing, she walked the last bit slowly. The letter would cause chaos and confusion, and Charlotte had promised herself to always be a force for hope in her family.

With feigned confidence, Charlotte entered her home and then the sitting room. Mama, Tabitha, and Lillian all looked up, seated on the sofa, precisely as they had been when she had left. Mama's eyes darted to Charlotte's hand, then back to her face.

Charlotte tried for a smile, but it was more like a grimace.

Mama took in a breath and nodded. "Bring it here, my dear."

Charlotte obeyed, then worked on removing her bonnet and gloves, trying to ignore how thick the air in the room was as Mama broke the seal and unfolded the paper.

"Dear Mrs. Mandeville," she read in a voice trying desperately not to shake, "I write to inform you of the status of our attempts to locate the heir to your late husband's estate."

Tabitha's hand reached for Charlotte's, grasping it tightly. No one valued Bellevue more highly than Tabitha.

"Unfortunately, the man believed to be the heir—the son of your late husband's cousin—was discovered to have died in Jamaica some months ago. As he was unmarried, the search continues. I will inform you, as promised, of any further developments. Your servant, John Marshall."

Mama's hand shot to her chest, and a trembling breath of relief passed her lips.

"He is dead," Tabitha cried out. "Thank heaven!"

"Tab," Lillian censured her, but there was little force behind it.

For her part, Charlotte felt weak with the sensation of deliverance. While the inheritance was still unsettled, the terms of the will allowed them to remain at Bellevue and receive a portion of the income. But there was no telling when they would be ousted from their beloved home.

She retired to her bedchamber, unable to fully put aside the utter helplessness she had felt upon being given the letter. How would they face what lay ahead when the dreaded letter arrived? The money she had saved from the caricatures was helpful, of course, and she was grateful for it. The diary had plenty of fodder for future caricatures, as well.

She pulled the diary from its place in the drawer, opening to the page she had left off, nearly halfway through. She had read until well past midnight, certain there was something about Anthony Yorke in those pages, as well—something he was desperate to keep secret. He claimed to wish for the diary on someone else's account, but that was precisely what a guilty person *would* say.

If only she could find his secret, perhaps she could persuade him to pay handsomely for it. The thought was distasteful, but sacrifices had to be made in these situations— even sacrifices of conscience.

But how much money would suffice when the future was so uncertain? How much would it require to support four women for an indefinite amount of time?

What they truly needed more than money were connec- tions—smart matches for Lillian and Tabitha, both of whom were fine young women deserving of love and support from equally fine young gentlemen. Charlotte was certain they would make a good account of themselves and capture plenty of interest if given the chance.

It was the opportunity to interact with eligible young men that they currently lacked.

Charlotte shut the diary, her intent gaze fixed ahead of her.

Perhaps this diary could change that.

6

ANTHONY

Anthony chose a table in the corner to take his afternoon refreshment, but even that did not save him from the glances of his fellow guests. Evidently, they had all seen the caricature.

He ignored the attention, focusing his mind on how to approach his visit to Miss Mandeville. He had gone after her when he had seen her leave the inn earlier, but it was obvious she had not wished to be found.

He would try his luck as soon as he could determine the best tactic to get her to bend to his will. Intimidation and threats? Kindness? Begging?

He was not confident he could manage the last two in a convincing way. Or a palatable one.

Miss Mandeville had tried to act as though she was unbothered by his threat of exposure, but he was highly skeptical. A revelation like that would put them firmly outside of Society circles, and if her family circumstances were what he understood them to be, that would be a grave blow indeed.

He took a last sip of ale, then rose from his seat and made his way out of the inn.

The village was less busy than it had been a few days prior, as most of those traveling to London had already passed through. Anthony did, however, see one acquaintance just outside the inn.

Mr. Jensen stood before the window, staring up at the caricature with an amused tilt to his mouth. He glanced over as the door to the inn closed, then bestowed a second, wide-eyed look at Anthony, as though he had been caught red-handed.

"A good likeness, is it not?" Anthony said.

Mr. Jensen mumbled an unintelligible response as Anthony tipped his hat and walked away. He had only passed the village baker when he spotted Miss Mandeville herself ahead, wearing a blue pelisse and the same straw bonnet she had worn earlier.

Her pace slowed briefly at the sight of Anthony, then she strode toward him more purposefully.

"Good day, Miss Mandeville," he said, thankful he would not be obliged to pay her another visit at home.

"Mr. Yorke," she said with a quick curtsy. "How fortunate. I was on my way to find you."

Anthony raised his brows. "Oh?"

She nodded. There was no pencil smudge on her face today, and he wondered whether she had felt embarrassed when she had discovered it. Unlikely. The girl seemed immune to such emotions. "I have a proposition for you. Would you care to walk with me?"

Curiosity sparked within Anthony, and he offered his arm to her. "It would be my great honor."

She hesitated—there was that streak of stubbornness— then took it.

"I have reconsidered the matter of the diary," she said as they walked back toward the center of Stoneleigh.

Anthony didn't speak for a moment. His heart was beating rapidly, but he had no intention of allowing her to see how relieved he was. At this precise moment, she held the reins, and if he didn't act wisely, he might find himself agreeing to ridiculous terms—or degrading himself with kindness or begging.

It would be best not to appear too eager. She should be made to feel herself in his hands.

"You take for granted," he said, "that I am still open to negotiating for it."

Her head whipped around. "Are you not?"

"I find myself less so after seeing the caricature you so obligingly drew of me."

She looked away quickly, but Anthony was almost certain it was to hide a smile rather than embarrassment. Impudent minx.

"In the future," he said, "you might reconsider making a spectacle of anyone with whom you wish to do business."

She opened her mouth to speak, but he cut her off.

"You may spare yourself, Miss Mandeville. I know you are the artist, and nothing you say will convince me otherwise, so let us waste no time on that. However, I *am* open to negotiating an exchange. As it turns out, I was on my way to see *you* and so happen to have the caricature on my person. And the thirty pounds."

"I will take the caricature, but it is not thirty pounds I wish for."

"I assure you, I do not have ten thousand pounds to offer."

She shook her head. "I want something else."

Anthony stole a glance at her profile. Her cheeks were tinged with pink, but her expression was determined. "And what is that?"

She stopped and faced him, meeting his gaze candidly. "I wish for you to introduce my sisters and me into Society."

Anthony's jaw slackened. "What?"

"I wish for you to introduce my sisters and me into Society."

He let out a laugh of scoffing amusement.

"Very well, then." She turned away. "Goodbye, Mr. Yo—"

He grasped her gloved hand, detaining her.

She faced him again, her lips flattened as their hands bridged the space between them. Her eyes darted to the side, as though she was looking for some means of escape without drawing too much attention.

"Wait," he said. "Surely you realize what you are asking. An unmarried and unrelated gentleman introducing three young women into Society? It would have the opposite effect you are seeking. And even if that were not the case, you have made abundantly clear that you have no high opinion of me. You think my sponsoring your sisters and you would do you credit?"

"Of course not."

He dropped her hand once he was satisfied she would not leave.

"But you have the power to arrange such a thing," she said.

"By riding roughshod over people with my carriage, for instance?"

The corner of her mouth twitched. "Something like that, no doubt. All it would require is an invitation to some exclusive party—and to make clear that you see us as deserving of acceptance by those in attendance."

Anthony's jaw shifted as he considered her words. His mind went immediately to Aunt Eugenia and the party she was hosting next week at her London house. He couldn't deny the wisdom of Miss Mandeville's request. It was far more valuable than thirty pounds. She was an enterprising young woman.

She watched him carefully. "I assure you my sisters and I

would be a credit to you and to whoever extends the invitation. Despite what you may think, I can be very amiable when I choose to be—and when confronted with other amiable people."

Anthony chuckled softly at the barbed comment.

"And Lillian and Tabitha are even more prettily behaved than I."

"You set my mind at ease, Miss Mandeville."

"Is that an agreement, then?"

Anthony hesitated, but why, he couldn't say. This was an easy request—and one that wouldn't cost him anything but a conversation with Aunt Eugenia.

"And the diary?" he asked.

"I will bring it to the party," she said. "To ensure you have held up your end of things."

He nodded, but his mind was exploring an unwelcome idea. "And can you assure me you will not make use of the diary's contents in the meantime?"

Miss Mandeville hesitated for a moment. "You have my assurance," she said firmly.

He studied her face, looking for any sign she might be lying. But he believed her. "We have an agreement, then."

Her mouth drew into a smile. "Very good."

"I will be in touch presently, Miss Mandeville."

"And I will be waiting, Mr. Yorke." She turned on her heel and walked away with that self-satisfied smile that he so detested—and that suited her so well.

"For the Mandevilles, you say?"

Anthony didn't like the knowing look in Aunt Eugenia's eye as she asked the question. He stood by the library fireplace in her London townhouse, while she sat in the sole wingback chair, a pot of steaming tea on the small mahogany table in front of her.

"Yes," he said, willing his expression to remain neutral.

"The same Mandevilles you asked me about the other day."

Blast. Until now, he had forgotten he had already broached their name.

The right side of Aunt Eugenia's mouth tilted up at the edge. "And there are three daughters?"

Anthony let out a sigh and refrained from answering. He could practically see the wedding bells in her eyes.

"I shall gladly send them an invitation." She arched a thin brow as she walked over to the large desk in the library and opened a drawer. "Or perhaps you would like to deliver it personally."

Anthony traced the round face of the clock that adorned the mantel. "That will not be necessary."

She kept her perceptive gaze on him as she pulled out an invitation. It was a testament to the strength of her hopes on his behalf that she saw anything but pure boredom as she watched him. "Very well. What are their names?" She took a seat and dipped her quill in the ink pot.

"Mrs. Mandeville, of course. Then Miss Charlotte Mandeville," Anthony said, "And Miss . . ." His brows pulled together. Confound it. What were the names of the two sisters?

Aunt Eugenia's head came up, her brows raised. "Charlotte and . . ."

It was no use, though. Anthony couldn't remember. He was certain Charlotte had said the names. He had even met the older one, but his mind had been too taken up by the fact that she was not the Mandeville he had come to see to take proper note. "Can you not simply address the invitation to the Mandevilles?"

"Or perhaps I should address it to Miss Charlotte Mandeville and her alone? Do we need the other two?"

"Yes," Anthony said, ignoring the implication in her tone and expression. "We decidedly do, dear aunt."

She dipped the quill again with a sigh. "Very well. To the Mandevilles, then. If it were not for the mountain of preparations still to be made, I would be wishing the party were tomorrow so I could meet this Miss Charlotte Mandeville."

"And her sisters."

Aunt Eugenia smiled as she finished writing with a flourish. "And her sisters, of course."

"And her mother."

"And her mother," Aunt Eugenia granted.

For Anthony's part, the only thing he was looking forward to was getting that diary in his hands and his brother home.

7

CHARLOTTE

Charlotte paused in front of the door to her home and stared at the letter in her hand, her heart skipping and stopping in turns. The script on the front was neat and the letter enclosed with a fine wax seal.

She knew exactly what it was, but she was finding it difficult to fathom that Mr. Yorke had been good for his word. She had half-expected him to find some other means of acquiring the diary—more threats, perhaps, or a Bow Street Runner, even.

Charlotte would have liked to meet a Runner. He would know all sorts of fascinating things that might prove useful.

It had been difficult for her to agree not to use the diary's contents, but if things went well with the invitation, she hoped she wouldn't need to continue the caricatures for much longer.

Charlotte was determined to make the most of the invitation. Both Lillian and Tabitha were handsome young women with good manners. Why should they *not* catch the attention of some respectable gentleman?

She opened the front door and strode inside, pulling off her bonnet. Mama, Lillian, and Tabitha were all seated in the parlor, needles in hand as they worked to darn stockings and other miscellaneous items.

Mama glanced up from her needlework with her characteristically kind smile. Her gaze dropped to the letter in Charlotte's hand, and the smile evaporated.

Charlotte hurried over to her. "It is an invitation, Mama."

Mama's brows drew together as she took the paper. It had been some time since they had received an invitation. At first, it had been due to Papa's death, but even once they had put off their mourning, the silence had continued. A deafening silence, in fact.

It made Charlotte's jaw clench just to think about. It grated her to accept an invitation to socialize amongst such fair-weather friends, but what was the alternative? She could not draw caricatures for the rest of her life to support her family. Neither did she wish to. Every interaction with Mr. Digby became more unpleasant until Charlotte's skin had begun to crawl at the mere sight of him. Though her skin crawled all the more knowing that her arrangement with him had caused her to join the *ton* in its low ways. Perhaps this party was her ticket out.

Tabitha lowered the handkerchief she was stitching and leaned closer as Mama broke the seal and unfurled the invitation.

Charlotte's own curiosity took her to Lillian's side, and four pairs of eyes examined the contents of the invitation. It was for Monday of the coming week—a dinner party to be held at Mrs. Eugenia Ashby's London house.

Mama blinked. "But why? I have never met Mrs. Ashby."

This was what Charlotte had been dreading—how to explain the invitation being extended at all.

"Is she not related to the Yorkes?" Lillian said, her gaze fixed on Charlotte.

To her dismay, Charlotte's cheeks filled with heat. She forced her expression into nonchalance. "I believe you may be right about that."

Lillian cocked a brow, but Charlotte studiously ignored her.

"Yorke . . . as in the handsome Mr. Yorke who came to see Charlotte?" Tabitha asked with a distinctly mischievous glint in her eye.

Mama's head whipped up again. She had yet to hear of the visit, and Charlotte had thought Tabitha ignorant as well. Evidently not.

"What do you mean?" Mama asked. "Is this *the* Yorkes? The ones related to the Duke of Rockwood?"

"It was nothing," Charlotte said, dampening Mama's visions of grandeur. "We had met at The Crown and Castle, and he thought I had dropped something there, so he came to return it to me."

"How chivalrous of him," Tabitha said, audibly impressed.

Charlotte couldn't stifle a scoff. Of all the words to describe Mr. Yorke, chivalrous would be the last she would use. Or perhaps ugly, but that was beside the point.

"It *is* chivalrous," Mama said. "Do you think he was the one who persuaded Mrs. Ashby to invite us? I cannot think of any other explanation for it."

Lillian and Charlotte did battle using nothing but their eyes, but Mama was not watching.

"Whatever the case," she said, standing with her eyes still fixed on the invitation, "I am grateful for it. We are overdue for a bit of good fortune, are we not?"

Charlotte could almost see Mama's mind whirring with hope and possibility as she paced across the floor in front of the hearth.

"We must put ourselves to work immediately to ensure all of you present the finest possible appearance. I will go into the village today to see whether Mrs. Clark can fit us up for the party. Of course, I can go without anything new—I would far rather put the little money we have into *your* dresses. Though, I fear my vision may be well beyond our means even then." She brought her thumb to her mouth and chewed the tip of the nail nervously.

"I need nothing," Charlotte said. "I have only worn my white satin twice. It shall do very well for me."

Mama shook her head decidedly. "Not for Mrs. Ashby's party, and certainly not if we mean to do everything in our power to further your acquaintance with the Yorkes. Which son was it, Charlotte? The oldest one is in line for the dukedom, you know."

Oh, heavens. This was getting out of hand quickly.

"It was not the oldest one," Charlotte said firmly, rising from the sofa, "and, given that the eldest is a distant fourth or fifth in line, the likelihood of Mr. Anthony inheriting is not much greater than that of *my* doing so."

"Well," Mama said, wrapping an arm around Charlotte and pulling her into her side, "I must say, I think you would do a fine job of being a duchess." She looked around at each of her three daughters with a bit of wistfulness in her eyes. "I am terribly proud of my daughters, and your father would be too. We may not be the smartest dressed at this party, but no one can say aught else against any of you. Kind, intelligent, and spotless reputations, each one."

Charlotte's stomach swam with guilt, but she forced a smile and leaned her head on Mama's shoulder. Her own reputation was not the unblemished thing Mama believed it to be, but at least they would be able to afford better dresses than Mama knew, using the money Charlotte had been saving.

Of course, Mama was unaware just where the money was

from. After Papa's death, Mama's grief had struck her low for weeks. Charlotte had offered to take up the task of communicating with the trustees regarding the estate. Whenever they received money, Charlotte merely added a bit from her own stores.

She hated to deplete their supply so much, but this party was an investment. The invitation could lead to other invitations, and their prospects would be greatly improved. Having their futures secured would, in turn, secure Mama's future. Charlotte merely needed to ensure her reputation remained intact long enough for Tabitha and Lillian to make their mark amongst high society.

"Perhaps we can be let down just here," Charlotte said, grasping the diary her reticule held as she looked at the carriages lining up in front of Mrs. Ashby's townhouse ahead. Not all the finery in the world could undo the sight of the Mandevilles stepping down from an outdated carriage with peeling paint. They so rarely used it that it had been gravely neglected since Papa's death.

The driver pulled to the side of the road, and the four of them descended one by one. Charlotte was satisfied with the appearance they presented—her sisters wore muted pastels. With Charlotte already twenty-three, none of them were in their first blush of youth, but they had never been properly presented. And though Charlotte would have preferred Lillian in a vibrant blue, to do so would have been to court comment, and that was something they could ill afford.

Charlotte had worn the satin dress, just as she had planned. She *had*, however, asked Mrs. Clark to embellish the sleeves, neckline, and hem with gold thread. She had promised

Mr. Yorke they would be a credit to him and his aunt, and she meant to be good for her word, even if it grated her to do anything with his interests in mind. In this one instance, their interests happened to converge.

Thanks to the talk the week's caricature had generated, Charlotte had learned a great deal about Mr. Yorke—or at least bits and pieces that presented a very disturbing picture indeed.

The Yorkes might be related to the Duke of Rockwood, but, if the gossip was to be believed, they were not exactly bastions of respectability. Naturally, Charlotte was not foolish enough to believe *everything* people said, but she did have enough experience to understand there was almost invariably a kernel of truth in gossip.

Mary's assertions about Anthony's brother were evidently true. He had killed a man and fled to France to escape his fate at the gallows. If his brother was capable of such brutality— and he the most likable of the Yorkes, according to many— who could say what Mr. Anthony Yorke might be capable of?

Was it completely irresponsible of her to deliver the diary into his hands? He had said a man's life was in the balance. She had assumed it was self-interest that motivated his desire for the diary, but now she couldn't help wondering if he intended to use the diary to *ruin* someone.

The four Mandevilles walked toward the lamplit entrance with Charlotte's gaze flitting from face to face of their fellow attendees. It only increased her nerves, for she recognized two subjects of recent caricatures. If they knew she was responsible for the drawings, the night would be ruined. There would be no further invitations, no marriage prospects for her sisters, and the future of their family would be in greater peril than ever.

The reticule with the diary hung heavy on her wrist as they passed through the doors. The entry hall was a veritable sea of faces—some familiar, but most unfamiliar. Even the familiar ones were not acquaintances of Charlotte or her family, though. They were simply known to her from having seen them at The Crown and Castle.

The Mandevilles were dressed well enough, but it was clear from the way their fellow attendees were dressed and the fineness of the furnishings in Mrs. Ashby's house that this was not their world.

"What do we do now?" Tabitha asked through a smile of clenched teeth as they stood in the entry hall. "Is your Mr. Yorke here?"

"He is not *my* Mr. Yorke," Charlotte hissed. But she would have been glad to see his face, if only to know one person.

"There," Mama said decisively, nodding down the corridor. A woman in vibrant green silk was talking with attendees beside the door. "That is Mrs. Ashby. Come. We should greet her."

Charlotte nodded, but inside, her heart was doing somersaults. She hadn't any idea whether this woman would even be aware they had received an invitation from her. Had Mr. Yorke informed her? Or had the housekeeper been ordered to send it?

Suddenly, this idea seemed complete and utter folly—a recipe for embarrassment that the Mandevilles would never have the opportunity to rise above. What if Mrs. Ashby resented having strangers at her party? It was entirely possible the woman was a harpy and would treat them like imposters they were.

"Be gracious but confident," Mama said in an undervoice as they approached their hostess. "You are daughters of a gentleman and have every right to be here."

Charlotte and her sisters straightened and took in steadying breaths as Mrs. Ashby turned toward them, the curiosity bred from unfamiliarity filling her gaze.

"Good evening, Mrs. Ashby," Mama said. "I am Louisa Mandeville, and these are my daughters, Miss Mandeville, Miss Charlotte, and Miss Tabitha. It was very kind of you to invite us." The three of them curtseyed in order, but Mrs. Ashby's gaze fixed on Charlotte.

"Miss Charlotte," she repeated, surveying her. Charlotte forced herself to meet the woman's eye with that delicate balance of confidence and modesty. "I have been eager to meet you."

"And I you, ma'am," Charlotte responded politely. In truth, she hadn't thought about Mrs. Ashby much at all until their arrival. Why Mrs. Ashby cared at all to meet a belatedly added guest was certainly a question flitting about Charlotte's mind.

For a long moment, the woman regarded her with unabashed curiosity, until Charlotte felt certain she was red from the roots of her hair to her bosom. Why did she not regard Lillian or Tabitha in the same manner? Did she know something about Charlotte? Had Anthony said something to warn her?

Finally, Mrs. Ashby turned to Mama and the others. "I am so pleased all of you could come. I shall hope for the opportunity to deepen our acquaintance over the course of the night. Now"—she looked about her—"where is—ah, there he is. Anthony!"

8

CHARLOTTE

Charlotte's heart rose into her throat as a man turned toward his aunt a dozen feet away. It took her a moment to recognize him, for he was smiling—an expression which faltered as he realized why he was being called upon.

Attired in a neat black tailcoat with a dark gray waistcoat, Anthony's gaze went to his aunt, to Mama, then to Charlotte. An arrested look came into his eyes at the sight of her, and she suddenly felt keenly aware of the awkwardness of her limbs. Did her arms always hang so strangely at her sides? Perhaps it was the weight of the reticule which made them feel so unwieldy.

She could only hope that the intent way he surveyed her was a good thing.

He was flanked by two men Charlotte could only assume were his brothers. Neither of them looked as severe as him, but the resemblance was otherwise unmistakable—heads of full, dark hair, sculpted jawlines, and the sort of confident bearing that came to those accustomed to giving orders and having them obeyed with haste.

"Miss Mandeville," Anthony said, his gaze on Charlotte as he bowed.

Beside Charlotte, Lillian fidgeted, and Mrs. Ashby cleared her throat.

"Miss Charlotte, that is," he corrected.

His aunt introduced him to the other members of the Mandeville family, then the Mandevilles to the other members of the Yorke family. Charlotte surveyed Anthony's brothers carefully. The oldest—William—was also the tallest. He held himself more rigidly than Anthony, but he hadn't the frown that came so readily to his younger brother. The youngest, Frederick, smiled broadly as he bowed. His hair was the lightest—glinting in a way that reminded her of caramel—and his face the most amiable. Charlotte already liked him.

"And the other brother?" Mama asked with a quick glance around, as though she was looking for someone else.

Charlotte's eyes widened as all three Yorkes *and* their aunt stiffened in chorus.

Mama seemed to realize her error, but there was nothing to be done.

"I fear you are mistaken, ma'am," said the eldest Mr. Yorke, his tone like flint. "It is only the three of us."

Anthony's gaze darted to William, his nostrils flared. He said nothing, though, as Mama apologized for the misunderstanding.

"If you will excuse me," said Frederick, "I must have a word with Lord Finsworth." He gave a quick bow, then made his way toward the baron.

"Frederick fancies himself a politician," Mrs. Ashby explained. She turned to Anthony. "You will introduce Miss

Charlotte and her family to whomever they wish to be introduced."

Charlotte's mouth twitched slightly. It gave her great pleasure to see a man accustomed to having his way be ordered around by someone else. Based on the tightness about his mouth, it grated him.

"Of course," he said.

Charlotte smiled widely at him and switched her reticule to the other wrist before taking his offered arm. "It was a pleasure to meet you, Mrs. Ashby," she said with a curtsy.

"Inform me without delay if he behaves with anything but the greatest chivalry, Miss Charlotte," she said, fixing Anthony with a hitched brow that might incinerate a less robust man.

Directed by a thoroughly diverted Charlotte, Anthony led them from group to group, introducing the Mandevilles to all the most eligible-looking gentlemen in the room as well as to those older men and women Charlotte recognized and knew to have respectable sons of marriageable age.

More than one of them appeared visibly impressed by Charlotte and her sisters, a fact which both relieved and thrilled her. She promoted conversation between the young men and her sisters, finding excuses to address Mama or Anthony to take herself out of the equation. She would far rather see her sisters' futures secured than her own, for she could fend for herself at need. The caricatures could feasibly continue to support her—particularly if there were more invitations to parties like this, where she could interact with members of high society and hear the gossip herself.

It was not the future she preferred, but she would pursue it if necessary.

"Has your thirst for introductions been quenched?" Anthony asked as Mama, Lillian, and Tabitha spoke with new acquaintances nearby.

"Not remotely," Charlotte said pleasantly. If she were wise, perhaps she would be afraid of Anthony, but she was not wise. And though she knew people considered him dangerous, for reasons she could not explain, she did not feel in danger with him. "Why? Am I keeping you from some lovely young woman here?" She went on her tiptoes to look around the room.

His thick brows drew together. "That is the furthest thing possible from my mind, I assure you."

"And what, pray, *is* on your mind?"

"The diary," he said without hesitation as he sent a glance at her reticule. "Allow me to take it off your hands."

"Perhaps later. If I gave it to you now, I suspect you would abandon me for the remainder of the evening."

"I would have thought that a desirable outcome for you."

"What, and forgo the opportunity to torture you more?" In truth, she had not intended to delay turning over the diary to him, but as the time approached, she felt more and more reluctant to do so. What would he do with it? If it was something unsavory, how could she forgive herself?

"You are mistaken," Anthony said, gazing over the crowd. "It is not torture to be with you."

Her heart jumped. Most women's hearts danced at poetic expressions of love. Apparently, Charlotte's was so susceptible that it could be set to galloping when a man said it was not torture to be with her. She had been deprived of male company for too long, it seemed. "The expression on your face says otherwise."

"When can I expect the diary?" he asked, ignoring her assessment.

She hesitated, fiddling with the strings on her wrist. "After dinner."

He gave a curt nod. "Do you see the balcony just outside of those doors?" He indicated the other side of the room with his head. "I will meet you there once the men leave their port for the drawing room."

"Very well," Charlotte replied as Mama approached.

She watched Anthony walk off, wondering whether she had been a fool to agree to put the diary in his hands.

Charlotte tapped an anxious finger on the stone balustrade of the balcony as she waited. She had slipped unseen from the drawing room once she felt enough time had passed that the men would soon be done lingering over their port.

Her wrist whined at the weight upon it, and she rested the reticule on the stone for a respite. Now that the evening was winding down and plenty of acquaintances had been made, Charlotte's conscience was making itself heard, whispering warnings in her ear, accusing her of selfishness.

Why should the future of her family matter more than the future of whoever Anthony meant to target with the diary?

Even in her own hands, the diary had the potential to harm a number of people. Now that she had met and conversed with many members of high society, she felt less confident in what she had been doing with the caricatures. It had been easier to justify when they were just names and faces.

The fact was, in the time since Papa's death, she had allowed resentment to grow up like a weed until it had begun to strangle her sense of compassion. He had worked so hard to take the small fortune he had and to grow it through careful investment. When he was persuaded by Lord Wadsworth to invest heavily in a new scheme, he had done it after only a great deal of thought—and with an equal amount of trust, for Wadsworth had a proven record of lucrative investments. But when Wadsworth had realized his scheme would not materialize as promised, he had withdrawn his own money while leaving Papa and the Mandevilles to feel the brunt of the failure.

It still made Charlotte sick with anger and hurt to think upon. And while it was true that there were members of the *ton* who would stop at nothing to achieve their ends—Anthony Yorke was one of them—she realized that did not mean that every member of the *ton* comported themselves in such a way.

She uncinched the string of the reticule and pulled out the diary. She had read enough of it to know what havoc it could wreak on the lives of some of those mentioned. The entries were not those of a man obsessed with gossip, though. In fact, the tone of Mr. Marlowe's writing was almost mundane, as though he thought little of what he was documenting. Most of it *was* mundane—bills passed in Parliament, comings and goings of merchant ships—but inevitably, there were tidbits that would cause a stir if they became public knowledge.

Did that sort of power belong in the hands of Anthony Yorke? Or of anyone, for that matter?

Charlotte doubted it. Mr. Marlowe could not have made such a record intending for it to become a weapon. Perhaps it would be better to get rid of the thing entirely.

Her eye caught on the hedges just over the balustrade. She could throw it into the bushes, but it would inevitably be found.

Her glance went to the torch at the end of the balustrade, and she took a step toward it, eyes fixed on the dancing flame. She could burn the diary. There would be no bringing it back from *that*.

It would be despicable behavior on her part after Anthony had held up his end of the bargain. But perhaps it was just as despicable to hand it over to him. Which was the lesser evil?

She held up the diary nearer the flame, letting the light

illuminate the plain leather cover as her heart pattered and raced. It would only take a single page catching fire, a simple accident—

"What are you doing?"

Charlotte whipped around, hiding the diary behind her back as Anthony strode toward her, his gaze intent and . . . angry.

"I was waiting for you," she said, heart charging against her ribs. "For far longer than I had intended."

The fire of the torch reflected in his disbelieving eyes. He stepped toward her until her back bumped against the balustrade, then he put out a hand for the diary.

Charlotte kept still, her heart leaping wildly as he loomed over her. Her fingers grasped the leather as her reluctance to surrender it to him loomed large. "What do you intend to do with it?"

"That is none of your concern," he replied, his hand still out insistently.

"I shan't give it to you unless you tell me."

His brows drew together. "You expect me to tell a gossip-monger what I intend to do with it?"

Gossipmonger. The word stung, but when she opened her mouth to refute it, no sound emerged. He was right. She *had* become a gossipmonger. "Do you intend to harm anyone using it?"

His jaw clenched, but he said nothing.

Charlotte's eyes widened. "You do."

"No one who is not deserving of it." He reached around her for the diary, but she pressed it between her back and the wall.

"And you think you are the best judge of that?" she asked, stalling as she tried to determine what to do.

He met her gaze squarely. "I do."

How could he be so unabashedly cold about doing someone an injury?

"We had an agreement, Miss Mandeville," he said. "I have done what I told you I would do. It is your turn now."

"If I give you this diary knowing you mean to harm someone using it, that makes me your accomplice."

Anthony let out an impatient breath. "Miss Mandeville, I have nothing against you. I don't particularly like you, but other than your aggravating stubbornness, I have no reason to wish you ill. However," he said with his eyes fixed significantly on hers, "we had an agreement. If you continue to refuse to hold up your end of it, you leave me little choice."

Charlotte's brows snapped together. "Is that a threat?" It was not a surprise, for it was not the first time he had employed such tactics.

"Without question." His gaze held hers. "Mr. Robbs seems quite taken with Miss Tabitha, does he not?"

Charlotte swallowed.

"Something tells me he will be less likely to pay her a visit if he discovers the rift between his parents is your doing."

Charlotte shifted nervously but kept her gaze fixed on his. Lamentably, Anthony was right, but she had no intention of letting him know that.

"Or," he continued, taking another step toward her, "Imagine if Lord Finsworth knew *you* were responsible for the depiction of his . . . cavorting—something he believes caused his bill to fail in Parliament this week. I doubt he will still see to it you and your sisters are invited to the *al fresco* party he mentioned."

Charlotte's skin pricked with guilt, but she raised her chin, defiant. "Is it my fault Mr. Robbs was untrue to his wife? Or that Lord Finsworth was engaged in unsavory endeavors?"

"No," he replied, "but surely you can see the irony of

lecturing me on harming others when you have been engaged in precisely that."

Charlotte's blood boiled. "You are all the same, do you know that? You behave despicably, but rather than take responsibility, you blame the person who brings your depravity to light."

His brow darkened. "And in what way am I accused of behaving despicably?"

Charlotte scoffed. "You cannot be in earnest! Since the first time I met you, you have threatened me, physically detained me, and insulted me."

"And *you* have thwarted me at every turn, made a public laughing stock of me, and used me for my connections."

Charlotte's chest rose and fell quickly as she met his gaze, again without a defense.

"Now," he said. "The diary. Before I lose my patience."

"Promise me you will not harm anyone using what is written within it."

Anthony took a final step nearer her, until their faces were just inches apart. "I do not wish to use force, Miss Mandeville, but I will if necessary."

"You wouldn't dare," she said, hatred for him bitter on her tongue.

He reached an arm around her until his fingers covered hers, grasping the journal. Their chests rose and fell against each other as they stared at one another mulishly.

"Men like you are everything that is wrong with this world," Charlotte spat.

"Men like me?" Anthony challenged, hovering over her so she was obliged to lean back to maintain even a few inches between their faces.

"Men like you," she repeated. "*You* are the reason my sisters and I must all but beg to be invited to a party like this, the reason I am, as you so politely phrase it, a gossipmonger. Nothing matters but your own selfish desires, and you trample anyone who stands in your way. Men like you," she said, shaking with mixed exhilaration and fear, "are the reason my father is dead—the reason we have nothing through no fault of our own."

His gaze flickered, and his hold on her hand and the diary slackened as his dark eyes searched hers. He was closer than Charlotte had ever been to a man, but there was no fear inside her. It was anger and anger alone that made her eyes sting.

She would rather die than cry in front of Anthony Yorke, however, so she clenched her teeth and stared at him, matching the intensity in his gaze.

"Charlotte?"

Their heads whipped toward the baffled voice. Tabitha stood in the doorway of the nearby balcony that led from the drawing room, her mouth open in surprise.

Behind her, Mrs. Ashby's head appeared. Once her gaze found Anthony and Charlotte, she pushed past Tabitha.

"Anthony!" she hissed.

But Tabitha's exclamation of surprise had drawn more attention, and other attendees began to appear in the doorway to see what the fuss was about—and why Anthony and Charlotte were pressed up against one another alone on another balcony.

Charlotte's heart beat against her ribs painfully.

This was the end. Whatever she and her family had accomplished tonight, it was all for naught now. Her reputation was in tatters.

Feeling sick to her stomach, she loosened her grip on the diary. It seemed so inconsequential now.

Anthony's gaze darted to hers, and she turned her head to avoid his gaze.

After a moment of excruciating silence, he pulled the diary from her hand. She released it willingly, no longer caring what he did with it.

He stepped back, his eyes still fixed on her.

"What is the meaning of this?" his aunt demanded.

There was something strange in Anthony's eyes, but Charlotte hadn't the heart to care. She had ruined everything.

All her work, all her saving was for naught.

"Aunt," Anthony said, stepping toward Charlotte so that they were shoulder to shoulder. "I beg leave to present to you my affianced wife."

9

ANTHONY

Swift intakes of breath rippled through the audience on the other balcony, followed by the hum of whispered chatter. Mrs. Mandeville and her daughters covered their mouths with hands.

"Your . . . affianced wife?" Aunt Eugenia repeated in a colorless voice.

Anthony gave a nod, switched the diary to his left hand, and reached for Charlotte's with his right. Hers felt limp and clammy as she stared at him absently, as though she was only half-present. "Miss Charlotte Mandeville has done me the honor of agreeing to marry me." Never had he felt so near to retching as a result of mere speech.

His aunt let out a strange, breathy laugh. "Well! This is beyond anything!" She turned to those behind her. "Did you hear? My nephew is engaged to be married!"

A few people congratulated her as Charlotte's nails dug into Anthony's hand. He squeezed back, and she stopped. The dream-like look on her face had been replaced by flared nostrils and an intensity that, quite frankly, frightened him.

But what else could he have done? The situation and position in which they had been found . . . the girl would have been ruined, not to mention that Aunt Eugenia would have disowned him. Had she not said she would countenance no more scandal amongst his brothers?

"I *thought* those two smelled of April and May," exclaimed a man jovially.

Good heavens.

Charlotte's nails dug more deeply into Anthony's hand until he was certain they would draw blood. The ungrateful vixen. If she had only given him the diary as she had promised, they would not be in this situation.

Anthony smiled at their audience. "Charlotte smells a great deal better than April *or* May, I assure you."

"Anthony, *dearest*," Charlotte said, her mouth arranged in the least convincing smile Anthony had ever seen, "may I speak with you in private for a moment?"

"Of course," Aunt Eugenia said before Anthony could protest. She positively glowed. "Come, everyone. Let us leave the lovers in peace."

Another wave of nausea crashed in Anthony's stomach as the crowd turned away, a few of them shooting knowing smiles at Charlotte and him.

"Not too terribly long now," Aunt Eugenia said with a little wink. "But make good use of the time." Before either of them could answer, she pulled the door closed behind her.

The latch click was deafening.

"Are you *mad*?" Charlotte seethed, wrenching her hand from his.

"I have been asking myself the same question for the past two minutes."

"What in heaven's name were you thinking?"

Anthony clenched his free fist. Did she not realize what an

enormous favor he had done her? Or how heartily he wished he could go back in time and redo the past hour? Nay, the past year. "I was *thinking*," he said harshly, "that I needed to save your reputation. Would you prefer I had allowed it to be ruined?"

"Yes!"

Anthony's jaw hardened. "Very well." He turned toward the doors, but Charlotte grabbed his wrist.

Reluctantly, he faced her.

She clamped her mouth and eyes shut, as though she was trying to summon patience. "I did not mean that. But . . . why, oh, why did you insist we meet *here*? Surely there was a better place—without an audience so near."

"Perhaps I would have had I known you would be so insufferably impossible! I thought we would be here for two minutes at most. I was not planning for a lengthy *tête-à-tête*." He spat the last words.

"Nor I for an engagement!"

He scoffed. "And you think I *was*? You think I am pleased about this?"

"You were the one who orchestrated it, so I certainly hope so! That would make one of us at least."

He began pacing, rubbing a hand over his chin. "Believe me, Miss Mandeville, marriage is the very last thing on my mind—to say nothing of marriage to *you*."

"A sentiment entirely reciprocated by me, I assure you," she said hotly.

He shot her a darkling look but continued his pacing. Of all the disastrous things to happen . . .

"What's done is done," he said. "We have no choice but to make the best of it now."

Charlotte's eyes widened. "Make the best of . . . you mean we must marry in earnest?"

"Of course not," he said with annoyance. Confound his sense of honor!

Men like you are everything that is wrong with this world. Nothing matters but your own selfish desires. Those words had stung, for were they not true? It was Anthony's selfishness, after all, that had led him to abandon Silas that night.

And the revelation that Charlotte's family was left with nothing, desperate for invitations? Sympathy had weaseled its way into his heart—a sympathy she clearly did not appreciate or deserve. It was the deuce of a situation.

"What, then?" she said. "We are to simply be engaged forever?"

"Would you care to help come up with a solution? Or do you prefer to point out—quite needlessly, I assure you—just how wretched all of this is?"

Her lips pressed together in a line, but she remained quiet. For a brief, heavenly moment, at least. "Can we not put an end to the engagement?"

"And have you labeled a jilt? A woman of unstable character and changing affections?" He let out a laugh and put out a hand, inviting her to go inside. "Be my guest."

She chewed her lip silently, apparently not fond of that option. Neither, in truth, was he. He would look a fool if she cried off immediately after he announced their engagement. It was the sort of scandal he had been trying to avoid in the first place when he had uttered those silly words.

He hit the diary against his palm, frowning. "We must bide our time."

"Bide our time?"

He gripped the diary firmly and met her gaze. "Yes. We carry on with the engagement for a few weeks, then quietly end things, claiming we have discovered we do not suit."

She scoffed lightly. "I discovered as much within a few *seconds* of meeting you."

He offered her a disingenuous smile. "Then you will have a few weeks to solidify the opinion." He set to pacing. "It will elicit some talk—that is inevitable—but less than if we ended it sooner." He glanced at her, and his tone turned dry. "No doubt you will manage to find some titillating piece of gossip to turn into a caricature, drawing everyone's attention away."

Charlotte blinked. "You mean to say you think we should carry on with the engagement for a few *weeks*?" She said the word as though it was synonymous with eternity.

"Shall I simply repeat everything I say? Or do you prefer to do it for me?"

"Forgive me," she said with nothing like the penance he thought the situation merited, "but I am still trying to grasp this . . . this . . . nightmare."

"Whilst I am flitting around like a contented butterfly in paradise?" He shook his head and resumed his pacing, his mind inspecting the circumstances he found himself in to determine the best path forward. There *was* no best path, though; there was only the least terrible one—the one that did both of them the least damage.

No matter how he looked at things, though, he came back to a prospect that made him want to throw the diary at the closest window. He released a resigned breath through his nose. "If we *are* to be engaged, we must act the part."

Charlotte shook her head immediately. "No, no, no. This" —she gestured between them—"is most certainly a marriage of convenience. People in such marriages often cordially dislike one another."

He stopped short. "Forgive me for speaking frankly, but, pray tell what convenience there would be for *me* in such a match?"

She swallowed, and he felt a sliver of regret for offering the insult to her pride, but he could tell his comment had hit home. If protecting their reputations was their aim, they needed to make this a credible engagement, and that meant—he could barely stand to think the words—a love match, for Charlotte Mandeville had neither money nor connections to make anything else reasonable.

"Miss Mandeville," he reasoned, "you wish for your sisters to make smart matches, correct?"

"Of course."

"Very well. Without wishing to sound arrogant, our being engaged may serve them well in that regard."

She laughed caustically. "By which you mean to say that a connection with someone as lofty as you will elevate us to a level more acceptable to Society?"

"Is that not the reason you insisted on my helping you obtain an invitation tonight?"

She met his gaze, her gloved hand fiddling with the fabric on her skirts. Somewhere inside—somewhere deep, deep inside—he felt a sliver of sympathy for her. This was the last thing either of them wanted, and yet here they were.

"Very well," she finally said. "We pretend to be well and truly engaged, and whatever that entails"—she nearly shuddered—"but *only* until I can find some piece of gossip to overshadow the talk that will result from ending the engagement." Her eyes grew suddenly wide. "What am I to tell my family?" She looked to him, as though he had the answer.

He lifted his shoulders. "Whatever you must to guard the secret." Anthony himself would have a great deal of explaining to do. A *great* deal. But that was a problem for him to address in the future. Albeit the very near future.

"But . . . but I cannot lie to them!"

"Are you not already? I gather they have no notion of your arrangement with Digby."

Charlotte stared at him, unmitigated dislike in her eyes. "Must you always be so . . . so—"

"Correct?"

"Intolerable," she spat.

"Let us hope you can find a way to tolerate me, or we will have much explaining to do—and your sisters may kiss their chances with anyone in attendance tonight goodbye."

She clenched her eyes shut.

Strange how he felt the same frustration and reluctance as she did to play the part required of him, yet seeing her struggle piqued his pride. He had never been hated so passionately.

"The longer we remain here, the more . . ." He faltered, but the way her cheeks tinged with pink told him she understood. The longer they stayed alone on the balcony, the more people would assume . . . things.

It seemed impossible anyone could assume the two of them to be doing anything of a romantic nature on this balcony. Charlotte was infinitely more likely to claw his eyes out than press her lips to his. And yet, they would have to give the impression of two young people in love.

This was *not* the distraction Anthony needed now that he finally had the diary in hand.

"Shall we go in?" he suggested.

She nodded and came up beside him, searching his face for a moment with an unreadable expression.

He offered her his arm, and with a large intake of breath Anthony might have expected from someone about to walk off a cliff, she accepted it.

10

CHARLOTTE

Charlotte was an engaged woman. An engaged woman walking into a drawing room on the arm of her affianced husband—a man she detested.

Oh, the cruelty of fate!

But if a temporary engagement to Anthony Yorke was what was required of her in order to ensure the happiness and future of her family, so be it.

"Where are you going?" she asked, pulling back on his arm as he tried to guide them to the left rather than the right.

"To the library," he explained. "I must put the diary somewhere."

Charlotte lifted her free arm, revealing the reticule, which hung limply, devoid of any contents now that the diary was in his hands.

He chuckled. "A valiant effort, but I think not."

He pulled her forward, and she relented, walking with him to the door farther down the corridor. It opened to a square room lined with painted bookshelves. In the middle sat a large desk with a colorful globe atop.

Charlotte released his arm as he chose a spot on the first available shelf, slipping the diary between two like-sized books.

"Do not even consider trying to come steal it," he said as he rejoined her.

"Why? What would you do? You wouldn't dare harm the woman you are madly in love with."

The corners of his lips pulled down at the sides.

"Our reputations are tied together now, Tony," she said, emphasizing his name.

"Do not call me that," he responded tersely as he offered his arm again.

"But you are my betrothed," she said.

He sent a gaze heavenward as if in silent plea for God to grant him patience. "If you *do* steal the diary, I will find other ways to make your life miserable, I assure you."

As she took his arm, she smiled up at him in a way she trusted would convey the sentiment *I would like to throttle you.* "How could I possibly be more miserable than I am now? If you must know, though, I have no wish to steal that diary. It has brought me enough trouble as is."

"Finally, some sense from your lips. Now, are you ready?"

"Of course I am. *You*, on the other hand, look as though you are marching to your grave. If people perceive our secret, it will be your fault, not mine."

He paused with his hand on the doorknob. "If I went into that room smiling like a buffoon, it would alarm everyone far more."

"A terrifying prospect," she agreed. "At least have the decency to look neutral, then."

He heaved a sigh, but the furrow to his brow lessened slightly.

She faced the door, preparing herself for what lay ahead. If he wished for her to play the role of a woman in love, she would exceed his expectations—and make him regret the day he ran into her at the inn.

The quick pause he took before opening the door of the drawing room betrayed his nerves and just how little he relished this. He had no one to blame but himself.

As he pushed the door open, she removed her hand from his arm and threaded her fingers through his.

He sent a quick glance at her, but there was no time for further reaction. The din of conversation diminished, and every eye turned toward them. They were immediately flooded with warm wishes and congratulations.

"We were beginning to think you would never return," said Mr. Naughton with a knowing raise of the brows.

"I admit to being tempted not to," Anthony said with a half-smile that communicated one thing to Mr. Naughton and a very different thing to Charlotte.

It was skillfully done, she had to admit. To herself, of course.

They received felicitations and such a smattering of eyebrow wags and comments about their future family that Charlotte felt quite warm by the time Mama and her sisters reached her.

Mama kissed her on both cheeks, then brought her in for an embrace. "My dear, sweet Charlotte," was all she could whisper in an unsteady voice.

The guilt nearly crushed Charlotte.

Watching Mama embrace Anthony and lovingly call him "her future son" made her feel sick in an entirely different way.

"You have much explaining to do," Tabitha whispered hurriedly in her ear as they embraced. "But, my, how handsome he is!" She pulled away with a sparkle in her eye, making way for Lillian.

"Well," Lillian said as she grasped Charlotte's hands and kissed her cheek, "you always *were* full of surprises."

Charlotte tried for a smile as Mr. Naughton emerged from the crowd. "I think we must hear the story—for a story there must be to have guarded your courtship so fully from so many."

Charlotte laughed breathlessly and glanced at Anthony, who looked as though he had just swallowed a rotten fish whole. Obviously, he could not be relied upon to save them. It was terribly disagreeable of him to put them in this situation, insist she agree to act as though she was in love with him, then to leave her to do the explaining.

If that was his game, she would play it. With gusto.

"Well," she said, entering into the spirit of it, "it would *not* have been such a secret if my Tony had had his way."

His hand tightened on hers.

"It may be difficult for you to credit," she pressed on, "for he is not wont to show this side to any but those he loves most, but he wanted to declare his love publicly. On the High Street in Stoneleigh."

Charlotte smiled as a number of people exchanged whispered comments, their eyebrows raised. Anthony's grip on her hand made her worry her bones would be crushed.

"I should have known something was afoot," his aunt said, smiling at him as though he was a mischievous little boy, "when you asked me if I knew her." She wagged a finger at him. "Shame on you for not telling me everything then."

Anthony opened his mouth, but Charlotte rushed in. "You must forgive him, ma'am, for I charged him with the utmost secrecy. I needed time, you see, to be certain of his character. I am ashamed to admit I had some doubts on the matter. Naturally, those have all been laid to rest." She turned toward him and conjured the most love-stricken expression she could manage. "My beloved Tony is the most upstanding gentleman in all of England, with never an ill thought or motive to cross his mind."

His smile struck a chord of exhilaration and fear within her, assuring her he would find his revenge upon her.

"I was so perplexed when he came to Bellevue," Lillian said, watching them bemusedly. "But it stands to reason, I suppose."

"Yes," Charlotte said, again preventing Anthony from speaking. "Tony could not restrain himself. He was forever finding excuses to see me or, failing that, to write me letters—always crossed twice."

"*That* is why you insisted on retrieving the post," Mama said as though experiencing revelation.

Charlotte nodded, though her conscience squirmed and writhed.

"When shall you marry?" an unfamiliar voice asked.

"If Tony had things his way, we would have eloped to Gretna Green weeks ago," Charlotte said with an indulgent look at him. It was met with a glittering, spiteful smile.

"I thought, mistakenly, as you can see," Anthony said, "that a woman who enjoyed such secrecy in courtship would also appreciate it in marriage. But my little pet"—he looked into her eyes—"is unlike any woman I or any of you have ever encountered."

Charlotte's smile became more forced, but determined as ever, she took the hand interlaced with hers and brought it to her lips, kissing it fervently to a chorus of tolerant appreciation.

"You have yet to answer the question, Anthony," his aunt said. "When are you to be married?"

Anthony's gaze lingered on Charlotte a moment longer, his eyes speaking with astonishing clarity of the terrible, horrible plans he had in store for her. "We did not expect to announce anything just yet, so the date has not yet been determined." He leaned over to Charlotte, smiling as much as Anthony Yorke could believably smile, and whispered in her ear. "Restrain yourself, ma'am. These people know me—better than you do, in most cases—and you are stretching the bounds of belief with these theatrics." He pressed a firm kiss to her cheek, which immediately burst into flames, then returned to his former stance.

The crowd's attention began to fracture, and conversations started amongst them, lessening the weight of scrutiny the two of them bore. It was for the best, for the kiss on the cheek had rattled Charlotte more than she cared to admit, even if it *had* been meant as more of a slap than an affectionate gesture.

As they conversed with people, Charlotte's eyes went again and again to Mama. Each time, her heart sank. *My dear, sweet Charlotte.* She couldn't remember when Mama had looked so happy or sounded so thrilled.

Charlotte was the most ungrateful wretch of a daughter to ever grace the earth. She deserved every ill that came her way.

But her family did not.

Was it possible this atrocious lie could lead to something good for her sisters, as Anthony had suggested? That was all Charlotte wanted—for those she loved to face a more certain future.

She and Anthony were soon separated by their conversational duties. Charlotte was content to see her sisters and Mama engaged in conversation every time she glanced at them. Surely, she could bear a few weeks of pretending for such a sight.

But the conversation was taxing and far less satisfying now that Anthony was not beside her to tease. Guests began to leave presently, and her gaze caught his from a dozen feet away. They shared looks of consternation. Evidently, they agreed at least that this was all very trying.

"Come, Miss Charlotte," Mrs. Ashby said, pulling her by the hand and walking to Anthony. She grabbed his hand as well and led them to Charlotte's family. "We are to be family now," she said, looking nearly as pleased as Mama. "I propose we have our own more intimate dinner tomorrow to celebrate and become better acquainted. What say you?"

Charlotte shot Anthony a pleading look. The more time they had to spend together in the presence of others, the more likely they were to make some error that would ruin everything.

"Oh, aunt," he said, clearly every bit as horrified by the prospect as Charlotte, "the Mandevilles live in Stoneleigh."

Mrs. Ashby waved a dismissive hand. "A matter of ten or eleven miles. I will gladly send my carriage."

"That is very kind indeed," Mama said, "but there is no need for that. We are spending the night at The Pelican—it will not be a problem to extend another night. Right, Charlotte?"

Charlotte forced a smile, but her mind was on the fact that it was Monday, and she needed to produce a new caricature by Thursday at very latest if it was to be posted Friday. She dreaded it more than ever now. What in heaven's name would she draw? How would she decide who deserved to be cast to the lions?

"Then it is settled," Mrs. Ashby said. "Shall we say half-past six tomorrow evening?"

An enormous wave was sweeping Charlotte toward a place she had no desire to go, and she had no one to blame but herself.

And Anthony. In fact, most of the blame belonged to him. Something about him had raised her hackles from the very first time they had met, making her do and say things she would not normally do and say.

Anthony and his aunt accompanied the Mandevilles to the door, where Charlotte thanked Mrs. Ashby for inviting them.

"Child," Mrs. Ashby said, "it is *I* who am grateful." She leaned in closer but looked at Anthony, who watched with mistrust in his eyes. "I was beginning to think he would never find a respectable young woman to sweep him off his feet. I am delighted to know you have managed it."

Charlotte's insides squirmed at hearing herself described as *a respectable young woman*. She doubted that any young woman, though, could sweep Anthony off his feet. But if Charlotte did get hold of a broom, she would far rather take the handle and hit him over the head with it.

"Now," Mrs. Ashby said, "the two of you may go off in that corner to say goodbye in whatever way you see fit"—she cocked a brow—"while the four of us face this way"—she linked her arm with Mama's and turned them toward the open door—"to admire the view."

The view was naught but a dark London street.

"Thank you, Aunt," Anthony said with anything but gratitude in his voice.

Charlotte walked to the corner his aunt had indicated. She would gladly take the opportunity to have a word with him before they separated for the night. After enduring everyone's congratulations and questions, she realized they had a great deal more to settle on if they were to pass things off. It was one thing to convince strangers and acquaintances of their engagement; it was another thing entirely to do so to their families: the people who knew them best.

"Are you content?" she asked, turning her back to the others and exposing Anthony to them—just in case their families chose to turn and look, which Charlotte had no doubt they would. Tabitha in particular would not be able to resist.

"Content?" he repeated in bemusement.

"With what you have done?"

He scoffed. "You are welcome."

Her brows shot up. "Welcome? For turning my world upside down? And shaking it violently?"

"For saving your reputation."

"Quite rich of you, is it not? You endanger my reputation and then demand thanks for saving it?"

He smiled suddenly and took her hand. Charlotte didn't need to turn to know someone was watching them. Anthony pulled her closer, keeping the smile plastered on his face.

"Allow me to remind you, Charlotte *dearest*, that you had already endangered it without any of my assistance."

"And yet *you* were the only one threatening to divulge the information that would have ruined me." That was not entirely true, of course. Mr. Digby had made a similar sort of threat.

The stakes were higher than ever now, for if Digby revealed her secret, it was not just her reputation or her family's that would be harmed, but Anthony's too. Not that she cared the snap of her fingers for *him*. But she liked his aunt. And Frederick.

"Enough arguing," she said. "What are we to do now? We will both face questions, and if our stories conflict . . ."

His lips pinched together. "Do your best tonight. Tomorrow evening, I will find time for us to converse in private, where we can sort out the details and make a plan for the coming days."

Charlotte nodded, rubbing her lips together nervously. She did not relish the task ahead of her. Any of the tasks.

Anthony's gaze flitted to the others, and Charlotte turned.

All four ladies watched with indulgent interest, the London street view evidently forgotten.

She turned back to Anthony. "Do something," she hissed through clenched teeth.

"Do what exactly?"

"Something a man in love would do."

After a moment of tortured hesitation, he leaned over ever so slightly and brought her gloved hand to his mouth. Brushing his lips across her knuckles, he looked up at her through his lashes.

Unexpected chills cascaded down Charlotte's neck as his dark eyes stared up at her as if to ask, "Am I doing it well enough?"

She blinked. This was the insufferable Anthony Yorke she was looking at. He was single-handedly ruining her life. Her reaction was merely a result of being unaccustomed to such behavior from a gentleman. Whether Anthony deserved to be described in such a way was a separate matter—and one of grave doubt.

Within minutes, they had bid Anthony and his aunt good-bye, and the door was shut behind them. The carriage awaited where it had left them earlier, down the street.

It was oddly quiet as they walked, until Lillian cleared her throat in an entirely unnecessary, highly theatric way.

"Yes, I quite agree," Tabitha said. "You have some explaining to do, Charlotte."

Mama squeezed Charlotte's arm and smiled. "I should give you four lashings for carrying on with him clandestinely—and four more for depriving us of the details as they were occurring —but I am far too elated to do that."

"I *knew* she was keeping a secret," Tabitha said, "but I cannot say this was the one I had expected. How in the world did you manage to capture his interest, Charlotte?"

"Tabitha!" Lillian said, horrified. "What an awful question to ask. It is quite natural that she would attract any gentleman's interest, of course."

Charlotte rather agreed with Tabitha on this count, but she didn't say so. It would have gone contrary to her goal of preserving the illusion of a bona fide engagement—a goal she hated with every bit of her.

"I was not trying to be rude," Tabitha complained. "But you must admit, Anthony Yorke is terribly handsome, and his family wealthy. I am sure he could have the daughter of a peer if he wished."

"Particularly given the family's connection to the duke," Mama said.

"Mama," Charlotte said on a sigh, "you must extinguish any hope that I may someday become a duchess." *Or even a Yorke, for that matter,* Charlotte thought.

Mama stepped into the carriage. "Perhaps, but you will, of course, be invited to ducal events."

"I think not. The Yorkes are not on the best of terms with Rockwood."

"Oh," Mama said, deflated.

Charlotte, on the other hand, felt hopeful for the first time that evening that perhaps Mama would now feel less thrilled about the engagement and, thus, less devastated when it ended.

"Well," Mama said brightly, "no matter. We need no dukes or even barons. I am content you have found an admirable gentleman to love. One who will care for you the way you deserve."

It was all Charlotte could do to smile unironically. The entire concept was ludicrous. Anthony, admirable? Charlotte in love with him? Him *caring* for her?

It conjured the picture of him kneeling beside her sickbed, holding her hand as he fought off tears.

He was more likely to try to finish her off.

Eager to steer the conversation elsewhere, Charlotte asked Tabitha about the man she had sat beside at dinner. Gregarious as she was, Tabitha needed little encouragement to talk at length, and soon enough, they were back at The Pelican, where prodding questions could be avoided with the task of preparing for bed.

But as Charlotte brushed her hair and plaited it, her mind was wrapped up in her problems, which were multiplying at an alarming rate. She needed an idea for a new caricature so that, when they returned to Stoneleigh, she could quickly execute it.

But what she needed more than anything was far less scandal in her own life and far *more* in the lives of the *ton*. That way, she could end this ridiculous farce of an engagement as soon as possible.

11

ANTHONY

"Well," Anthony said as soon as the door had shut behind the Mandevilles, "I should be getting home."

"Not so fast." Aunt Eugenia restrained him with a hand above his elbow.

"Yes, not so fast," Frederick said, appearing around the corner with William behind him. The expression on his brother's face told Anthony he was likely to heartily detest the next few minutes. It was a look of utterly delighted mischief.

Anthony was forced into the drawing room, then into a wingback chair near the empty fireplace. His aunt took a seat nearby, while his brothers went to the liquor cabinet and poured drinks from the crystal decanters there.

"Well?" Frederick said.

"Well?" Anthony parroted back.

"Oh, don't be perverse," Frederick said, taking a relaxed seat on the chair of the sofa. "I thought you had sworn off women."

"As did I," William said.

"No man swears off women," Aunt Eugenia said testily. "They may *say* something of the sort, but they never mean it."

Anthony bit his tongue. He certainly *had* meant it. None of them knew the reasoning, of course. They had no idea Anthony was meant to be with Silas and Langdon—and that if he had been, Lord Drayton would not have been able to get away with murder. No woman was worth the pain Miss Baxter had brought Anthony and Silas.

Both William and Frederick believed Silas guilty of the charges brought against him. His unhappy history with Langdon —borne of their own conflict over a woman in addition to Silas initially suspecting Langdon as the one responsible for the business's decreasing profits—and his flight to France had been enough for them to believe Drayton's story. Both of them resented Silas heavily for it. Frederick's resentment was not just borne of the feeling of betrayal but of the way the scandal tainted him by association, making it more difficult to gain the respect he needed to achieve his goal: becoming a Member of Parliament.

William, on the other hand, had been against Silas's investments from the beginning, disliking the way they tainted the family name. He had always thought Silas impulsive.

"How did it happen, then?" Frederick asked. "How did my ornery brother fall head over heels into love?"

Anthony swirled the brandy in his glass, thinking of his first meeting with Charlotte. If only he had snatched the reticule from her wrist right then and there. "Oh, you know how love is," he said, keeping his eyes on his drink. "One minute, you are minding your business, and the next thing you know, it barrels into you, turning your life upside down and making you wonder how you ever lived without it."

Happily. That was how he had lived before Charlotte Mandeville's antics had upended his entire existence.

"Gads," Frederick said, staring at him blankly. "You *are* in love."

"And set to beat you to the altar," Aunt Eugenia said significantly.

Frederick shrugged a shoulder. "I am in no hurry."

"Even for five hundred pounds?" She cocked a brow.

"Ah, yes," Anthony said. "I had meant to tell you, Frederick . . ."

"Tell me what?"

"I am giving five hundred pounds to the first between you to marry." Aunt Eugenia smiled as she waited for this information to sink in. Her gaze flitted briefly to William. "Not to you. You need no more money."

William chuckled and tossed back the rest of his drink. "How discerning of you."

It wasn't entirely true. William was certainly better off than the rest of them, but the sizable estate in Kent came with hefty debts and obligations.

"Forgot to tell me, did you?" Frederick said to Anthony. "Or thought you'd get a head start?"

Anthony didn't deign to respond. He hadn't bothered to tell Frederick because he had known neither of them were interested in marrying.

"Hush now," Aunt Eugenia said. "I told Anthony less than a fortnight ago, but I like things fair. You have that long, Frederick, to catch up. A grace period."

He scoffed. "A fortnight to engage myself to someone? When I am in the middle of trying to make headway amongst the MPs?" He shook his head. "No. I am sorry, aunt, but I cannot possibly play this game of yours. There is too much at stake, and women are too much of a distraction."

"I could not agree more," Anthony said. The silence that

followed brought his head up. Everyone was looking at him, confused. "A pleasant distraction, naturally."

Not naturally.

He stood. "If the inquiries are at an end for the night, I am for bed."

"The inquiries are *not* over," Aunt Eugenia said, "but they can wait for dinner tomorrow. You are all coming." It was an order rather than a question.

William frowned. "I suppose I could."

"As long as I am not required to watch Anthony swooning over the hand of his betrothed." Frederick winked at him.

"I will attempt to restrain myself," Anthony said as he left the room, happy to escape further interrogation.

Once the door was closed, he let out a long, slow breath. Charlotte had been right; they needed to make their stories cohesive, preferably before dinner tomorrow.

He was exhausted, but sleep was not on the horizon. When would this madness end?

He slipped into the library to retrieve the diary, half-thinking Charlotte would have managed to steal it back somehow. But it was where he had left it—an entire book full of Marlowe's observations and knowledge.

Anthony had heard of Marlowe, of course, but it was Harris who had informed Anthony that, in addition to having family connections in various quarters of Society, the man had kept a highly detailed diary—one with a specific entry that had the potential to clear Silas's name.

Harris had been in discussions with Marlowe when Marlowe had died suddenly. Apoplexy, reports said. But Harris had managed to get his hands on the diary despite that.

And finally Anthony had it.

He went to his apartments on foot and, after shrugging out

of his coat, sat with the diary at the escritoire and began to read it from the first entry.

It was not until nigh on three o'clock when he reached the final pages.

His eyes ran over the last lines of the diary until he reached the signature at the bottom of the last page. He stared at it for a few seconds, then slammed the book shut, and threw it at the wall.

Not a single mention of Lord Drayton in the entire thing. Nothing at all he could use as evidence of what had truly happened that fateful night.

Anthony sat back in his chair, shut his eyes, and ran his hands through his hair.

How could this happen? Harris had been certain the diary contained evidence Anthony could use to exonerate Silas. Perhaps this was Anthony's just desserts for trusting anything that outlandish man said. He had been so desperate, though, to believe there was a path forward to bringing Silas home.

He opened his eyes, and they shifted to the diary, sitting on the floorboards next to the wall. That little book had turned his entire life on end. He had spent weeks trying to get his hands on it and now found himself engaged, of all things, to a woman he detested—all in pursuit of the information inside.

Information that was *not* inside. He was no closer now to clearing Silas's name than he had ever been.

He kicked at a leg of the desk, and pain shot through his foot.

He didn't care. Anything was preferable to this frustration, to this despair. He would have taken Silas's place in France in a heartbeat if it would have made a difference. From his mother's death, Anthony had promised himself that he would watch over his younger brothers. When it became clear that Silas's and William's temperaments and passions were too different to be conducive to a close relationship, Anthony had reaffirmed that promise.

He and Silas had attended Cambridge at the same time, lived together afterward, invested in Lord Drayton's company together.

But Anthony had failed when it had counted the most. And now, the one certain way to clear Silas's name turned out to be useless. Without it, Silas would be stuck in France indefinitely.

That was a prospect Anthony couldn't bear. He *had* to bring Silas home. But how?

Anthony pushed through the door of The Pelican. It was a respected establishment, even if not among the finest. Perhaps the Mandevilles were not in such financial trouble as Harris had given him to believe. That would be welcome information, for he didn't particularly relish the prospect of sending rumors flying that he had wooed and then jilted an impoverished young woman.

"How may I help ye, sir?" a maid asked, wiping her hands on her apron.

"I am looking for Miss Charlotte Mandeville," he said.

"She's in the parlor, sir." She indicated the second door on his left, and he thanked her before marching toward it. He stopped short, though, at the sound of voices within, for he recognized Charlotte's. He shifted so he could see through the small gap the just-ajar door afforded.

Charlotte and her mother were seated beside one another at a table. In front of them, were two teacups and plates with nothing but crumbs remaining. Mrs. Mandeville took her daughter's hand, looking at her with an affectionate smile. "I cannot tell you how pleased I am for you."

"Thank you, Mama."

"No. Thank *you*. You cannot know this, but I have been at my wit's end of late, unable to sleep for fear of the future, dreading that ghastly letter informing us the heir is on his way to oust us from our beloved Bellevue. But now . . ." She squeezed Charlotte's hand.

She was trying valiantly to match her mother's emotion.

"But now," her mother continued, "our fortunes have changed. *Your* fortunes have changed, and no one could be more deserving."

Charlotte looked away. "Mama . . ."

"I mean it, Charlotte. No one has been a greater force for hope in the family since Papa died. No one has encouraged us as you have to believe in a joyful future despite our adversities." Her voice faltered, and they both dashed away tears.

Anthony's conscience pricked him, and he knew he should draw back, but Mrs. Mandeville's whisper had him drawing nearer instead. "I am unspeakably proud of you. Indescribably happy for you. For you and your Anthony."

His heartbeat quickened.

"And Tabitha is right, you know," Mrs. Mandeville said with an enigmatic smile. "He *is* dashing."

Anthony's mouth quirked at the edge. Charlotte must be itching to set her mother's view of him to rights.

But behind his amusement, there was something else. A heaviness.

Heaviness at the realization of the burden their lie required of Charlotte. Anthony had no desire to speak untruths to his brothers or aunt, but there was an obvious intimacy between Charlotte and her family that he had failed to recognize until now.

There was more heaviness at the recognition of the pressures the Mandevilles were facing as a family—and Charlotte's attempts to see them through. That must be the reason behind the caricatures.

And dash it all if it didn't make it harder for him to detest her with as much force.

The continuing silence brought him toward the gap in the door again. Charlotte and her mother were embracing, and the way Charlotte's head rested on her mother's shoulder, he had a full view of the tears and misery in her face.

When they pulled back, though, she had formed her lips into a trembling smile, the sight of which pulled at Anthony's heartstrings.

It was the last thing he needed.

"We shall come about, Mama." Charlotte stared deep into her mother's eyes. "No matter what we face, no matter how terrible it may seem, we shall come about. I will make sure of it."

Was it Anthony's imagination, or was she trying to prepare her mother for when the engagement was broken off?

Frowning, he shifted his weight to his back foot, eliciting a loud creak from the floorboards.

Charlotte's head whipped around, and her gaze met his.

12

CHARLOTTE

Charlotte couldn't decide whether to turn aside to dash away the tears on her cheeks or to wear them defiantly. Anthony was looking at her so strangely—almost . . . sadly.

Mama smiled and rose to her feet. "How good to see you again, Mr. Yorke. Please do come in. We were just taking tea. Would you care for some?" She strode to the door and opened it wider for him to pass through.

"It is kind of you," he said, "but no. I merely came to see how you are getting on—and to perhaps take Charlotte for a drive in the Park. If you have no objection, of course, Mrs. Mandeville."

Charlotte's eyes widened. A ride in the Park, as though this was a real and true engagement rather than a sham. What in heaven's name was he about? He must be up to some mischief —revenge for last night, most likely.

Mama smiled at Charlotte. "I think it would do her good to take the air. Go on, then, my dear."

Charlotte rose, angling her body away from them on the

pretense of adjusting her skirts, while she used one hand to brush away the tears on her cheeks. It was very much like Anthony to appear at the moment she least wished for him. And that was saying something, indeed, for there were no moments she *did* wish for him.

She arranged her mouth in a smile and turned back to them. "I must fetch my gloves and bonnet, but I shan't be above two minutes."

"I shall await you in the yard," he replied.

Charlotte hurried up the stairs, retrieved her things, and returned to the entry way, where Mama awaited, looking as pleased as anything.

Charlotte was tempted to ask if Mama would rather take her place, but she did not.

"It reminds me of when Papa took me out in his new carriage when we were courting," Mama said as she helped Charlotte with her gloves. "There. Enjoy yourselves now." She had no notion how impossible such a thing was.

Charlotte walked through the archway and into the galleried yard, where Anthony was seated in a phaeton, holding the reins of two bays. It annoyed her just how dashing he looked, to use Tabitha's description, with his well-tailored blue coat, dark green waistcoat, and polished topboots. Was Charlotte dressed smartly enough to deserve a seat beside him? She had put a disheartening dent in her savings to let a room at The Pelican, to say nothing of adding a second night. In any case, she had not dressed for the day intending on riding through London's most frequented park, where everyone strutted like peacocks. It was one thing to attend a party to impress the Yorkes; it was quite another to live up to the expectations people would have of someone *engaged* to one.

Anthony looked at her with a slight frown to his brow, but

his expression was otherwise unreadable as he handed the reins to the ostler. He hopped down with ease and offered Charlotte a hand of assistance.

Why did she never wish to accept it from him? Something about him brought out all her most childish tendencies. Including, she hated to admit, a tendency to stare. But not admire. Never admire.

Taking his hand, she stepped up into the phaeton, aware that *something* was different between them. She could guess quite easily: he had seen her cry, and there was no coming back from that. Would he think her a poor creature now, easily over-set, needing to be handled with kid gloves?

Anthony took his seat and navigated the phaeton out of the yard and onto the streets of London.

"I was not expecting you," Charlotte said.

"No, how could you have?"

"You might have sent a note informing me of your intentions."

"I thought you might disappear if you had warning."

She opened her mouth to retort, but closed it immediately. It was entirely possible she would have chosen to take a walk precisely when he was meant to arrive, if only to irritate him.

Charlotte could not decide how to feel toward Anthony. Part of her hated him for forcing her into this conundrum and wished to thwart him whenever possible. From the beginning, he had seemed to take for granted that she would obey his every wish. And now, she was expected to go along with this engagement. What would happen when he ceased to see her use? Would she be discarded as easily as Papa had been discarded by Lord Wadsworth?

The other part, however, recognized that she owed Anthony—dared she admit it?—gratitude. He might have thrown her to the wolves last night, for it was not his reputation which would have suffered most. He would have faced criticism for the way they had been found, certainly, but it was Charlotte whose reputation would have ultimately suffered.

But instead of allowing such a thing, he had done the unthinkable.

It was intolerable to feel gratitude toward someone she so disliked, and since she sincerely doubted he would appreciate her thanks, she relievedly shut it away.

"Is this the way to the Park?" she asked as they turned a corner.

"It is."

She grimaced. "Must we go there? Surely, that will only serve to advertise our engagement, making its end all the more scandalous."

"I assure you, news of our engagement was enough of a surprise that it has likely traveled as far as Botany Bay already."

Charlotte let out a scoffing laugh. "So, you choose to feed the fire by parading us about?"

"Do you have a better plan that enables us to speak privately? Perhaps I should hand the reins off to you." He offered them to her, and she pursed her lips.

She hadn't the faintest idea how to drive a carriage, much less a high-perch phaeton with two energetic horses. "Might we not ride somewhere else?"

"Such as?"

She shrugged. "Some dark alley where there is no one we know?"

"Yes," he said dryly, "an unmarried gentleman and an unmarried lady driving down a dark alley is precisely what your reputation needs."

"No doubt you are infamous amongst London's dark alleys and would be immediately recognized."

He laughed—the first true laugh she had heard from him

—and it caught her off guard. Her pulse quickened at the sight of his genuine smile, which brightened his countenance in a way that made him more handsome than ever.

Perhaps she had better *not* make him laugh moving forward.

"Your ideas of me are fascinating," he said.

"As are yours of me."

"Which is why we are here in this carriage. If we are to be convincing, we had better know more about one another."

"We could hardly know less. Pray, what *do* you know of me?"

He glanced at her but said nothing as he guided the horses onto Rotten Row.

"You needn't fear offending me," Charlotte said knowingly. "I am not so poor-spirited as that."

"Poor-spirited is precisely what I thought you."

She smiled serenely and looked around at the trees. "You shan't have the pleasure of getting a rise out of me, Tony."

"Very well. What do I know of you?" He paused. "Your name is Charlotte Mandeville."

"Bravo. Have you considered taking up with the Bow Street Runners? They could use a man of your perceptivity."

He cleared his throat significantly. "As I was saying . . . your name is Charlotte Mandeville, and you are the second of three daughters. You are a talented artist and well-informed—by methods I have not yet grasped—about the antics of the *ton*, using which knowledge you create—"

She grasped his arm in warning, glancing at two young gentlemen walking nearby.

He waited until they had passed to continue. "You hate the wealthy, yet when given the opportunity to demand something from me, you most wished for an invitation to a dinner replete with precisely such people, which gives one to assume that your hatred is more of a resentment than anything, connected, given what you have said, to your father's death."

Charlotte stared at him, speechless. Had she been so very transparent?

Anthony stole a glance at her. "You see? I *have* offended you."

"You have not." The fact that he had called her a *talented artist* had almost made her blush—until his assessment of her feelings toward the *ton*. It was an aggravatingly accurate assessment.

"Am I correct so far?"

She hesitated before nodding reluctantly.

"Good. Let me see, then. What else do I know?" He thought for a moment. "You are eager to marry off your sisters, while you yourself seem to take no interest in that blessed state, which leads me to believe you either cordially dislike both marriage and your sisters, or you are, for undetermined reasons, attempting to secure their interests before your own."

"I am very fond of my sisters."

"Then why the rush to marry them off?"

Charlotte gritted her teeth. She had no desire to tell Anthony of her family's current situation, but there was no avoiding it. If she left him ignorant, he would undoubtedly say something to humiliate her—or both of them.

"Bellevue is entailed," she explained.

"I know."

Her head whipped around. "How?"

He cocked a bold brow.

His aunt's words came to mind—*when you asked me if I knew her.* "You made inquiries about me."

He shrugged. "I needed the diary, and your unwillingness to give it to me obliged me to discover more about you."

"So that you could use it against me."

"Yes."

His willingness to admit his depravity took the wind out of her sails. "What *do* you need the diary for?" The guarded way he looked at her made her quickly add, "You said we needed to know more about one another, did you not?"

"That, I assure you, is not knowledge that will be necessary for you. Besides, the diary was useless."

"What do you mean *useless?*"

"It does not contain what I was looking for." He said it colorlessly, but by the tight set of his jaw, she was disinclined to believe it was a matter of indifference. Of course it wasn't. He had gone to great lengths to obtain it.

"Now," he said, "why do you harbor so much resentment toward the *ton?*"

"That is not knowledge that will be necessary for you," she parroted back.

"Given that you accused *me* of being responsible for your father's death, I must disagree."

"Not *you*. Men like you." She debated for a moment, torn between a need to keep her secrets and to explain herself to Anthony. "If you must know, my father spent the last decade of his life making careful investments to grow the little he was left by *his* father. He was a skilled and conscientious investor, and over time, his hard work was fruitful. He had plans to hire apartments in London in the coming Season to introduce us to Society."

Anthony was quiet, listening with his ever-furrowed brow, nodding now and then to a passing acquaintance.

"He was approached by a wealthy, well-known gentleman, who persuaded him to invest heavily in a scheme of his with promises of a life-changing return. When the man realized the scheme was going awry, he sold his shares and left Papa to feel the full weight of the investment's failure." She swallowed and directed her gaze toward something to her left to hide her face from Anthony. "The financial loss was staggering and deeply humiliating. All those years of scrupulous work were suddenly for naught. But even more staggering a loss was Papa's rapid decline and death shortly thereafter." The unsteadiness of her voice persuaded her to leave the narrative there.

The only sound was the crunch of the gravel beneath the wheels.

"I am sorry," Anthony said.

Charlotte stole a glance at him, for the words were unexpected from his lips. Unexpected but genuine.

"But surely," he continued, "you overgeneralize by directing your anger at the entire *ton* for the actions of one miserable man."

"Do I?"

"It is my opinion, certainly, and I believe others would agree."

"Tell me, then . . . have you not seen such disregard for others amongst your acquaintances, such willingness to view those supposedly below you as disposable?"

He did not respond immediately, but the muscle in his jaw flexed. "I have."

"As have I. At first, they were trivial matters—the way those passing through Stoneleigh treat the villagers, or the way they demand service immediately at The Crown and Castle without regard to anyone else's needs or claims. But since then, I assure you, I have found plenty more grievous examples."

"Like my running roughshod over anyone in my way?" His voice was laced with irony.

Charlotte forced herself not to shift in her seat. If anyone knew she was the one behind the caricatures—and that one in particular—it would make their engagement far more difficult to explain. That was one reason she was not looking forward to seeing Mr. Digby—not that she ever looked forward to that. But he would want an explanation, certainly.

Charlotte's silence must have confirmed to Anthony the truth of his statement. His interactions with her had indeed been a prime example of how the *ton* interacted with those lower than them.

"Brave of you to come out in a carriage with me," Anthony said, breaking the silence, "when you know the dangers."

"But I am not afraid of you," she pointed out.

He glanced at her. "Evidently not."

"You think I should be?"

He let his gaze travel over her face for a few seconds, then returned his eyes to the road. "Perhaps."

"Perhaps it is you who should be afraid of *me*."

He chuckled. "Because you intend to humiliate me at every turn?"

"You could use a bit of humility, you know."

He gave a scoffing sort of laugh. "Thank you for that assessment. Does it not occur to you that, by making me look a fool, you also injure yourself? We are inextricably connected now, Charlotte."

Her heart gave a little quiver at the sound of her name on his lips and the words *inextricably connected*. An image stole into her mind: her arms wrapped around Anthony's broad back and his around her waist as their lips met.

Cheeks and body warm, she looked away, as though the image was before her rather than a figment of her rogue imagination. That was not what he had meant by *connected*. She was still accustoming herself to this level of intimacy with a man. The novelty would wear off with time. In three or four weeks, her mind would not force such unwelcome images before her.

Or perhaps the images would intensify.

"Oh, *Tony*," she said, forcing herself to remain present—
beside the man whose imaginations of a 'connection' with her
likely consisted of boxing her ears. "I only wish that everyone
knew just how passionately in love with me you are, and *that*
cannot harm me."

"Imagine my relief," he said drily.

"Speaking of which, we should turn back if I am to have
sufficient time to dress. I must look the part of the esteemed
Anthony Yorke's affianced wife."

"We have not yet discussed how to answer people's questions, which was the purpose in coming out together in the
first place."

"But we have," she countered.

"You mean you will say whatever makes me look like a
lovelorn sap?"

She smiled and patted his arm. "You are not as slow-witted
as I had thought."

"Nor you as harmless as my aunt thinks. What shall we say
when people inquire as to how we met?" He guided the
equipage toward the archway that led out of the Park.

She lifted her shoulders. "We tell the truth—we met at the
inn. It is best, I think, to keep as close to the truth as possible."

"Is that what you call your story about a planned trip to
Gretna?"

"Oh, no. I call that embellishment. And a dash of revenge."

13

ANTHONY

After taking Charlotte back to The Pelican, Anthony made his way toward precisely one of those dark alleys she had wished to drive down together. He left his horses and some coin with the ostler at the nearest inn, then went the rest of the way on foot.

"And ye're sure there was nothin' inside?" Harris asked once they were seated at a corner table at The Rook's Nest.

"Entirely certain," Anthony gritted through clenched teeth.

Harris frowned, hand on his tankard of ale.

"You think I am lying to you?" Anthony asked.

"No, no. It's only . . . the information I had was from Marlowe himself." His lips pressed together, and his forehead furrowed. "Very nearly got hanged *myself* gettin' that diary."

He brought his gaze to Anthony's again, determination there. "We'll solve this case yet. No need to be in the doldrums."

"I have every expectation you will set this aright."

Harris nodded quickly. "Aye, and I shan't accept a farthin' until I've brought you somethin' you can use."

That was certainly a relief, for Anthony's pockets were increasingly light. So much so that part of him wished to marry Charlotte just for the five hundred pounds his aunt had promised. Would it be so terrible to be married to her? It would be a lively marriage, certainly, which had its merits. And perhaps she was not so very prickly as she seemed—the moment he had witnessed with her mother seemed to support such an idea. Not that he wanted a weepy wife—or any wife at all.

But, in theory, if he were to marry at some future date, he would wish for a wife who loved him down to her very bones, despite all of his flaws; a woman who felt the full range of human emotion, who would fight for him and be loyal to him the way he would fight for and be loyal to her.

But he was not convinced such a woman existed—or that he would recognize her if she did. He had thought Miss Baxter the pinnacle of feminine perfection, but when he lost the money he had invested in Drayton's scheme, he had lost her attention along with it.

As for Charlotte Mandeville, she was as far from loving him down to her bones as she could be. He had claimed they were engaged to safeguard her reputation, but by the time they managed to break off the betrothal, it was Anthony's reputation that would be injured beyond help. She was determined to make him out as some sort of Byronic figure.

It made him sick. But he intended to give as good as he got.

Anthony took a last sip of ale and rose to his feet.

"Ah," Harris said. "Forgot one thing."

"What?"

Harris smiled broadly, displaying a couple of missing teeth. "Congratulations on your engagement, sir."

Anthony nearly turned on his heel and left without another word. But even Harris couldn't know of the ruse. Anthony

might have asked how he was already aware of the engagement, but he didn't waste his breath. The man had ears everywhere. It was why Anthony had hired him.

"Thank you," Anthony said with effort.

"Hadn't pegged you as the marrying kind."

"Nor had I," Anthony replied truthfully. "Now if you will
excuse me, I have a dinner engagement to prepare for."

"With . . . *her?*" He raised his brows significantly, a knowing
smile trembling at the corner of his lips.

Anthony nearly told him the whole truth then and there, if
only to wipe that ridiculous expression from his face. "Yes." He
tossed a coin on the table. "You know where to find me when
you have any information at all."

He strode out of the public house, sincerely hoping Harris's
determination would lead him to something they could use.
Lord Drayton was so dashedly well-connected, so aggravatingly wealthy that it was nigh on impossible to get anyone to
inform on him. It was why they'd had such high hopes for the
diary. It was supposed to contain Marlowe's written record of a
conversation where Drayton had essentially admitted to what
he had done, thereby clearing Silas's name.

But alas. It had been too good, too convenient to be true.
Why Marlowe had claimed such a thing was a mystery to
Anthony. But the man was dead, so a mystery it would remain.

Harris had counseled Anthony not to be in the doldrums,
but his impatience was growing, and along with it, the fear
that perhaps he never *would* be able to clear Silas's name.

The thought didn't bear entertaining. Failure was simply
not an option.

"How *did* you become acquainted?" Tabitha asked as the Mandevilles, the Yorkes, and Aunt Eugenia ate from the array of desserts on the table. "We have not attended any parties or events in an age."

Anthony shot a glance at Charlotte, wondering whether it would be wisest to take charge of answering.

"We met at the inn," Charlotte said before he could utter a response. She was looking more than usually handsome this evening, with a small pink ribbon threaded through her dark hair. Her clothing was neat but simple, leaving the attention to be centered, rightfully, on her face.

It seemed strange that the two of them had gone out earlier and were now dining in this intimate setting, when, in a matter of weeks, they would part ways and perhaps never speak again.

"Outside of the inn, to be more precise," Anthony said, intent on participating in the narrative this evening—if not taking hold of it entirely.

Charlotte's gaze flitted to him.

Anthony tried to make his smile look like the indulgent type an enamored gentleman might wear. "She was on the pavement when I first saw her from across the road. I immediately took note of her—how could I not?—but it was when she darted into the road that my attention was well and truly caught. Without regard for her own safety, she rushed in front of several carriages and carts."

Eyebrows went up around the table, and everyone stopped their eating. Even without looking at her, Anthony could feel Charlotte's eyes fixed on him.

"She was saving a kitten that had wandered into the street."

"A kitten?" Lillian Mandeville paused with her utensils

suspended over her plate, directing her baffled gaze at Charlotte. "You detest cats."

Charlotte shot Anthony a look that told him she would wring his neck when they were next alone. Why did that prospect send a little thrill through him?

"I cannot say I blame you," Aunt Eugenia said as she reached for more sauce for her pudding. "Temperamental little things, aren't they? You never know whether they will curl up on your lap for an interminable nap or send their claws through the gauze of your new gown."

"I can't abide the creatures," Frederick said. "What induced you to risk your life for it, Miss Charlotte?" Despite his dislike of cats, he was evidently impressed by her selflessness.

Anthony fixed his gaze on her, the ghost of a smile on his lips. "Yes, what was it?"

She took a long drink before responding. "I suppose it was how utterly pathetic it looked. I seem to be drawn to such creatures." Her gaze flitted to Anthony.

"In any case," he continued, the delight of revenge coursing through his veins, "I rushed after her, narrowly avoiding a cart stacked high with barrels as I brought her and the kitten to safety."

"Sadly," Charlotte interrupted, "the little critter was entirely ungrateful. She left me with more than a few scratches. A mean little thing she was, intent on doing me harm."

Another significant and unamused glance at Anthony had him suppressing a smile with difficulty. "I helped tend to Charlotte's wounds in the inn, and the rest, as they say, is history."

"Then you owe your life to this good man, my dear," Mama said, looking at Anthony as though he was an angel just dropped from heaven.

"So," Tabitha said, her eyes narrowed as she looked at

Charlotte, "your insistence on fetching the post was, in fact, because you were going to meet *him*."

"I confess I find it all a bit baffling," Lillian said. "Charlotte saving cats and carrying on a clandestine courtship . . . I feel I hardly know you."

"We often assume we know more of our family members than we truly do," William said.

Anthony had no trouble identifying what was implied by his brother's comment. William harbored a great deal of resentment toward Silas. The two of them had never seen eye-to-eye, and the divide had grown since their father's death, when William had taken it upon himself to protect the family legacy—something Silas had little patience with.

"Indeed," Anthony said in a hard voice.

It grated him more than anything that he couldn't correct everyone's opinions about Silas. But this was Anthony's battle to fight. He was the one responsible, and he was the only one who believed Silas. Once he had evidence his family couldn't deny, he would prove what had truly happened that night. But until then, secrecy was of paramount importance. If word spread, Drayton would take measures to ensure any existing evidence of his wrongdoing was destroyed. Anthony needed to lull him into a false sense of security by saying nothing to defend Silas.

Aunt Eugenia set down her spoon and looked around. "What do you all say to a bit of dancing? We have three young men and three young women."

"And no music," Frederick commented.

Aunt Eugenia raised her brows until they risked disappearing beneath her scarlet turban. "Do we not? I still play quite proficiently, I'll have you know. And if Mrs. Mandeville is willing to turn pages, we will get along quite well."

"More than willing," Mrs. Mandeville confirmed.

"Then it is settled," Aunt Eugenia said, rising from her seat.

"After port, then," Anthony said.

His aunt waved an impatient hand. "No port. You drank my reserves dry last night. Besides, who needs port when there is dancing to be had?"

"I do," Anthony said, but perhaps Aunt Eugenia was beginning on the road to deafness, for she gave no sign of hearing him.

She led them into the drawing room, instructing Anthony and his brothers to move the few chairs while two servants were summoned to roll up the rug.

Aunt Eugenia spread out her skirts as she took a seat at the piano, Mrs. Mandeville standing beside her.

"Now," Aunt Eugenia said, "what shall we dance to?" Her smile grew. "Ah, I know just the thing." She rifled through the sheets in the mahogany cabinet beside the piano as Anthony moved the final chair out of the way. "A waltz. It is becoming all the rage, you know."

Anthony paused with the chair legs hovering over the floorboards. His gaze darted to Charlotte, whose face was full of chagrin. This was as unwelcome a development to her as it was to him.

It was just like Aunt Eugenia to make a choice that would force all the young people in the room into intimacy. She positively delighted in helping others tiptoe along the line of propriety.

Aunt Eugenia ordered Lillian and William to be partners, and Tabitha and Frederick to be partners, and the six of them took their places in the middle of the floor.

By then, Charlotte seemed to have resigned herself to the task at hand. Across the set, she smiled at Anthony in a way that made him narrow his eyes in suspicion. Before the music began, she walked over to him, went on her tiptoes, and whispered in his ear, "I just wished to remind you that you are madly in love with me." The words tickled his ear and made something strange course through him.

"A needed but not entirely welcome reminder," he whispered right back.

She wore the same smile as she stepped back to her place in the small set, but he was beginning to recognize that Charlotte carried her mischief in her eyes.

Anthony bowed, and she curtsied, and before he knew it— or was prepared for it—they were pressed together in a way that made it all but impossible to look anywhere but those mischievous brown eyes.

"I wanted to give my personal thanks," she said, "for that gripping story you recounted at the dinner table."

Pain shot through his toes as she crushed his shoe with the heel of her slipper.

"Oh dear," she said, eyes wide as an innocent babe's. She was anything but that. "Forgive me."

He smiled through gritted teeth. "I couldn't allow their ignorance of your heroics to continue when *you* were so kind to inform them of the depth of my feelings for you."

"And yet you fashioned yourself the hero of the cat story in the end, as well, didn't you? Saving the poor creature and me from all those carriages."

He slipped his arm around her waist, and she followed suit as they began twirling, their faces a matter of inches apart.

"What can I say?" Anthony said. "I was as moved by your helplessness as you were by that of the cat. Much about your description felt . . . familiar. What did you say? About the cat being entirely ungrateful and leaving you with scratches? A mean creature, intent on doing you harm? Something like that, was it not?"

She struggled against a smile, making victory flash through him like lightning.

"I still possess evidence of my run-in with those claws," he said, pulling back his sleeve enough to show the faint marks which remained from her nails.

Her cheeks tinged with pink. "Perhaps you should take more care. You nearly undid us with that story," she said, though there was no rancor in her voice. "My sisters are well-aware, as you heard, that I have no liking for cats."

"As are my *brothers* well-aware that I am not the type of man to throw himself at the feet of a woman and stalk her like prey."

"Perhaps not motivated by *love,* but you did appear at my door unannounced and unwanted, threatening me unless I conceded to your demands, all of which made me *feel* very much like prey."

"I was desperate," he said, annoyance pricking him at the reminder of how little good any of it had done him.

"Speaking of which," she said, drawing even nearer. "I need your help."

He tried to ignore the sweet scent that enveloped him with every movement she made. "And what, precisely, do you call the service I rendered you last night?"

She pulled back. "You mean claiming we were engaged?"

Through the corner of his eye, Anthony glanced at the others to see whether they were watching. "You are in love with me, remember?"

Her nostrils flared, but she regained control of her expression, smiling without humor. "You truly do fancy yourself a hero. And I your little kitten."

"With the claws of a tiger," Anthony replied.

She gave a scoffing laugh. "Very well. If you are such a hero, you will help me with the subject of my next caricature."

Anthony's face screwed up.

"Madly in love, remember?" she said.

With a sigh, he adjusted his expression to something more pleasant. "Why do you need my help?" They began to spin about the room again, each with a hand around the other's waist, one hand held above their heads. "You have done well enough without me before now."

Charlotte took a moment before responding. "I need your help because I only wish to target those who deserve it."

Anthony searched her face. Did she think he merited the caricature she had drawn? He could only assume so. She made no secret of how little she thought of him.

"Surely," she said, "you can think of someone who deserves that their dealings or foibles should be made more widely known."

Anthony's mind went immediately to Drayton. No one deserved to be publicly flogged more than that man. Of course, Anthony wanted a great deal more than for the man to simply be humiliated. He wanted Silas's freedom. But that was not within reach—nor was he certain it was even possible anymore. Why not use the resources he had to hit back at the devil?

But no. Anthony couldn't settle for such a paltry victory. Neither did he wish to alert Drayton to the fact that he was being watched.

"Give me a moment to think," he said.

Charlotte nodded as they finished the last figures of the dance.

Aunt Eugenia insisted on another song, and another one after that. Before she could command a fourth, Frederick insisted he must say goodnight on account of wishing to be present to watch the proceedings in Parliament first thing in the morning.

Charlotte capitalized on the opportunity to plead their excuses, as well, pointing to their journey back to Stoneleigh in the morning.

They all bid farewell to one another and safe travels to the Mandevilles, and Anthony walked them to their awaiting carriage.

"Well?" Charlotte said to him as her sisters climbed in. There was no stated question, but Anthony knew what she was asking.

He hadn't yet given her any information for her caricature.

"I will write to you," he said, pushing the matter off until some later time. Feeling the gazes of his aunt and Miss Mandeville upon him, he took her gloved hand and brought it to his lips. He pressed a kiss there, then straightened and looked at it with a small smile, brushing his thumb along the covered nails. "My little kitten."

Charlotte tried and failed to suppress a smile as she pulled her hand away. "Goodnight, Tony."

He chuckled softly as she stepped into the carriage, and soon, she was gone.

Good riddance, he thought. But he didn't truly feel it.

"I mislike her returning home," Aunt Eugenia said as they watched the carriage turn and disappear at the end of the street.

"Why?" Anthony asked. Misgiving suddenly crept into his stomach. What would be expected of an engaged couple, madly in love? Stoneleigh was not so far that Anthony had an excuse to go a fortnight without seeing his betrothed. Should they be spending a great deal of time together?

"I want her near so I can keep an eye on things. It would be like you to make a muddle of things somehow, and I like Charlotte."

Anthony's brows pulled together. "Do you?"

She gave a definitive nod as she availed herself of his arm to help her up the steps. "Almost better than I like *you*."

"Well, that is not saying much, is it?"

But it was. Aunt Eugenia could be both exacting and eccentric in her taste, for clothing, food, and people.

And yet she liked Charlotte.

That made one of them, at least.

14

CHARLOTTE

Charlotte should have known there would be no post at The Crown and Castle. At least not the post she wished for. She should have known by the reluctance Anthony had exhibited that he would not give her information for a caricature.

These were the people he interacted with at parties and balls and the opera. He was far too much like them to wish to make their indiscretions or foibles public.

She took the two pieces of post from Mary and slipped out of the inn before Mr. Digby could catch sight of her.

Charlotte envied Anthony—not his association with the *ton* but the fact that he was not obliged to find some bit of provocative information to satisfy Mr. Digby and the gossips. She had almost forgotten what it felt like to live without worrying about such things.

She kicked at a patch of weeds growing on the side of the road that led to Bellevue, wishing she could give Anthony a piece of her mind. Did he not care whether she was exposed?

Perhaps not. As a gentleman from a well-to-do family, his

reputation could withstand great blows. Charlotte's, on the other hand, could suffer from a soft breeze. Not to mention he was not even aware of Digby's threats.

What would she do now? She had nothing but inconsequential trifles about the eccentricities of the wealthy, and Mr. Digby wouldn't be satisfied with those.

Charlotte wished she could simply run away from it all—from the caricatures, from her engagement to Anthony, from the lies it all required. It had all started out so innocently, with noble aims, even. How had it come to such a pass as this, where she was lying to those dearest to her and desperate for the veriest morsel of gossip?

She removed her bonnet as she stepped inside her home, setting the post on the table in the entry before making her way up the stairs to her bedchamber. There was no more time to waste. She needed a caricature if she wished for Mr. Digby to pay her. Perhaps if she thought hard enough, she could remember something someone had said at Mrs. Ashby's house the other night. She hadn't been focused on amassing gossip at the time, for her efforts had been targeted upon pursuing her family's interests, but she was beginning to regret that.

Not that she wished to cast aspersions on the characters of anyone she had met. They had all been shockingly pleasant.

Half an hour later, she was seated at her escritoire, not even a hint of ink on the paper in front of her, when she spotted someone walking briskly toward Bellevue. She narrowed her eyes and watched as the boy drew nearer.

"Focus, Charlotte," she said, forcing her eyes back to the paper. Lord Preston boarding up half of his windows was simply not interesting enough. "Think!"

But the knock on the door, the muffled voice of Tabitha as she spoke to the boy, and the subsequent thud of footsteps on the stairs were too distracting.

"Letter for you, Charlotte," Tabitha said from outside of her door. "From *him*."

Charlotte shot up from her seat and rushed to the door.

Tabitha smiled at her knowingly, letter in hand.

Charlotte reached for it, but Tabitha pulled it away, turning to inspect the front. "I have always wished to read a letter between two real lovers. What sort of things do you say to one another?"

"Give it to me, Tab, or I shall tell Mama you escaped to the balcony with Mr. Robbs the other night." Under no circumstances could Tabitha be permitted to read what was inside that letter. But *not* because it would be full of poetic declarations of love.

Tabitha sighed and handed it to her. "You did not used to be so secretive, you know. I think I prefer the old version of you." She strode off toward her own bedchamber.

Charlotte swallowed, her gaze remaining on her sister's door even after it had closed. She preferred the old version of herself too. She missed the openness she used to enjoy with Tabitha and Lillian.

But that time was past, and there was little she could do about it. Anthony was the only one she could confide in now, and that was a very lowering thought indeed.

She opened the letter and hurried through its contents, breathing out relief at the information there. He *had* given her what she needed: reports of Sir Geoffrey Hamilton paying for the smuggling of Catholic relics and artifacts, among other things.

"Bless you, Anthony," she whispered, bringing the letter to her chest in an embrace.

She set the letter on the escritoire and picked up the quill again, letting the feather brush against her temple as she stared out of the window and decided exactly what to draw.

Charlotte followed Mary into Mr. Digby's office, where he sat behind a desk, a host of papers scattered before him. He glanced up and gathered them up hastily.

"A knock would be appreciated, Mary," he said testily.

Charlotte focused on the papers, her curiosity immediately piqued at his suspicious behavior. What was he afraid they might see? It did not surprise her that the man harbored more secrets than hers, but she wondered what sort they were.

"Miss Mandeville," Mr. Digby said as he straightened the papers, then set them in the drawer of his desk, "I understand we are to offer you felicitations."

Charlotte had prepared herself for this, and she smiled. "Thank you. It is very kind of you."

"Felicitations?" Mary asked, looking between them.

"Miss Mandeville is betrothed to Mr. Anthony Yorke."

Mary's jaw slipped open.

Mr. Digby smiled at Mary. "I had a very similar reaction, for I could have sworn it was less than a fortnight ago that Mr. Yorke was here, asking your name. My, how quickly Cupid shoots his arrows."

Charlotte disliked the glint in his eye. She let out a trilling laugh. "Anthony is so diverting, is he not?"

Mr. Digby and Mary shared mystified glances.

"I charged him with the utmost secrecy about our courtship," Charlotte continued, "and it seems he was vigorous in his respect of my wishes, going so far as to pretend we did not know one another. In any case, I am grateful for your congratulations, but that is not why I am here." She pulled the caricature from inside her pelisse and handed it to him.

Mr. Digby unfolded it, letting his eyes run over the art. His mouth lifted at one corner. "This is . . . very good."

"Thank you." Charlotte was feeling more confident in herself today. Perhaps it was because she was pleased with the caricature, or perhaps she felt less afraid of Mr. Digby now that he knew she was engaged to a man with a reputation for being ruthless.

Either way, she found herself full of an unusual courage. "Perhaps we can settle the matter of payment."

Mr. Digby glanced up from the caricature, his gratification suffering slightly.

"It has been three weeks rather than two, after all," Charlotte added, keeping a pleasant smile but a firm gaze.

"Of course," Mr. Digby said, passing the caricature to Mary. He opened a drawer and pulled out a wooden box, which he opened with the small key retrieved from a chain around his neck.

Charlotte's eyes fixed on the abundance of notes as he counted out a few of them and some coins besides. How much of the money in this secret trove was ill-gotten gains from taking advantage of desperate people like Charlotte?

Whatever the source, Mr. Digby was clearly quite plump in the pocket. Charlotte, on the other hand, couldn't help but lay awake at night, wondering what would come of her family once her engagement to Anthony ended. They might wait until the most propitious time, but they couldn't possibly avoid *all* scandal, and it would attach more vigorously to Charlotte.

Mr. Digby straightened the notes remaining in the box, then shut the lid and handed her the money.

As she took it, Charlotte's boldness took flight in her chest. If there was any time for bravery, it was now, when Mr. Digby was pleased with her work and newly aware of her connection to the powerful Yorke family. "There is one other matter I wished to discuss with you," she said before she could lose her nerve. "No doubt you have noticed the growing reluctance of your customers to convey gossip within the walls of The Crown and Castle. While business has grown for *you* as a result of the caricatures, my part in our arrangement now requires a great deal more ingenuity. Enough that I believe an adjustment may be merited."

Half of her hoped he would agree to it, while the other half hoped he would tell her their arrangement was at an end.

Mr. Digby stared at her, his jaw working, his face slowly but surely taking on a redder hue. "An adjustment?"

"Yes. It is my name at risk, after all, and I am certain you agree that my compensation should reflect that. Perhaps a guinea per piece?"

The vein in his forehead throbbed behind his mottled skin at the near doubling of her price.

Charlotte waited with as pleasant and unhurried an air as she could manage, even though her heart felt ready to burst with the force of each beat.

Mr. Digby opened the box again, and her heart soared as he pulled out eight shillings. He shut the lid again, then locked the box, and set it back in its place.

Rising from his desk, he walked over to Charlotte and met her gaze.

She could hardly believe he had agreed so readily to her demand, but she itched to take the money from his hands, eager to add to the reserve which had dwindled from their time in London. But Mr. Digby had not yet extended it to her.

"I wonder," he said, "if Mr. Yorke is aware of your . . . endeavors here." The words were harmless enough, but the way he watched her intently as he fiddled with the coins was anything but that.

He was becoming increasingly threatening, and Charlotte was tiring of it. "He is fully aware, of course."

Mr. Digby cocked a brow, as if he was skeptical.

Charlotte suddenly wished Anthony was there with her. Would he stand by her, she wondered.

He would. For all their disagreements, she knew that with almost perfect certainty.

"And what was his opinion of the caricature you drew of *him*?" Mr. Digby asked. "It was hardly the sort of thing a man would appreciate from his betrothed."

Charlotte laughed softly, though it was the question she had dreaded the most. How was she to explain the motivation behind the drawing? "You will have to ask him when next you see him, for it was his idea. He worried people might suspect the truth about us, you see, and feared rumors would spread before he could explain his intentions to his aunt. Mrs. Ashby is so particular, you know."

Heavens. She was becoming far too adept at untruths.

Mary was staring at her, brow furrowed and something very much like hurt in her eyes. It made Charlotte's stomach twist and churn.

"I see," Mr. Digby said slowly, but she was not at all certain he *did*. He began shaking the coin in his palm gently. "It is only that, well, it has been my understanding of the Yorkes that they place high value on propriety and reputation. I cannot imagine they would be pleased if the truth of your undertakings here became public knowledge."

There it was again—the heavily implied threat. She could not let Digby see even a sliver of fear. She held his gaze firmly as she spoke. "Fortunate, then, is it not, that it is only Anthony and the three of us who know that truth?"

Mr. Digby nodded. "Fortunate indeed. Though, a tongue

can slip . . ." A coin between his fingers fell, but he caught it deftly in his other pudgy fist.

Charlotte's teeth pressed together with such force that her head began to ache. But she smiled despite it. "It can. But I trust it will not. As you said, the Yorkes are particular about their reputations, and Anthony is even more so about guarding mine. He would not allow it to be sullied without grave consequences to the responsible party."

Heart thudding against her chest, she put out her hand for the money.

Mr. Digby looked at her for a moment, then reluctantly gave her the coins, which she slipped into her reticule. She could hardly believe her own gumption—making threats on Anthony's behalf. Threats she wasn't entirely confident would be carried out if her reputation *did* become sullied. Perhaps Anthony would grasp at the excuse to end the engagement, pleading ignorance of her vulgar occupation. Then, she would be well and truly ruined.

She could only hope Mr. Digby found her story credible enough not to put it to the test.

"Mary, would you walk me to the door?" Charlotte asked.

The maid, who hadn't said a word since Mr. Digby had offered his congratulations to Charlotte, quickly nodded and followed her out.

Neither of them spoke until they were in the bustling inn yard, where the call of ostlers and drivers and the clomping of hooves were enough to cover their conversation.

Charlotte's eyes fixed on a small boy, holding the reins of a horse that towered above him while the ostler tended to the bridle. "Who is that?"

Mary followed her gaze. "Patrick?" Her lips flattened as she watched him draw back nervously as the horse pawed the cobbles impatiently. "'Tis Digby's nephew come to work here. His mother needs the money."

"But he cannot be above six years old."

"Five, miss," Mary replied darkly, shaking her head. "He's become Digby's boy-of-all-work, but the task he's charged with most often is wandering amongst the guests to elicit sympathetic coin."

"Of which Mr. Digby swiftly relieves him?"

Mary nodded as the ostler took the reins and shooed the boy impatiently. Patrick scurried off toward the door and disappeared inside.

Pulling her eyes away, Charlotte reached into her reticule and took out a few of the coins. She took Mary's hand and set them in her palm, closing the maid's fingers over the cold metal. "There is your portion of the earnings."

"But, miss," Mary said with round eyes as Charlotte released her hand. "'Tis far too much."

"Nonsense." Charlotte cinched her reticule strings. "You deserve every last penny."

"But I did not even help with this week's drawing."

"And yet, without you, I could not have done any of the others. You have been a true friend to me in all of this, Mary, and I thank you for that."

Mary clenched her hand into a fist around the money, eyes shining with gratitude. "No, miss. Thank *you*." Her gaze became more somber, and she glanced around to ensure no one was listening. "What was all that about, though, miss? Are you truly engaged to Mr. Yorke?"

Charlotte did not respond immediately. It was one thing to lie to Mr. Digby, but Mary . . . Mary had been there when Anthony and Charlotte had met. They had spoken about him enough that she would not easily believe the untruths Charlotte had told.

"If I tell you this, Mary," Charlotte said, "you mustn't tell a soul."

"Of course not, miss," she said with wide, earnest eyes.

Pulling her farther from the few people in the yard, Charlotte recounted what had happened in the past week—the diary and the visit from Anthony, then the ball and the sudden, unwanted engagement.

"But that's awful," Mary cried.

"It is," Charlotte replied. "But there is nothing to be done. At least, not yet."

"But are you not afraid of him? What do you think he wants with that diary?"

Charlotte chewed her lip, shaking her head. "I do not know. But whatever it was, he did not find what he wanted."

"How terrified you must be, having to spend time with him like that."

Charlotte smiled slightly as she thought on Anthony. "I am not afraid of him, Mary. I can manage. But Mr. Digby mustn't know."

"He won't, miss. Not from me."

They bid one another goodbye and parted ways, Mary toward the inn, and Charlotte toward the street.

When Charlotte caught sight of Patrick standing just inside the open inn door, however, she reached inside her reticule and took out a few of the last remaining coins. Looking for any sign of Mr. Digby, she crouched down in front of the boy.

"Patrick, is it not?"

He nodded, his round eyes watching her warily.

"If I give you something, can you make sure your mama gets it?"

He nodded again.

"You mustn't give it to anyone else, not even your uncle. Do you understand? I wish very particularly for it to go to your mama."

"Aye, miss."

She revealed the coins she was holding, and his mouth opened wordlessly in surprise. "Do you have somewhere to put them?"

He fumbled with the pocket of his patched coat, opening it to show her.

She slipped the coins inside. "Remember. Those are only for your mama."

"For mama," he repeated.

"There's a good boy, Patrick." She rose to her feet, offered him a last smile, and strode off toward Bellevue.

15

CHARLOTTE

Charlotte counted the money in her box a third time. It was a respectable amount, but not nearly as much as she would like it to be. Would it ever be enough?

Her mind had explored every possible scenario of the future, from her exposure and ruination to Lillian and Tabitha making matches. In the first event, this money would certainly help, but only for a short time. Charlotte would have to find another way to make a living.

In the event that Lillian and Tabitha both wed, the money would ensure Mama could live comfortably on some of it, in addition to whatever Tabitha's and Lillian's husbands could spare.

And if Lillian and Tabitha wed *well*, Charlotte's sisters *and* Mama would be completely taken care of, and Charlotte could use her saved money to start some new endeavor of her own.

Ironically enough, as an engaged woman, marriage for herself felt like a distant and unlikely option. Who would want her after she had been discarded by Anthony Yorke? Perhaps someone, but would Charlotte want *him*?

"Charlotte!" Lillian's voice called from downstairs.

Charlotte hurried to conceal the box under the loose floorboard, then went to open her door and peer down the stairs.

Lillian held a letter. "This just came for you. Private messenger." She cocked a brow.

Charlotte's stomach tumbled and turned as she went down the stairs. Anthony had written her again? The last letter had only been sent because he had assured her he would give her information for the caricature. What reason could he possibly have for writing a few days later?

"The best part about the amount of post you are receiving," Lillian said, "is that Mama has stopped worrying quite so much over *the letter*."

Charlotte retrieved the letter, and Lillian went back to her book on the parlor sofa. Charlotte rather thought Mama's lessening fear of the dreaded letter was centered in the fact that she believed her second daughter to be on the verge of marrying a gentleman. How little did she know.

Charlotte broke the seal and unfurled the paper, then frowned. It was *not* from Anthony; it was from his aunt.

Her eyes raced curiously over the fine script.

Tabitha's head peeked around the doorway from the dining room, and her gaze went straight to the letter. "What is it?" she asked, coming over to look over Charlotte's shoulder.

Charlotte shifted to prevent her from seeing the letter, and Tabitha went still.

"Ah," she said, the warmth in her manner all but disappeared. "Another secret letter from Anthony, is it?" She walked toward the sofa and took a seat next to Lillian.

Charlotte shut her eyes. The distance between her and her sisters grew ever wider. The entire purpose to everything she was doing was to protect them, and yet somehow, their friendship was suffering more than ever.

"Here." Charlotte took a seat beside Tabitha and handed her the letter. "It is from Anthony's aunt."

Tabitha searched Charlotte's face, then took the paper. Her gaze flew over the lines, and her eyebrows crept up.

"What, all of us?"

Charlotte nodded.

"Mama!" Tabitha called. "We are to go to London again!"

Charlotte snatched the letter right back. "*That* is why I keep secrets," she hissed, "for *you* certainly cannot."

"May I see?" Lillian asked.

Charlotte reluctantly handed her the letter.

"Why should I not tell Mama?" Tabitha asked. "She must pack just as the rest of us must."

"Because I am not at all certain we should accept," Charlotte said.

"Why ever not?" Tabitha asked.

Charlotte had no ready response for this, for she could not say the truth: she hardly thought Anthony would appreciate having to devote more time to keeping up the appearance of their engagement—and Charlotte agreed with him. Mostly, at least.

"I see no reason not to accept, either," Lillian said, handing the letter back. "It is a very generous offer, and naturally, you must wish to spend more time with Anthony."

"Naturally," Charlotte said in what was surely the least natural voice she had ever used. She *had* enjoyed being in London, though, despite the chaos of everything that had happened. If it had not been for the stress of the caricature, she might have even been a bit sad to come home.

But the more time she and Anthony were required to spend amongst their families and the *ton*, pretending to be in love, the more likely they were to make an error—or strangle one another.

Mr. Digby had not been wrong when he had said *a tongue can slip*, and such a slip from Charlotte or Anthony would have grave consequences.

"But what an imposition we would be," Charlotte said, grasping for an excuse.

"If that were so," Tabitha said, "why would she have made the offer in the first place? Come, Charlotte." She grasped her sister's hands. "Do not deprive us of a month in London over such a qualm."

"What qualm?" Mama asked from the doorway.

"Charlotte wants to turn down a perfectly kind and warm letter from Mrs. Ashby inviting us all to stay with her for a few weeks, because the girl worries about *imposing*."

Mama's brows went up, and Charlotte sighed before handing her the letter to read for herself. So much for private correspondence.

"Kind and warm indeed." Mama said as she reached the end. Her brow furrowed as she looked at Charlotte. "Do you not wish to go?"

"It is not that," Charlotte lied, "but it seems such a long time for her to feed and house us. And what if important post were to come while we were away?"

Mama smiled. "Oh, Charlotte. Of course we will have any important letters sent on to London. As for the length of the stay, I cannot think she would have offered if she felt it would be a burden. She does not seem the type of woman to put herself in a position she would dislike."

Charlotte could not argue with that. Nor could she argue at all unless she wished to cast suspicion upon her feelings for Anthony. What woman in love would not jump at the opportunity to spend time nearer her beloved?

Besides, to decline would be an act of selfishness. Her sisters clearly desired to go, and it was the perfect opportunity for them to pursue the acquaintances they had made at the party—and develop other promising ones.

Charlotte forced a smile. "Very well, then. I shall respond favorably."

Tabitha stood. "That is well, for I would have taken you forcibly if you intended to refuse. Though, why you would need persuading to accept an invitation that will bring you and your dear Anthony nearer, I cannot fathom."

No. She could *not* fathom, nor could Charlotte tell her.

Loaded with an alarming number of valises and portmanteaux, the Mandeville carriage rolled to a stop in front of The Crown and Castle.

"Must we truly stop here?" Lillian asked.

"Perhaps," Tabitha said with a glint of mischief in her eye, "Anthony has been so long away from his beloved that he intends to travel to London *with* us."

"I trust not," Lillian said, "for we are cramped enough as it is."

"Do not be ridiculous," Charlotte said testily, pulling the hem of her skirt from under Tabitha's foot as she worked her way toward the door.

"It is *not* ridiculous, though," Tabitha insisted. "Did you not say he came to the house because he could not help himself after too long away from you?"

Charlotte's hand paused on the door handle. She was feeling irritable today, but she needed to compose herself. "I only meant it would be ridiculous of him when we shall be in London later today."

"Then why stop here at all?" Lillian asked again.

She and Tabitha were both eager to be in London again.

Heaven help Charlotte if everything went awry and she had given her sisters a taste for London, only for it to be snatched away from them when their family name was dragged in the mud.

Charlotte thrust her pride all the way down to the soles of her half-boots. "I am expecting a letter from him, if you must know."

Tabitha covered a laugh with a hand.

"Ridiculous for him to come," Lillian said with a cocked brow, "but not ridiculous for him to send a letter when you shall see one another in two hours?"

Mama smiled indulgently. "Go on, Charlotte."

Nostrils flared, Charlotte opened the door and stepped down. She would have not a shred of dignity left when all of this ended.

Mr. Digby was just inside, conferring with a manservant, and his brows went up at the sight of Charlotte. He dismissed the servant and smiled at her, inviting her to his small office. How she hated that false smile.

"What can I do for you, Miss Mandeville?" he asked.

"Nothing at all," she said. "I only wished to inform you that I shall be in London for the next few weeks."

"London . . ."

She nodded.

"And what of our agreement?"

The caricature of Sir George had generated a great deal of talk as well as an increase in custom for the inn. One piece of gossip inevitably generated more, and people were eager not only to discuss it accompanied by food and drink, but to see if they could garner more information from fellow guests.

"I shall send them by post," Charlotte said, keeping her chin up. She might not think much of Anthony, but others apparently did, and a woman engaged to him should hold her head high.

Mr. Digby frowned. "And how am I to be certain I shall receive them?"

The last thread of Charlotte's threadbare patience snapped with a twang. "Because I am giving you my word that you shall."

The man stared blankly at her.

Through her gloves, Charlotte's nails pressed into her palms, giving her a bit of sympathy for Anthony. "Would you prefer I send Anthony to provide *his* word? He will do it, but I cannot vouch for the pleasantness of the visit."

"No, no, no," Mr. Digby said hurriedly. "That will not be necessary. Enjoy your time in London, Miss Mandeville."

"You can be sure I will." She held his gaze a moment longer, then turned on her heel and left.

16

ANTHONY

"*Another* diary?" Anthony repeated, staring at Harris with incredulity.

They stood in the small alley between two buildings on a dark and dingy street. Dark alleys couldn't help but bring Charlotte to mind, but this one smelled of rotten fish, and, for all her faults, Charlotte did *not* smell of rotten fish. She smelled of violets, and he would have given an arm and a leg to transport her here this instant, pull her into his arms, and bury his face in her neck.

His brows drew together at the unexpected thought and the way it quickened his heartbeat.

"Aye, sir," Harris said with great energy. "Apparently, Marlowe kept the same sort of records for years. There are a whole host of diaries. Surely the man wrote down in *one* of them diaries what he told me."

Anthony said nothing for a moment. After their last efforts had come to naught, he was skeptical, but he couldn't quash the bit of hope Harris's words brought. He was desperate for news of anything that could prove helpful for Silas.

"And where are these diaries?" he asked.

"Still workin' to find that out, sir, but I've a meetin' with a man in two days. He should be able to tell us what we need to know."

"And this is the extent of what you have found that might help us?"

Harris's eyes darted to a man passing by. He watched until the man disappeared. "For now, sir. 'Tis our best hope, I think. Drayton ain't an easy man to take down."

That was certainly true. Of one thing Anthony was certain: the incident with his brother was far from Drayton's only sin. If he could have asked and been given honest answers, most members of the House of Lords and a good number of those in the Commons could undoubtedly have told tales on the man.

But that was not a path Anthony could pursue. The fear and awe in which Society held Drayton meant they would not only come up empty-handed, but those they questioned would likely alert the cur. That would not only injure their investigation but could well prove dangerous. Fatal, even. It only reaffirmed Anthony in his determination to keep his pursuits to himself. No one else should suffer for something he bore responsibility for.

"Keep me informed," Anthony said. "The minute you know anything."

"Of course, sir," Harris said.

"Is there anything I can do?" Anthony asked. "To speed things along, I mean."

Harris's mouth turned down at the ends, and he took a number of seconds before responding. "Ye're a member of White's, are ye not?"

"I am."

"So was Drayton until a few months ago. Do ye think ye

could get your hands on the old betting books? See if his name comes up anywhere?"

"I will look into it. Thank you."

"I won't let you down, sir."

Anthony gave a nod and strode out of the alley and in the direction of his apartments. It was unlikely there would be anything of use in the betting books, but he was eager to do *something*, and one never knew where information could lead.

When he reached his apartments, he had not even removed his gloves when he spotted a letter on the silver tray in the entry. Noting his aunt's script on the front of the letter, he tossed his gloves on the table and opened it.

Anthony,
Please come with all due haste.

He frowned, his heartbeat quickening. Was she ill? Perhaps he had been wrong when he had teased her about not being on death's door. She certainly wouldn't be the first person to hide an ailment from the public.

He pulled the bell just inside the parlor and instructed his carriage to be brought around immediately.

Within ten minutes, he was on his way, his mind vacillating between Silas's problems and his aunt's message. The carriage had not even come to a complete stop when he jumped down and ran to her door, using the brass knocker.

There seemed to be some sort of commotion inside, for the hum of voices met his ears—and then laughter. It faded quickly, though, and he frowned. Had he imagined it?

The door opened. "Good morning, sir," the white-haired butler said. "Please come in. She is expecting you."

Anthony stepped into the house, allowed Saunders to divest him of his hat and gloves, then followed him through the corridor. He was not being taken to Aunt Eugenia's room, which was a sign she was not on her deathbed, at least.

Saunders stopped at the morning room, turned the handle, and moved to the side as he opened the door.

Anthony nodded his thanks and stepped forward, only to stop short at the sight within. Aunt Eugenia was upright, looking very much alive and well as she spoke with all four Mandevilles.

All eyes turned to Anthony, and the talking ceased.

With a smile that stretched from ear to ear, Aunt Eugenia came toward him, arms out. "Surprise, surprise, nevvy."

He blinked as he received her into his arms, still trying to grasp what exactly was happening.

"Surprise?" Charlotte asked, meeting Anthony's blank gaze with her own confused one.

Aunt Eugenia pulled back, putting her hands on his shoulders. "I have invited Charlotte and her family to stay with us for the next few weeks. It seemed a terrible shame for the two of you to be apart when there is so much space in this house."

Anthony tried to laugh, but all that came out was a strange, staccato breath. "Staying with *us*, you say?"

"Yes, *us*. Of course you are coming too. Now, close that fly trap of yours"—she used a finger to shut his mouth—"and greet your bride."

Aware that the gazes of Charlotte's mother and sisters were all upon him, waiting for him to do as he had been bid, Anthony did his best to hide his dismay and strode over to Charlotte. The expression of chagrin on her face might have been comical if it hadn't so perfectly matched his own feelings.

He took one of her hands in his and stretched his mouth in a performative smile. "A surprise indeed, my dear." He leaned in and pressed a kiss to her cheek. It was soft—and warm with embarrassment.

He inhaled in spite of himself.

Gads, her scent was divine.

"I had no idea," she hissed into his ear, her grasp on his hand urgent and tight.

"A likely tale," he whispered back, pulling away before he could lose his head in that intoxicating scent.

The look of affront on her face faded the moment she saw his teasing eyes. Perhaps it was Harris's news that they had simply got their hands on the wrong diary before, but Anthony was feeling less put out by the Mandevilles' presence than expected.

He knew his aunt well enough to see her hand in all of this.

"Are you certain we are not too much of a burden?" Charlotte asked Aunt Eugenia. "You will miss your peace and quiet terribly."

"Aunt Eugenia detests peace and quiet, my love," Anthony said.

Charlotte's gaze darted to him at the form of address. Apparently, *my dear* was acceptable, but *my love* was simply too much. He was to be *madly in love* with her without using that word. They would have to clarify what her expectations of him were in all of this. They seemed to be very particular.

"It is true," Aunt Eugenia said. "I was never able to have children of my own, which is why I have made it my business to host and attend boisterous parties as often as I may—to drown out my loneliness. Shall we get you all settled? Your bedchambers have been prepared, and once you have freshened up, there will be meats and cheeses in the garden."

Aunt Eugenia linked her arm through Anthony's, preventing him from staying behind as she escorted the Mandevilles upstairs and to their respective bedchambers, all divested of Holland covers and looking neat as a pin. Exactly how long had she been planning this surprise?

"And finally," she said as they reached the second-to-last bedchamber in the corridor, "here is where you will sleep, Miss Charlotte."

"The Mandevilles are overrunning your entire house, ma'am," Charlotte said ruefully.

"Nonsense," she replied. "Anthony is not a Mandeville, and he will be in the bedchamber next to yours."

Anthony, who had been surveying the portrait of his late uncle which adorned the wall, whipped his head around. Aunt Eugenia ignored him, however, reminding Charlotte to take her time but not to forget about refreshments in the garden.

Anthony craned his neck, peering into Charlotte's bedchamber. His betrothed closed the door with a smile at his aunt and a quick glance at him. But before she had done so, his suspicion had been confirmed.

"What?" Aunt Eugenia asked him, acting innocent as a newborn lamb.

"Adjoining bedchambers? I thought you wished to avoid scandal, not encourage it."

"Oh, hush. I know what it is to be young and in love. The minutes apart feel like days, and those together like mere seconds."

Anthony shook his head at her as they walked toward his bedchamber. "And here I came as fast as can be, thinking you were violently ill."

"I wrote nothing to put such a notion into your head. It was quite silly of you to think it, for you know I am strong as an ox."

"And stubborn as one too," he muttered.

"I heard that. *Someone* must get things done in this family. Now, are you not forgetting something?" She raised her brows expectantly at him.

"Like the fact that I haven't time to help you play host to

the Mandevilles at the moment? I may be engaged, aunt, but I still have obligations and *other* engagements to—"

"You mean with that grubby man I found you with in the Park? Let us have no more of that. What could you possibly prefer over spending time with your betrothed and her delightful family?"

Almost anything, Anthony nearly said. "Nothing at all, of course."

She smiled at him, pleased. "Good. Now, for that final thing . . ."

"And what final thing is that?"

She extended her cheek toward him and tapped it.

Anthony chuckled softly and leaned in. "Thank you, aunt, for the delightful surprise."

She beamed. "See that your belongings are fetched, and make yourself more presentable before coming outside for refreshments." And with that, she left him in the corridor and went off to—Anthony could only assume—meddle in someone else's affairs.

Anthony was certain he would be the last outside, for it took more than an hour for his belongings to arrive. But as he entered the small garden behind the townhouse, only Mrs. Mandeville stood present, and even she seemed to have arrived only shortly before him.

She turned at the sound of his approach and smiled with relief. "How glad I am to see you. I worried I had missed it entirely."

"I had the same fear," he replied. "But as the refreshments have not been touched, I think it is safe to assume otherwise." He took a plate from the small stack at the edge of the table and handed it to her.

She thanked him warmly and began choosing from amongst the options Aunt Eugenia had provided: cold cuts, various cheeses, and some sliced bread. Anthony followed her example, using the opportunity to observe Charlotte's mother from the corner of his eye.

She was a handsome woman, with light brown hair and a genuineness to her expressions that made her easy to like. Anthony estimated her to be near five-and-forty, though the wrinkles she wore made her look older. Little wonder for a woman tasked with settling three daughters in the world without the support of a husband.

"Your aunt is thoughtfulness itself," Mrs. Mandeville said. "I sincerely hope she shan't regret her invitation. I love my girls dearly, but they are a . . . vivacious trio."

"Which will suit my aunt very well, I assure you, ma'am."

She looked up at him, smiling appreciatively. "You are just as good and kind as she." She set her plate down and faced him, a bit of hesitation in her soft eyes. "We know each other only just, Mr. Yorke—"

"Just Anthony, if you please."

"Very well. Anthony, then. Despite how little we know one another, I must tell you how pleased I am that you and Charlotte found one another. She would dislike my saying this, but since my husband's death, she has taken a great number of our burdens upon her. Whenever the rest of us grow sullen, or whenever I have quaked at the prospects before us, she has been the one to remind me not to lose hope. She is the best of daughters, and I have no doubt she will make the best of wives —and you the best of husbands. She wants nothing more than to ensure the happiness of those she loves."

Anthony could not bring himself to meet Mrs. Mandeville's gaze and instead ran his finger along the edge of his plate. His experience of Charlotte was a far cry from the one her mother described, but he had seen her stubbornness and tenacity firsthand, and he was beginning to understand that it was on her family's behalf that it was all exercised.

"I have embarrassed you," Mrs. Mandeville said with chagrin. "Forgive me. I merely wished to thank you."

He frowned. If only she knew the truth: he had threatened her daughter and all but forced her into an engagement that was certain to damage her reputation if anything went awry. And even if it did not, the termination of it would see her name bandied about in a way no parent wished for. "Thank me for what, ma'am?" He forced himself to meet her gaze.

Her eyes shone with the threat of grateful tears, though her mouth was pulled into a trembling smile. "For loving my Charlotte."

He broke his gaze away again. How was it that he could tell a blatant lie to pursue Silas's freedom, but he could not even bring himself to meet the gaze of a near-stranger?

"She tries to appear independent and self-sufficient," Mrs. Mandeville continued, "and she puts everyone else's needs before her own. But behind the façade—"

They turned at the sound of a door closing.

The three sisters were walking toward the refreshments, laughing together. Anthony's gaze fixed on Charlotte in the middle.

The sight of her with such a carefree smile, flocked by the people she was doing everything in her power to make happy, held him momentarily transfixed. What would Mrs. Mandeville have said if she had been able to finish her thought? What *was* behind the façade? And why did Anthony suddenly wish so fervently to break through it?

The Mandevilles *were* a vivacious family. As they became more comfortable and more confident that they were not expected to keep quiet or simper, their laughter became more frequent.

Anthony watched with a growing feeling of envy. The Mandevilles' interactions reminded him vaguely of the sort of relationship he had once enjoyed with his brothers. Silas's escape to France had changed that, though. The scandal had rocked the family to its core, cracking the foundations. The secrets Anthony kept had only deepened that divide.

Once the refreshments had been eaten and everyone had returned indoors to rest and prepare for dinner, Anthony paced in his room. He had yet to speak in private with Charlotte, and it had become more apparent than ever during the time in the garden that they sorely needed to discuss their plan. They could not spend hours on end with her family and his aunt without such a thing.

He glanced at the door that led to her adjoining bedchamber. He *could* simply knock on it—it would be easier to be private with one another that way. But somehow, he doubted Charlotte would appreciate the presumption on his part—or the intimacy. He couldn't forget the way she had looked when he had called her *my love*.

With a sigh, he turned his gaze from the adjoining door and strode to the one that led to the corridor. He would do things the proper way.

He opened his door and stopped short at the sound of Mrs. Mandeville's voice nearby. He pulled the door most of the way closed again, stopping before it could make the *click* that would alert her to his presence.

"You look splendid, my dear," Mrs. Mandeville said as she stepped out of Charlotte's bedchamber and into the corridor. "No wonder Anthony whisked you off to that balcony t—"

"Mama!" Charlotte's scandalized whisper made Anthony smile.

Mrs. Mandeville begged forgiveness in hushed but unapologetic tones, and the sound of her light and retreating footsteps followed.

Anthony waited a few minutes until he was satisfied there was no danger of her returning, then he left his room to knock on Charlotte's door softly. The door creaked, opening slightly, not having been properly shut.

Charlotte was seated upon her bed, a handkerchief in hand. Her head came around at the creaking, and she stared in consternation at him through eyes that glistened.

She turned her head aside. "Go away." Even had he not seen the tears, the quality of her voice would have alerted him that she was crying.

After a moment's hesitation and a quick glance down the empty corridor, Anthony slipped inside and shut the door, his heart feeling odd and heavy.

"Not until you tell me what is wrong."

"Nothing. See?" She turned toward him with a forced smile, but her pink nose and cheeks, her glistening eyes, and the way her lashes stuck together betrayed her.

He strode over and took a seat on the bed beside her. "We are engaged, Charlotte. You should be able to tell me what ails you."

She turned to look at him, her eyes brimful of tears but her brows turned down in frustration. "Our engagement *is* what ails me, Anthony." She shook her head and stood. "I cannot do it anymore. I cannot continue lying to Mama or Tabitha or Lillian. I *cannot*."

Anthony stayed silent, frowning as he watched her walk to and fro. Her mother had been right. She looked beautiful, even in her sorrow. Or anger. Anthony wasn't entirely certain what to call it. All he knew was that seeing her in this vulnerable state was quickly evaporating whatever dislike for her remained in his heart.

"Mama asked when we plan to be married," she said, "and what could I say?"

"What *did* you say?"

She scoffed, dashing a tear from her eye. "That we cannot agree which parish to be married in—the most ridiculous thing. I am surprised she believed me. And yet I am not, for I am not accustomed to lying to her. Or I didn't use to be." She clenched her eyes shut and brought her hands to her forehead, pressing her fingers against it.

She was distressed—that much was certain. And if he had not walked in, Anthony could only imagine she would be crying silently rather than trying to guard her pride with anger toward him. The façade, as her mother had called it.

Anthony rose and walked over to her. "Naturally, we will be married in *my* parish."

She dropped her hands and stared at him, the incredulity in her eyes contrasting sharply with the tears there. "This is all *your* fault"—she jabbed her finger into his chest, and he caught her by the wrist—"and yet, you stand there and tease me, as though it was a laughing matter?"

"I would rather see you laugh than cry," he replied.

She stared at him, her gaze hard and her nostrils flared so that he thought she might slap him with her free hand. But then she swallowed, her eyes filling with tears as she stared her hatred at him until her chin began to tremble and Anthony's own throat began to feel thick.

He knew what it was to lie to one's family and to bear a burden too heavy. It was lonely. So terribly lonely.

He stepped toward her and, heart beating with a painful

ferocity, released her wrist, wrapped his arms about her, and pulled her toward him.

She pummeled his chest with her fists, but she did not pull away.

"It is all your fault," she said, punctuating each word with a hit.

Anthony did not fight the blows; he merely held her.

"I am sorry," he whispered.

Her thrusts grew weaker until they stopped altogether, her hands coming to rest on his chest. Her head slowly lowered to his shoulder as her chest rose and fell with silent sobs.

"You do not understand how terrible it is," she said into his coat, "lying to everyone about *everything*."

"I know better than you might think," he said softly.

There was silence for a moment.

"Tell them the truth, Charlotte."

Her breathing stilled.

"But . . ." she said.

"It is a risk," he said, his nostrils filling with the scent of her. "But if it will make you happy, and if they can be persuaded to guard our secret . . ."

She shook her head, a silent laugh shaking her shoulders. "Tabitha cannot keep a secret to save her life."

Anthony smiled into her hair. "I cannot say I am shocked to hear it." There was a pause as he took in a breath, but each time he inhaled, his arms itched to pull her closer. "You have my permission to tell them the truth. If you wish to."

"No," she said firmly, still holding fast to him. "You were right when you said we must wait a while longer, then find a way to end the engagement."

A sense of relief flooded Anthony, for if Charlotte told her family the truth, it would lead to questions about the reasons for the ruse—questions he could not yet answer. Not until he had the diary. Supposing this time it contained what Harris claimed it did. "I promise I will do whatever I can to ensure the least damage possible to your reputation."

"And to yours," she said, a smile in her muffled voice.

His lip quirked up at the edge. "Most especially to mine."

She let out a long, slow breath as they stood there, Anthony's arms around her.

"I still hate you," she said into his chest.

"And I you," he replied against the lump in his throat.

17

CHARLOTTE

The brushing of silks, the brilliant light from the scores of candles hanging on chandeliers, and the hum of chatter filled Charlotte's senses.

"This way," Anthony said, guiding her to the right.

Mama, Mrs. Ashby, and Charlotte's sisters followed behind as they made their way through a sea of people to Mrs. Ashby's private opera box. Above their heads, wispy feathers from headbands and turbans fluttered gently about, mesmerizing Charlotte.

"Yorke," a man said jovially, halting their progress. "Didn't think to see you here, but I'm glad to be wrong." He dipped in a quick bow as Anthony responded in kind, then urged the others to go ahead without them.

The man's eyes shifted to Charlotte, and his brows hitched. "Is this the bride I have heard so much about?"

Charlotte willed her cheeks to stay cool. Would she ever accustom herself to being called Anthony's bride?

"Bride-to-be," Anthony corrected, as though the distinc-

tion was of the utmost importance, which, to be fair, it was.
But not to others.

Smiling at the stranger, Charlotte jabbed Anthony with an
elbow as inconspicuously as possible and regretted it instantly.
She might as well have elbowed a statue. And yet, a statue's
arms could not have held her the way Anthony had held her
yesterday. Since their strange embrace in her bedchamber, she
had been taking notice of new and unwelcome things about
Anthony. The strength of his shoulders, for instance, and the
cut of his jaw. Or, just now, the unyielding firmness of his
body.

"Allow me to introduce you," Anthony said. "Charlotte, this
is Mr. Whittlesworth. Mr. Whittlesworth, this is Miss Charlotte Mandeville."

"Well *done*, Yorke," the man said as Charlotte curtsied.
"When are you two off to church, then?"

"Soon," Anthony replied noncommittally.

Mr. Whittlesworth slapped Anthony on the back. "What
are you waiting for, man? Better shackle that leg to yours
before she's whisked off by someone else." He winked.

"Your concern is noted," Anthony said.

"It's been an age since I last saw you," the man said, oblivious to the lack of Anthony's eagerness to pursue conversation
with him. "Not since before your brother ran off to France."

Anthony stiffened, and Charlotte stole a glance at him. She
still knew precious little about the Yorke family, but one thing
she was beginning to notice: any mention of Silas inevitably
made the air feel as thick as gruel. It was certainly maladroit of
Whittlesworth to mention the topic as casually as he had.

"If you will excuse us," Anthony said tersely, "we do not
wish to miss the opening."

Charlotte offered Mr. Whittlesworth a warm smile as she
ceded to the insistent pull on her arm.

"That was not very civil of you," she said.

"Neither was the way you jabbed my ribs."

"For good reason," she said. "If you insist on correcting everyone who calls me your bride, no one will believe this a love match much longer."

"You are *not* my bride," he said in a low voice as they threaded through more people in the corridor.

"I am," she said, matching his volume to prevent anyone from hearing. "It can refer to a woman shortly to be married, you know."

"Which you are not."

She shot him an annoyed look, but he was not looking at her. "Thank you, *Tony*. I am well aware of that. But the entire purpose of this miserable ruse is to ensure no one *else* knows it."

They reached the door to the private box, and Anthony opened it for her, forcing his mouth into a smile. "After you, my little kitten."

Charlotte offered a saccharine smile of her own, then laid a hand over his on the door handle, letting her fingernails press against it through her glove. She could hardly believe she had spent time in this man's arms yesterday. Agreeable time, no less.

Mrs. Ashby and Charlotte's family were already seated in the box, and Anthony and Charlotte joined them just as the opening act of *Il barbiere di Siviglia* began. Charlotte couldn't decide whether to direct her gaze at the stage or at the equally enticing view of those seated in the other boxes and below.

What would she have thought if she had known a few weeks ago, scraping for gossip about the *ton*, that she would be rubbing shoulders with them in a place like this? With a quick surveyal of those in the boxes opposite them, she counted three people who had been subjects of past caricatures. Now that she had the opportunity to observe them firsthand, she realized she had not done justice to Lord Muxton's figure or to Mr. Oteley's foppishness.

Her gaze settled on a woman in one of the boxes opposite. She was dressed opulently in a gown of violet, with a black gauze overdress and a matching black feather in her golden hair. Her eyes were fixed on—Charlotte followed her gaze—Anthony. It was not a gaze of passing curiosity but intent scrutiny. Familiarity, even, as though she was willing him to look at her.

Beside her, a handsome man in his forties, with streaks of gray near his temples, leaned in to say something and the woman broke her gaze away to respond.

Charlotte's eyes lingered until her own attention was claimed by the events unfolding on stage.

During the opera, they received more than one visit from people they had met at Mrs. Ashby's recent dinner party, and Charlotte watched with quiet pleasure as her sisters rekindled friendships with a few of the ladies and gentlemen from that evening.

When she happened to look back to the woman in the box opposite, she found the same steady gaze focused on Anthony again.

Charlotte glanced beside her, trying to understand what could be drawing the woman's attention.

Anthony's dark hair had been brushed to the side and his cravat tied in the Mathematical style. His lip pulled up at the corner as the audience laughed at something on stage. Charlotte was forced to admit that he *did* look more than usually handsome this evening. It might explain the woman's attention, she reluctantly admitted.

But when Charlotte's gaze returned to her, it was not Anthony but rather Charlotte herself who was the focus of her gaze. She forced herself not to shy away from it, and after a few seconds, the woman directed her attention to the opera.

"Who is that?" Charlotte asked, too curious to stop herself.

"Who?" Anthony asked.

"The woman across from us in the purple dress. She keeps staring at you. And at me."

His brown eyes searched until they settled on the woman. The muscle in his jaw jumped.

Charlotte's curiosity ignited. "Who is she?"

Anthony stared at the woman for a moment, something strange but unidentifiable in his eyes. "My greatest mistake."

An unfamiliar feeling flashed within Charlotte, and she frowned as she inspected the emotion and tried to put a name to it. But it simply made no sense. Why in heaven's name would she feel jealous?

She was becoming mixed up by the events of the past weeks. On some level, her mind must truly believe her to be engaged, which was what was making her feel this odd and absurd possessiveness toward Anthony.

His interactions with women were no business of hers, mistake or not.

The words had been bitterly said, though, and Charlotte couldn't help wondering what lay behind them. Had the woman rebuffed Anthony? Chosen the man beside her instead? Had she broken his heart?

The torture in his expression as he looked at her made Charlotte's stomach swim and her heart ache for reasons she didn't understand.

"And the gentleman seated beside her?" she asked.

Anthony's jaw tightened, and when he spoke, the words were quiet but harsh. "He is no gentleman."

"Who *is* he, then?"

"No one you need concern yourself with. I shan't let you within a dozen feet of him."

The savage protectiveness in his tone caught her off guard, sending a cascade of butterflies into her stomach. It should have angered her for him to act so managing, but it did not. It pleased her.

"As if you could stop me," she said, unsure whether she was being defiant for her own sake or because she was curious whether he was in earnest.

The blaze of fire she encountered in his eyes made her breath catch in her chest. "You can be certain I could. And would."

"Thankfully," she said, trying to maintain her composure amidst the mishmash of feelings within her chest, "I have no *desire* to come within a dozen feet of him. Will you not tell me his name, though? Or hers?"

"Enough of this, Charlotte. Did we come to ogle people or to watch an opera?" He turned his head toward the stage, his message unmistakable: the subject was not to be pursued.

Charlotte's interest was fully aflame now, but she forced her focus onto the man and woman singing at the top of their lungs on stage. Her gaze wandered again and again to Anthony, though.

She knew so little of her betrothed. He was a man full of secrets—secrets Charlotte wished valiantly she could pay no heed to, but her questions buzzed about like a swarm of bees trying to gain entry to a crowded hive.

What had happened between him and that woman? Was his hatred of the man a result of jealousy? And, the most persistent question of all: what had he wanted the diary for?

When it came time for intermission, all six of them vacated the box and made their way for the refreshments. Tabitha linked her arm through Charlotte's as they left the room.

"You will forgive me, won't you, Anthony?" she said. "For stealing my sister from you for a bit?"

Anthony chuckled softly as he held the door open. "Impossible."

And for the flash of a second, Charlotte wished he was serious.

She was carried away on the tide of Tabitha's conversation, for her sister was eager to discuss the events of the evening thus far. Charlotte glanced over her shoulder and found Anthony engaging Lillian in conversation.

Drink in one hand and a small berry tart in the other, Charlotte listened as Tabitha recounted her interaction with the gentlemen who had come to their box shortly after the opera had begun. Lillian soon joined them, and Charlotte's eyes searched for Anthony.

They found him with shocking ease, as though they had never truly lost sight of him. Charlotte paused with the drink at her lips at the sight of who he was with.

"Hold this," she said, handing her drink to Tabitha without even looking. Gaze fixed on Anthony, she picked her way through the crowd, her heart beating quickly.

Whatever Anthony's flaws, however much Charlotte claimed the blame lay with him for her recent misfortunes, he had come to her rescue when he had claimed they were engaged. He, too, was in an unsought betrothal, and it wasn't until this moment that she had considered what it was costing him—or who he might have wished to be betrothed to if circumstances had been otherwise.

It cost her nothing to come to his aid just now.

She reached for his hand as she approached, and Anthony's gaze shot to hers.

She looked into his frowning countenance with all the

admiration she could muster. "Here you are," she said, nestling up to his side. "I was looking for you."

His gaze searched hers, and Charlotte feared he would humiliate her by pulling away.

Instead, his frown lightened as his eyes stared into hers searchingly.

Charlotte's heart fluttered at the intensity and wonderment in his gaze, as though he was seeing her properly now.

Taking better hold of her hand, he brought it to his lips and pressed a kiss to the back of her glove, his eyes never leaving hers. "Forgive me, darling."

Charlotte's knees quivered, but she forced herself to finish what she had come to do. She let out a breathy laugh and looked at their audience. "How very rude of me. I hadn't realized you were in the midst of a conversation."

The woman in purple looked at her with those steady, blue eyes.

She looked to Anthony for an introduction, and the frown returned to his brow. "Lord Drayton, Miss Baxter, allow me to present you to Miss Charlotte Mandeville, my bride."

Charlotte sent a quick glance at him, but there was no time to decipher his motivation for using the word. The women curtsied, and Lord Drayton gave Charlotte a shallow bow.

"If you will excuse us now," Anthony said, "we only planned to stay until intermission."

Charlotte did her best to look unsurprised by this blatant falsehood. "It is sad but true. It was a pleasure to meet you."

"And you," said Miss Baxter, while the man only nodded.

Anthony guided Charlotte toward the door.

"Are we truly leaving?" she asked.

"Yes."

"What of your aunt and my family?"

"I shall send the chaise to fetch them home." He spoke with

a servant, instructing him to have their carriage brought around, then inform the people in Mrs. Ashby's box that Charlotte had gone home with a headache.

"A headache?" Charlotte protested, but when he set her hand back on his arm and guided them to the door, she made no move to resist.

They waited in silence until the carriage was brought around, at which point Anthony handed Charlotte up into the chaise, then followed her in. The moment the door was closed, Charlotte could keep silent no longer.

"I can only assume you forced us to leave early so you could take the opportunity to explain all of that to me."

Anthony stared through the window, his fist covering his mouth as the light of the passing lamps cast shadows across his brooding features. "You assume wrongly."

Charlotte watched him, trying to decide what to say and how far to push for answers. She didn't truly mind being made to leave the opera early, but how could he have known that? And yet, here he was, taciturn and giving every indication he meant to speak of it no further.

The sight of Miss Baxter must have affected him deeply for him to leave so suddenly. She sensed now was not the time for combativeness and conflict. Anthony had comforted her yesterday; perhaps that was what he needed just now.

"Anthony," she said.

His gaze flicked to her.

She swallowed. Somehow, it was more nerve-wracking to speak kindly to him than it was to say things calculated to ruffle his feathers. "You can confide in me." She smiled slightly. "We are engaged, after all."

Anthony held her gaze for a moment, then looked away. "Thank you."

The silence continued, and with it, her embarrassment and the feeling of rejection grew.

"You think me untrustworthy," Charlotte said, more as an explanation than a challenge.

He turned toward her finally. "Charlotte, you sell people's secrets."

"Not yours."

The muscles in his jaw shifted. "Truly, it is nothing about you. I do not confide in anyone. Not anymore."

There was that dashed enigmatic language he insisted on using. Who had he been accustomed to confiding in? Silas? Miss Baxter? "Perhaps you *should*. I promise you can entrust me with your confidences."

"And how forthcoming have you been with me about *your* secrets?" he challenged her.

"You *are* my only secret."

His gaze intensified.

She hadn't meant to say it precisely that way, but when she tried to correct herself, she found her lungs bereft of air. She swallowed, then spoke more quietly. "What I mean to say is that you already know my only secrets. You are the only man in the world who knows them."

They stared at one another across the dark of the chaise as it rocked from side to side over the cobbled streets. Anthony's gaze, usually so guarded and resolute, softened as he looked at her, as though searching for something in her eyes.

Whatever he was searching for, he must not have found it, for he turned his head to the window again, and the moment was gone as soon as it had come.

But Charlotte couldn't give up.

She chose her question with care, not wanting to begin with the subject that was weighing him down most. Heart beating at a clipping pace, she leaned forward and reached for his hand. "Anthony, what happened with Silas?"

His hand clenched inside hers.

"Surely, you know that," he replied.

"I know what people say," she agreed, "but I also saw the pain in your eyes when William refused to claim Silas."

His hand balled even tighter, and he pulled it slowly but firmly from her grasp. "I have no wish to speak of it, Charlotte."

She stayed where she was for a moment, her chest growing heavy with frustration. She leaned back on the squabs as the chaise came to a stop in front of Mrs. Ashby's lodgings.

Anthony opened the door and stepped down, then offered her his hand, his expression stern and unyielding.

She took his hand and descended, facing him as the horses pulled the chaise toward the mews. "I am only trying to help."

"Thank you," he said. "But I need no help."

She held his gaze for a moment, then gave a nod and turned away, refusing to let him see her disappointment.

18

ANTHONY

Anthony flipped through the pages of one of the betting books at White's, keeping a thumb on the page of the most recent wagers. He searched the names, looking for one in particular.

His eyes caught on Lord Drayton's signature, and his heart tripped as he hungrily read the names of the other parties, the stakes, and the subject of the wager.

His shoulders dropped. It was nothing but a bet over how long a pigeon would stay on a branch of a nearby tree.

With a sigh, he kept looking, flipping through page after page, slowly but surely losing hope he would find anything he might use against Drayton. Not that he had harbored any great hope when he had started.

Drayton came up a few more times, but none of the bets were anything out of the ordinary. The man was too smart to put his name to anything unsavory on paper. It was precisely why the diary had been so integral to Silas's case. Without that, they were unlikely to find anything incriminating. Certainly, such records must exist—financial records, for instance—but those who held them would naturally be in Drayton's pocket. They either stood to gain too much from his continuing success or to lose too much if they betrayed him. Both, perhaps.

Anthony cursed under his breath, shut the book, then strode out of the club. He pulled a paper from the inside of his coat pocket, unfolded it, and read over the short contents.

The street Harris had mentioned in the note was only a few minutes' walk, and Anthony traversed the distance more quickly than usual, for he was restless, eager for news.

Harris, on the other hand, was nearly a quarter of an hour late, and Anthony's temper was fraying at the edges when he finally appeared, wide-brim hat pulled low so it took a moment for Anthony to be certain it was him.

"Might you not simply tell me a quarter-past-three rather than saying three o'clock and obliging me to wait?"

The way Harris's mouth stretched into a grin sent a shock of hope through Anthony—one he refused to pay heed to until there was good reason. They had followed too many trails that had led nowhere.

"A quarter of an hour will prove well worth your sacrifice today, sir," Harris said.

Anthony raised his brows, waiting for Harris to elaborate.

Harris grinned, tipping his hat up slightly. "I've located the other diary."

Anthony's heart skidded to a halt. His gaze went to Harris's hands, but they were empty. "Where? Where is it?"

Harris's self-satisfaction flagged slightly, and he hesitated.

"You say you have it," Anthony said. "Then, where is it?"

"I said I *located* it," Harris clarified with a grubby finger.

Anthony stared, his impatience returning with force. "Meaning?"

"I don't have it, but I know who does."

"Who?"

Harris's hesitation returned.

"Who, Harris?"

He watched Anthony carefully as he responded. "Drayton, sir."

There was utter and complete silence.

Drayton had the diary they needed to prove that it was him and not Silas who had killed Langdon.

"But now that we *know* he has it," Harris said, "we can get our hands on it."

Anthony's teeth gritted together, his hope dashed to bits. "You're a fool, Harris."

"Perhaps. Or perhaps not."

"There is no *perhaps* about it. If Drayton has the diary, it is because he knows its value—he realizes it could ruin him. There isn't a chance he will let anyone get their hands on it. He has likely destroyed it already." Anthony turned aside, running a rough hand over his chin, despair beginning to rear its ugly head inside. Would Silas be forced to live the rest of his life an exile?

"Now, that is where you are wrong," Harris said. "Well, not about him not wanting anyone to get their hands on it, but about destroying it."

"And how would you know that?"

Harris grinned again. "I make it my business to know these things."

Anthony waited, jaw clenched.

"Servant talk, sir. The diary's been seen in a particular drawer of Drayton's at Barrington Hall. Apparently, he recognizes the value of the other information within it."

"And who is to say he has not ripped out the pages we need and burned them?"

"I thought of that, sir, and my informant assures me the diary is intact."

"And why did the servant not bring the diary to you himself instead of simply providing you with this information?"

Harris shot Anthony a significant look. "Because he knows what's good for him, sir. Drayton is a hard master, and he's been known to dismiss every maid and footman in the house when something's gone missin'."

Anthony shook his head and turned away again. "It is irrelevant. If Drayton has the diary, he may as well have burned it for the good it will do us."

"Unless you manage to make a visit to Barrington Hall," Harris said enigmatically.

Anthony whirled around. "Are you mad? The man would never invite me to his estate. Is this all you have to offer?"

Harris swallowed, then gave a reluctant nod.

Anthony's impulse urged him to scream out every profane word in his vocabulary. Instead, he clamped his teeth together and strode off.

Head in his hands, Anthony stared at the place where the grass and the stone intersected beneath the bench on which he sat in his aunt's garden.

He hadn't felt this defeated, this hopeless and alone since the night Silas left for France. Today was the first time since then that Anthony truly considered whether there was any way to bring his brother home, any way for him to atone for what had happened that night.

He simply couldn't live the rest of his life with this guilt in his heart or this burden on his shoulders. He would go mad.

The squeak of a door sounded, bringing his head up.

Charlotte stopped short in the doorway to the garden, her eyes on him.

She had been distant with him since the opera last night, and he couldn't blame her. She had tried to be kind to him, and he had been a cur in response. He had wanted to confide in her, had been on the verge of doing so, desperate to unburden himself to someone.

But then the memory of that night had returned. The last time he had trusted a woman, she had disappeared—to Drayton, apparently—and his life had turned into a shambles. His decision had hurt those he loved most. It was *still* hurting them, though Aunt Eugenia and William would never admit it.

"Forgive me," Charlotte said. "I hadn't realized anyone was in the garden." She turned and opened the door again to return inside.

"Wait." Anthony's voice came out rough as gravel—and almost pleading.

Charlotte paused on the threshold, then turned her head toward him.

He didn't want to be alone, and though his mind told him not to trust Charlotte, his heart told him she was worthy of that trust.

"Will you sit with me a while?" he asked. More difficult words he had perhaps never uttered—a cry for help. The help he had refused just last night.

Charlotte's gaze searched his long enough that he thought she might refuse, just as he had refused *her* last night. But she finally nodded, closed the door, and came to sit beside him.

They sat in silence for a time, Anthony leaning forward with his elbows on his knees as he gathered the courage to speak the words he had been keeping within him for months and months, unable to confide in anyone but Harris—and the man was hardly the sort of confidant one wished for.

Charlotte remained silent, reluctant, he could only imagine, to say anything after the way he had gone about things last night.

"Silas is innocent." A rush of nerves surged in his chest as Charlotte's head turned slowly toward him, her gaze alert and steady.

He kept his own fixed ahead as he continued. "Silas and I and another man—the one who was killed—had invested in Drayton's shipping business a few months after he created it. Things went well for a time, and we began to see profits. Promising profits. Then, profits began to decrease, and our largest competitor began to thrive—beating us to ports with similar shipments, pricing in ways that made it difficult for us to recoup our costs. At first, Silas suspected Langdon, for he was the one handling the books. But a confrontation between them made it clear that it was Drayton. The three of us decided to meet with Drayton and give him a chance to explain himself. Drayton agreed to meet after a party that same night."

Anthony shut his eyes and clasped his hands together rigidly as the memories flooded back. "In the weeks leading up to that night, I and many other men had been eager for the attention of Miss Baxter. But no one had yet been successful in capturing her attentions. On the evening in question, I attended the same party as Drayton. Miss Baxter was there, and for the first time, she chose to bestow her *precious* attention upon me." His nostrils flared. "When the hour for the meeting came, she begged me not to leave, and, like a fool, I submitted to her pleas, thinking Silas and Langdon could manage on their own. What need had they of me for a simple conversation?"

His clasped hands tightened, his knuckles going white.

How was it simultaneously so difficult and such a relief to speak these things? "When I returned home that night, it was to find Silas gathering his things in the dark, insisting he needed to reach Dover without delay. It was not until we were on our way there that he told me what had happened. Langdon was dead—shot by Drayton. Rather than kill Silas too and bring suspicion upon himself, Drayton claimed he and Langdon had confronted Silas for cheating the company, and that Silas had killed Langdon and fled. He told Silas to leave England and never return unless he wished to meet his end at the gallows. Silas took the next packet across the Channel, and that was the last time I saw him."

Charlotte's hand covered Anthony's. He stared at her delicate skin for a moment, then turned his hand in hers to hold it. It was soft and warm, everything the past year of his life had not been.

"But he cannot do that," Charlotte said. "Ruin another man's life for a murder he himself committed?"

"You of all people should understand the power a man like Drayton holds, Charlotte. He has title, money, influence. Not long after Langdon's death, he sold the company to our competitor, gaining majority share in their enterprise. There is precious little he cannot do."

"Perhaps that is true, but he shan't get away with it in secret." She squeezed his hand. "I have decided the subject of my next caricature, Anthony." Her eyes were bright and determined.

He turned toward her, grasping her hands in his. "You cannot, Charlotte. It is not enough and too much, all at once. If you expose him without evidence, he will come after you, and Silas will be no nearer to exoneration."

"Is that why you needed the diary?"

He nodded.

Charlotte clenched her eyes shut. "And I made it all but impossible for you to get it."

"It did me little good. The records inside were not recent enough to provide what we needed."

"What *do* you need?"

He lifted his shoulders. "Record of a conversation Marlowe overheard and recorded—Drayton admitting what had happened that night to one of his closest friends. But it is not in the diary you gave me. Evidently, Marlowe kept dozens."

"But then there is still hope! We need only obtain the right one."

Even in Anthony's despair, the way she said *we* brought a hint of a smile to his lips. There had been no *we* in all of this. Not really. William and Frederick couldn't be convinced of their brother's innocence. Silas could do nothing from where he was and seemed to have accepted the futility of trying. As for Harris . . . he was not helping Anthony for any motivation other than money.

It was Charlotte's sense of justice that put that look of indignant determination on her face. He understood better now what her mother had said about the burdens she had carried since Mr. Mandeville's death. Charlotte was not the sort of woman to sit back and let things happen.

But she didn't understand the gravity of the situation or the utter futility of her suggestion.

Anthony let out a sigh, and, realizing he had been stroking his thumb along Charlotte's, he stilled his hand. "Perhaps we could retrieve the diary, were it not Drayton himself who possessed it."

Charlotte's eyes widened, and she held Anthony's gaze. "He knows."

Anthony nodded, glad she realized the significance of the information. "He keeps the diary in a drawer at his estate outside Town. I have no doubt he is making good use of its contents to bend other people to his will."

"We must get it, Anthony."

He shook his head. "Impossible."

"Difficult and impossible are not the same."

"Charlotte . . . you do not understand Drayton's influence. *Everyone* stands in awe of him. His servants are terrified of him."

"*I* am not."

Anthony faced her so that their knees touched. Suddenly, a new fear filtered in around the heavy despair he felt. A fear for Charlotte's safety. "You should be. He killed a man. I have begun to suspect he was behind the death of Marlowe too."

"But he cannot get away with it, Anthony."

"I agree. Believe me, Charlotte. It is all I have thought about for months. You cannot understand how desperately I wish for Silas to return home, for everyone to know that it is honor rather than dishonor he deserves."

She nodded quickly.

"But Silas's freedom will have to be achieved some other way—how, I wish I knew."

Silence fell again between them, and the birds chirped merrily, utterly oblivious to the mood in the garden.

Despite the bitter taste of the reality he had to face, Anthony felt less despair than he had when he had first taken a seat on this bench. He let his gaze travel to Charlotte. She was staring straight ahead, her eyes bright and alert.

"All we need is a plan," she said.

He smiled slightly, touched by the depth of her devotion to the cause of Silas—a man she had never met. "I have realized that plans are harder to come by than I had previously thought."

She turned toward him, her body teeming with energy. "I will do it."

Anthony's brows pulled together. "Do what?"

"Obtain the diary."

"Charlotte . . ."

She took his hands again, as though trying to gather up every bit of his attention. "I need time with Lord Drayton. Can you help me with that?"

Anthony watched her warily, ignoring the way his body recoiled at the thought of her coming near the murderer. "He leaves in less than a fortnight."

"Leaves? Where?"

"Like many members of Parliament," Anthony said bitterly, "Drayton requires frequent respite from his burdensome duties. He has invited a dozen or so people to join him at his estate outside of London."

Charlotte smiled. "Perfect."

Anthony directed her with an expression meant to bring her back down to earth, for he could see precisely what she was thinking. "It is not a public assembly, Charlotte. It is a private party."

She raised her brows and smiled enigmatically. "You think me unable to gain an invitation to such a gathering? I can be quite charming, you know."

Anthony was coming to know that more and more each day he spent with her. "It is not your charms I doubt but Drayton's willingness to extend an invitation to an utter stranger."

"Not a stranger," she said, a finger up to correct him. "We are now acquainted—and I plan to pursue that acquaintance with vigor." She wrinkled her nose, as though realizing she had chosen the word poorly. "With . . . persistence, rather."

Anthony's mouth twitched.

"Are you laughing at me?" she asked with narrowed eyes.

He shook his head, but he could not contain his growing smile.

She kept her suspicious gaze on him for a few seconds, then continued. "What I need is an opportunity for me to pursue my acquaintance with Lord Drayton."

"With vigor?"

She shot him a look and ignored his comment. "If I have at least the opportunity, that will be sufficient. Can you manage it?"

Anthony's smile dissipated. "Charlotte, you cannot be serious."

She met his gaze, her own clear and unflinching.

"What, then? You gain an invitation for yourself to Drayton's estate, where you will promptly bamboozle him?"

"An invitation for *us*," she corrected. "We are engaged, remember?"

"Drayton falsely accused my brother of murder. If you think I will ever be amongst those he chooses to entertain in his home, you belong in Bedlam, not at Barrington Hall."

"I don't see why you shouldn't be invited."

Anthony gave a nod. "Bedlam it is."

She stood and began pacing in front of him, the hem of her dress grazing the grass and making the blades tremble as they emerged from beneath her skirts. "It seems to me that the general consensus is that your brother is, indeed, guilty. Even your aunt and brothers seem to think so, do they not?"

Anthony grimaced. "They do. Silas and Langdon had a strained relationship, and people were aware of it. And then, when Silas fled . . ."

"It made him look guilty," Charlotte finished with a grimace. "Well, it shouldn't be difficult to persuade Lord Drayton that you are of the same opinion. Perhaps you can even apologize to him for—"

"I would rather die."

Charlotte stopped her pacing, and their gazes held. "I understand your reluctance, Anthony, but if we are to obtain that diary and vindicate your brother, is it not worth a bit of sacrifice?"

Anthony's jaw worked and worked. She was right. He knew she was. But his pride balked at the thought of trying to ingratiate himself with Drayton.

What other option did he have, though? He had no promising avenues to explore. And, even supposing Harris found anything new to pursue, who was to say it wouldn't end in failure, just as their other hopes had?

"It is dangerous, Charlotte," he said, frowning deeply. "I cannot let you take that sort of risk."

She came to sit beside him again, smiling slightly. "I thought that might be an incentive to you. If things were to go poorly, the ensuing scandal would be an easy way to rid yourself of me."

His brows snapped together. Did he wish to be rid of Charlotte?

"But if you would rather," she said, "*you* can go in search of the journal. I can be the pretty face required to gain entrance." Her eyes twinkled at him, daring him to contradict her.

He couldn't help a soft chuckle.

"If he leaves as soon as you say, though," she said, "time is of the essence. I need enough opportunity to persuade him to extend us an invitation."

Anthony's heart began to beat more quickly. Charlotte was determined, already planning and plotting. He couldn't help but be carried along on the wave of her boldness and resolve. Something told him she could achieve whatever she set her mind to, no matter how mad.

Could they truly manage this plan of hers? Just as importantly, could they do it and keep their own reputations intact?

He had to believe they could.

Charlotte rose, returning to her quick pacing. Anthony's heel tapped anxiously on the ground, and he stood too, trying to think through the strategy such a plan would require. Much rested on Charlotte's shoulders, for Anthony had no confidence at all that, left to his own devices, he could manage to elicit an invitation from Drayton.

It would be difficult enough to play his own part. But for Silas, he could swallow his pride. Silas deserved that from him.

"If the house party is in less than a fortnight," Charlotte muttered to herself, "and we are there"—she looked to Anthony.

"A week," he said.

"A week. That leaves but one *more* week until our return to Stoneleigh. News of Drayton's crimes will be all over London by then, of course, which"—her eyes brightened—"will provide the perfect distraction from—" Her footsteps halted, and their eyes met. "The end of our engagement," she finished.

They stood a few feet apart, gazes fixed on one another.

"Yes," Anthony said, speaking past the odd blockage in his throat. "The perfect distraction, as you say." Why, then, did he feel a sliver of regret at the prospect?

Charlotte swallowed, nodding. "Then, we are agreed."

"We are," he said, ignoring the way he felt.

These emotions, they were only there because he had finally unburdened himself to someone. It was only natural his heart would revolt at the prospect of losing that confidant so quickly. It had nothing at all to do with wanting to be engaged.

As long as the end of their betrothal coincided with the end of Silas's exile, all would be well. Better than well. It would be everything Anthony had been wishing for.

It *had* to be all he wished for.

19

CHARLOTTE

Hair coiffed as close to perfection as possible and wearing—unfortunately—the same dress she had worn at Mrs. Ashby's dinner party, Charlotte's pencil flew in all directions across the paper on the escritoire.

She sat back and surveyed her work, her nose wrinkling. It was always difficult to decide precisely how to go about a caricature—what parts of the person to accentuate and exaggerate, what the scene should be, and how to best convey the secret. The feat felt more difficult than ever today as she attempted to draw a person she had never seen.

With a sigh, she stood, setting down her pencil and making her way toward the door. She had turned the small lock beneath the knob to ensure no one could enter from without, but she unlocked it, entered the corridor, and went to the door of the last bedchamber in the corridor: Anthony's.

After a moment's hesitation and a quick glance down the corridor, she knocked softly. Within a few seconds, muffled footsteps sounded inside the room, coming in her direction.

The door opened a few inches, and Anthony peered back at

her, his hands at his throat, doing up the button there. His shirt was tucked into his breeches, but he wore no waistcoat and no cravat. His hair was damp and uncoiffed, with locks falling haphazardly over his forehead.

"Charlotte," said in surprise, brushing his hair back with his fingers in a way that held her momentarily mesmerized.

She forced her eyes to his, refusing to let them explore. "Forgive the disturbance, but I require a bit more information from you."

His brows drew together as he fiddled with the button again. "Information?"

"I am trying to sketch the scene, and I realized I know far less than I had first thought. Did you say Mr. Higgins was at Vauxhall when it happened?"

"Yes," he said, extending his head through the gap in the door and looking down the corridor. "Outside."

"Very good, thank you." She gave a little curtsy, then walked back to her bedchamber before her eyes could take in more of her betrothed. *Pretended* betrothed.

But within minutes, she found herself at his door again. This time, his cravat was draped over his shoulders and his waistcoat on but not yet buttoned.

"Yes?"

"The girl he was with," Charlotte said. "Was she a performer, or did you say she was serving the food?"

"A violinist," he said decidedly.

"Perfect. Thank you." She curtsied again and walked to her door.

"Charlotte."

She paused, hand on the handle, as she met his gaze questioningly.

"If you have another question, you may simply use the door that connects the rooms."

Her heart skittered. Silly, really. It was just a door—not so different from the one he looked at her through right now, in fact. But she had caught herself staring at it a number of times since yesterday.

"I shan't need to," she assured him, "but thank you." Using that ridiculous door felt like an intimacy with Anthony she could not afford. They could pretend to such familiarity in public, but it was another matter in private.

He cocked an incredulous brow. "If you say so." He smiled slightly, then disappeared behind his door again, leaving her with a hint of regret that she would never again enjoy the sight of Anthony Yorke in a state of half-dress.

Contrary to her assertion, however, within minutes, Charlotte needed him again. She refused, however, to surrender to the need, until she had been sitting, staring at the paper, for nearly ten minutes.

Her gaze flitted to the door that, if opened, would lead to Anthony's bedchamber. "It is just a stupid door," she said. Rising from her chair, she strode over to it determinedly, then rapped upon it three times.

Within seconds, it opened, and Anthony smiled pleasantly back at her, a glint of amusement in his eyes. His cravat was still untied, draping over his shoulders, but his hair had been brushed into order and his waistcoat buttoned.

Regrettably, Charlotte's unruly mind said.

"I can only assume this is you *not* having a question," he said. Had his smile always been so roguishly handsome? She could have sworn it had used to be arrogant and annoying.

"It is only that I have never *seen* Mr. Higgins," she defended. "And now I fear no one shall recognize him in the caricature because I have not captured his essence."

"If you simply draw a large pile of horse manure, that should suffice."

Charlotte couldn't stop a smile. "That would certainly be much simpler."

Returning his own smile, his gaze shifted behind her. "Is that it?" He nodded to indicate the escritoire.

"It is."

"May I see?"

Charlotte hesitated. No one had ever seen her work before it was complete, and she felt sudden anxiety at the thought of Anthony, of all people, witnessing the messy process.

But she needed him.

Heavens, that was an admission to make to herself.

She went to retrieve the paper, only to discover Anthony following her. Into her private bedchamber.

Which did not matter in the least, for they hated each other, naturally.

It was pure, unmitigated hatred that made the blood thrum in her veins as he came up beside her.

He looked over the messy drawing for a moment, his arm pressed against hers in a way she found utterly distracting. So she sat down.

There. That was much better.

"You have his hair all wrong," Anthony said, pointing to the pencil strokes above Higgins's forehead. "He parts his hair on the side. Quite far, in fact."

Charlotte took a new piece of paper and hurriedly sketched the shape of a new head while Anthony watched. This time, she placed the parting of his hair to the side—down near his ear. "Is that better?" She glanced up at Anthony, whose lips drew into a smile. A regrettably handsome smile that, since meeting Miss Baxter, Charlotte had come to realize was likely the downfall of plenty of women.

"Much better," he replied. "Even without facial features, he is already recognizable."

Charlotte's chest filled with satisfaction. "What of his eyes, though? Have I done them justice?"

Anthony's brows drew together as he looked at the last sketch. "The eyes are well enough. But his brows are more distinctive. Far thicker than what you have."

Charlotte's pencil went back to work, making the crude outline of wide brows on the new face.

Her pencil slowed when Anthony rested his hand on the escritoire, leaning over to observe the strokes more closely. Charlotte kept her hand moving, trying to ignore his sudden proximity and the warmth he brought with him.

He pointed a finger to the brows. "They curl up near the center. Just there."

"Like this?" She scooped her pencil upward, and Anthony's breathy chuckle tickled her ear.

"Precisely. As though they were about to take flight."

They worked on the nose and mouth, laughing in turns as Charlotte took Anthony's descriptions and embellished them.

Once she had finished the full top lip, she surveyed the result of their work, then glanced up at him, smiling. Her breath hitched, for he was nearer than she had realized, his own lips mere inches from hers.

Their gazes caught and held. The heat of the room suddenly felt oppressive. What in the world was happening?

Was this how hatred felt?

No. Charlotte knew what it felt to hate, for she had hated the man responsible for Papa's death for some time now. This feeling was nothing at all like that.

She turned her head to the drawing. "That should do well enough, don't you think?"

"It will do better than *well enough*. Anyone who has ever seen Higgins will recognize him immediately. You have conveyed him to perfection."

"Only with your help," she replied, allowing herself the briefest of glances at him.

He was looking at her, his expression impassive. What she wouldn't give to know what was in that mind of his just now.

He stood straight. "Well? Shall we move to the body?"

Something told Charlotte it would be unwise to allow Anthony to remain in her bedchamber any longer—and particularly not if they would be discussing *bodies*.

"I think I can do well enough with what you have told me," she said.

Anthony nodded and glanced at the small clock on the mantel. "We only have half an hour before we must leave."

"Half an hour will suffice, for I am already dressed—but for my gloves, of course."

As if to verify her words, his gaze ran over her, stopping at her back. His mouth opened, then shut again immediately.

"What?" Charlotte twisted to look over her shoulder.

"Your buttons," he said. "Two are undone."

Charlotte's cheeks heated, and she stood up, stretching her hands behind her to try to reach them. "Those confounded things!" When she'd had the dress embellished before the dinner party, she had also changed out the buttons. But the ones she had chosen were slightly smaller than the original ones, making situations like this one a constant risk.

Anthony watched her struggles with ill-concealed and growing amusement as she reached her arms over her shoulders, then up behind her back with no success at all.

"Would you care for some assistance?" he finally asked, his hand covering his mouth in a way that failed to cloak the lines of laughter beside his eyes.

"You are abominable," she said somewhat breathlessly, but she turned her back toward him. Time was of the essence if she wished to finish the caricature.

Her skin prickled the moment Anthony came up behind her. When his fingers took hold of the top button, grazing her skin, a shiver ran down her spine—one significant enough that it was impossible he had not noticed.

"Your fingers are cold," she lied.

"Forgive me." He cleared his throat, and there was silence as he fastened the other button.

She shut her eyes and pressed her lips together in an attempt to take hold of her wandering thoughts and emotions. But the second her eyes closed, the image of Anthony's hands stealing around her waist pressed itself upon her.

She whirled around the moment the second button was fastened. "Thank you. I shall be down shortly."

With the veriest narrowing of his eyes, Anthony nodded and saw himself out of her bedchamber and into his.

"That wretched door," Charlotte muttered, giving her hands a shake to rid herself of the crackling energy coursing through her.

Charlotte had found her mind wandering to Miss Baxter a number of times—and to Anthony, wondering what they had shared and what remained of it. The bitterness with which he spoke of her made it clear that Anthony, at least, had not moved past it.

Knowing his heart was soft enough to be so hurt, realizing the motivation behind all he had been doing and that it was not selfish, as she had thought, but rather entirely self*less* . . . it cast him a new light, making the shadows fall away. And without shadows, Anthony Yorke was an entirely different man. A man Charlotte wasn't sure how to pretend to be engaged to without being just a bit curious what it would be like to truly be his.

And that would not do.

She might be engaged to Anthony Yorke, but she could not

fall in love with him on any account.

"Are you ready?" Charlotte asked Anthony as they strode toward the ballroom three-quarters of an hour later. Her arm was tucked into his, and she looked up when he didn't answer immediately.

His jaw was set, the shadow it cast on his cravat sharp from the candles lining the corridor.

Her heart twisted, for what she was asking of him was far from easy or simple. The difficulty of it was evidence of his love for his brother, and she almost wished she could return to the time when she had thought him arrogant, selfish, and hard instead of a man crumbling under the weight of his guilt.

If she were in his shoes, would she be able to face the man responsible for Papa's death and pretend she harbored no ill-feelings toward him?

Just shy of the ballroom door, she stopped, her hand on Anthony's arm keeping him from moving forward. She allowed her family to pass, then tugged Anthony toward the wall where the open door offered them a bit of privacy.

"We do not have to do this, Anthony," she said.

"We do," he replied, his brows knit together and his jaw set.

"Even so, it does not have to be tonight. We can wait if you would rather." For the last two days, she had pestered Anthony with questions about Lord Drayton, trying to gain a clear picture of what it would require for her to seek his favor. From what Anthony had conveyed, the man was a stickler when it came to genteel behavior, having no patience for any degree of vulgarity. It was a trait which would require every bit of Charlotte's deficient training and experience to live up to.

Her one hope had been Anthony's contention that Lord Drayton was susceptible to flattery. He put great value on those whose admiration and adulation were within the limits he deemed appropriate. That was something Charlotte could use to her advantage if she was careful enough.

Anthony's dark and determined eyes met hers, and they softened, as did his voice. "Silas has waited long enough. I am ready."

Searching his face, she nodded, and they proceeded to the ballroom.

Charlotte's eyes swept over the room, searching for Lord Drayton. Tonight, her objective was simply to deepen her acquaintance with him, but for Anthony, it would require a difficult conversation.

"He is over there," Anthony murmured. "Speaking with Lord Tysdale in the far corner."

Attired in a neat dark brown tailcoat, Lord Drayton sipped from the drink in his hand as he laughed at something Lord Tysdale said. Charlotte watched him carefully, her chest filling with indignant determination. He looked so at ease, so carefree in his guilt, while innocent Silas Yorke did his best to make his way in France. It was despicable.

"I find myself utterly parched," she said, focus still on Lord Drayton.

"Let us find you some refreshment," Anthony said, his voice determined.

They made their way around the ballroom floor, but their progress was halted as they waited for four gossiping women to take note of them and move.

"Well, if it isn't the man himself," Anthony said under his breath. "In the flesh."

"Who?" Charlotte asked, trying to follow the direction of his gaze. The word no sooner left her lips than her eyes caught on a man taking his place in the forming set. His sparse hair was parted deeply, while his full brows turned upward in a distinctive curl. Her hand flew to her mouth, but her laugh escaped, drawing the attention of the nearest woman.

"Do try to compose yourself," Anthony said, but he was smiling just as much as she at the sight of Mr. Higgins.

The crowd of women shuffled aside, allowing them to pass, and their humor gave way at the sight of Lord Drayton, who finished his conversation with Lord Tysdale just as they approached.

The muscles in Anthony's arm tightened under Charlotte's hand.

"For Silas," she whispered just before Lord Drayton's gaze turned to them. "Lord Drayton! How happy I am to see you again." She dipped into a curtsy as he inclined his head. "We were disappointed not to have more time to converse at the opera the other night."

"Were you?" Lord Drayton's gaze shifted to Anthony.

The silence lasted long enough for Charlotte to wonder if she should have put her foot down and insisted they wait until Anthony was truly prepared for this interaction. It was entirely possible that his response to Lord Drayton's question would be to throw a glass of ratafia in the man's face.

Her clutch tightened on Anthony's arm.

"Indeed we were," Anthony said, drawing a suppressed sigh of relief from Charlotte as he covered her hand with his.

Lord Drayton took a moment to respond. "Forgive me, Yorke, but I was under the impression you had no liking for me."

The fingers of the hand Anthony had used to cover Charlotte's curled around hers, gripping it. She glanced up at him and noted the tightness of his jaw, the slight flare to his nostrils.

She wanted to wrap her arms around him and assure him his sacrifice would all be worth it in the end, but instead, she merely returned the pressure of his fingers.

"You are mistaken, my lord," Anthony said. "If I have seemed cold toward you, it must be a mixture of my unfortunate tendency to look severe combined with an assumption that you harbored ill feelings toward my family. In truth, I have been trying to gather the courage to speak with you these months and more. To apologize."

Lord Drayton's brows rose. "Oh?"

"Yes." There was a pause, and Anthony's hand tightened around Charlotte's until she clenched her teeth from the pain. "For the words and actions of my brother."

Lord Drayton's gaze intensified, but he said nothing, waiting for Anthony to continue.

"I understand he meant to bring accusations of a serious and highly offensive nature against you. Accusations meant to cover his own underhanded dealings. I gather the unfortunate result of all of this was the failure of your business as well as the death of Mr. Langdon. Please accept my belated apology on behalf of my entire family."

Lord Drayton's gaze rested on Anthony for another moment, and Charlotte held her breath.

His mouth stretched into a sympathetic smile. "There is nothing at all to forgive *you* of. You believed in me enough to invest in the business, and I heartily regret that you, too, suffered a financial loss as a result of that disastrous affair." He extended a hand. "Let us shake hands and put it all behind us, shall we?"

Charlotte's heart soared as she smiled at Lord Drayton, watching Anthony out of the corner of her eye. This was better than they could have hoped. Never had she thought the man would so readily accept an apology.

Despite Charlotte's anxieties, Anthony released her hand and took Lord Drayton's.

"It is benevolent of you, my lord," he said.

"Nonsense." Their hands clasped, then released. "I know as well as any that a man cannot control the actions of his family. Some men are just bad apples."

The vein in Anthony's temple pulsed, and Charlotte's heartbeat sped.

"Ah!" she exclaimed. "Look. Another set is forming! Will you not ask me to dance, my lord?"

Lord Drayton looked at her with a smile. "Gladly, if you will accept." He put out a hand, and she placed hers in it with a quick glance at Anthony—a glance that reaffirmed to her that it was time to put distance between Lord Drayton and him.

Lord Drayton led her to the middle of the ballroom floor, where they took their places amongst the still-forming set.

"It was very magnanimous of you, my lord," she said as they stood across from one another. "With your words, you have relieved a great burden from his shoulders."

"It was my pleasure." As the music began, he lowered into a bow. "Almost as great a pleasure as it is to dance with you."

Charlotte's cheeks grew warm, but she tried to take the flattery with good grace. She wanted him to like her well enough to invite her to his party, after all. She simply had to ignore the fact that she was dancing with a murderer and the man whose conspiring and disregard for anyone but himself had put her in the impossible situation she was in.

"My sentiments precisely," she lied as they drew together for the first figures of the dance.

Her lies continued as they spoke whenever the dance allowed it. She attempted a few subtle compliments, and the result convinced her of what she had suspected: like so many men in positions of power, Lord Drayton was inclined to surround himself with those who made him feel as important and remarkable as he found himself.

Perhaps it would not take so much time before she could elicit an invitation.

She chanced a glance at Anthony for a dose of encouragement. He still stood near the refreshment table, his hard eyes watching the two of them in a way that made her eager to engage Lord Drayton in conversation. If he glanced at Anthony just now, nothing Anthony could say would persuade him he was not detested.

"Tell me, Lord Drayton," she said. "Shall we be fortunate enough to see you at Astley's next week? I have been assured that everyone who matters will be in attendance, which tells me you must be at the top of the list." The levels her flattery had reached nauseated her, but she persisted in spite of it, for she had a goal to achieve.

Lord Drayton kept his eyes fixed on her as they clasped hands and turned in a circle. "Almost you convince me to postpone my engagements. I might have delayed them had I been aware of your intentions."

"Might you not still?"

He chuckled. "I rather think the guests I have invited to my estate would miss their host, so I will *not*, regrettably, have the pleasure of seeing you there."

"How disappointing," she replied, arranging her expression into something pitiful and disappointed. "How long shall you be away?"

"Ten days, perhaps," he replied. "Barrington Hall is not so far."

"Barrington Hall?" she repeated. "Is that *your* estate?"

He nodded.

She laughed wonderingly. "I have heard many tales of its marvelous sculpture garden—often enough that I tried to persuade my aunt to see whether we might have a tour when we were last passing."

The gratified expression she had become familiar with over the course of the dance graced his face. "I am delighted to know you enjoy sculptures, Miss Mandeville, and, supposing I was there at the time, I sincerely regret that your aunt did not indulge your fancy. I would have gladly offered you a tour myself."

"I shall never forgive my aunt. She was adamant it would be an intrusion at best."

"I could never regard you as an intrusion," he replied.

She smiled, though her hands itched to slap the man. How could he adopt such ingratiating manners in the bright light of a ballroom while committing such heinous deeds in the darkness?

"Well," she said as they performed the final figures, "I quite envy you, for a stay in the country sounds sublime after the crowds of London."

The implicit request in her tone was glaringly obvious, and the moment the words left her lips, she regretted them, for Lord Drayton's smile flickered.

She had gone too far, become too bold. Refined woman of Lord Drayton's acquaintance would never say something so desperate or tasteless. They did not seek invitations, for they came in abundance.

The violins drew out the last notes of the song, and it was everything Charlotte could do to keep her head held high as they bowed and curtsied to one another.

"I find this dancing has tired me, Miss Mandeville," Lord Drayton said. "Shall we forgo the second song of the set?"

Charlotte nodded with a smile plastered on her lips, but as Lord Drayton led the way back to Anthony, she knew she had misstepped, putting their plan in jeopardy.

20

ANTHONY

Anthony couldn't decide whether to be relieved or anxious at the sight of Charlotte and Drayton coming toward him. Anthony had danced dozens of cotillions in his life, but they had never felt as long as the one he had just witnessed. Neither, he was certain, had the ones he had participated in required so much holding of hands or touching.

But things could not have gone well if they were skipping the second dance of the set.

How much of his violent reaction to watching Charlotte and Drayton was rooted in a hatred of the man versus the continuing shift in his view of Charlotte, he didn't know. Or didn't *want* to know, perhaps.

They were not truly engaged—at least not in the way everyone believed them to be—which made it all the more confusing how much Anthony hated watching her smile with Drayton.

But she was not smiling as the two of them approached.

The shape of her brows and the glint in her eyes was apologetic, and Anthony's heart began to thump.

"As promised, Yorke," Drayton said, extending the arm Charlotte's hand rested upon as an offering to him. He drew it back suddenly, though, smiling in a way that made Anthony want to pull off his cravat and strangle him with it.

"Just one thing," Drayton said. "As I am returning Miss Mandeville to your care before my promised time with her has been enjoyed, I hope you will offer me something in return."

Anthony could think of a dozen things he'd like to offer Drayton, but he forced a smile. "And what might that be?"

"To accept an unfortunately belated invitation to a small party I am hosting at Barrington Hall."

Anthony's gaze flew to Charlotte's, but the wideness of her eyes told him it was just as much a shock to her as to him.

"Naturally, had I known of Miss Mandeville's interest in Barrington Hall or of the true nature of your sentiments toward me, Yorke, I would have thought to extend an invitation in a more timely manner. Is it too much to hope you will accept despite that? As a gesture of goodwill, let us say."

Anthony could have kissed Charlotte right then and there. He restrained himself, however, pulling his gaze from her and clearing his throat. "We would be delighted, my lord. It is very gracious of you."

He hesitated. Drayton had not mentioned anyone else in the invitation. Being engaged, he and Charlotte did not require a chaperone, but given the impending end of that betrothal, it behooved them to protect her reputation in whatever ways he could. "My lord, I hesitate to ask such a thing after your profound generosity, but would it be possible for my aunt to join us? As a chaperone of sorts."

Drayton laughed. "I would have thought you would be eager to shed such constraints now that you are able."

Charlotte laughed with a hint of nerves. "It is all so new, you see."

Drayton smiled knowingly. "Rest assured, there will be more than enough married women present to act in that capacity—should you wish for it." One of his brows quirked, and Charlotte's cheeks filled with color.

She smiled despite that, thanking him.

Anthony did not feel himself able to press further. It would have to do.

Drayton smiled and held out his arm again, allowing Charlotte to thread hers through Anthony's.

They bid him good evening and watched him walk a few feet before he was stopped by an acquaintance.

Before Anthony had the opportunity to ask Charlotte how in the world she had managed to garner an invitation within a quarter of an hour of her first real conversation with Drayton, they were interrupted by a man asking if Charlotte would do him the honor of dancing with him.

Anthony did his best to take this unwelcome development with good grace. He sipped from his glass of ratafia slowly, letting his eyes wander over the lines of dancers. All too frequently, they settled on Charlotte.

She was so different from what he had first thought her, with a ready smile and so little of the biting banter she had subjected him to from their meeting at Bellevue House.

She was kind and loyal to her family—more so than they knew or might *ever* know. She accepted Aunt Eugenia's antics with good humor. And, beyond all that, she was putting herself at risk for Anthony.

No. Not for Anthony.

For Silas.

It was not her affection for Anthony that led her to plan and strategize. It was her sense of justice, her need, he had come to believe, to avenge her father in some way.

He would be a fool to make anything more of it.

When Charlotte's hand was claimed for the following set and then the fourth and final set of the evening after *that*, however, Anthony's patience began to wear thin. Was a man not permitted to dance with the woman he was pretending to be engaged to? How could they keep up the appearance of being in love if every other gentleman present spent time with Charlotte while Anthony sat and watched?

But his pride prevented him from intervening. Charlotte wished for her family to become better connected. Naturally, she would marry someday, and it would be entirely selfish of him to monopolize her attention given the situation.

He was coming to well and truly hate that confounded situation.

With Tabitha's need to discuss all the events of the evening, there was no chance for conversation on the short carriage ride home. Anthony sat beside Charlotte, trying to ignore the press of her body against his. He focused his efforts instead on dissecting why he was in such an ill humor when they had accomplished their very goal.

Once he was in his bed, restful sleep evaded him. He tossed and turned, flitting in and out of dreams about an alternative house party, where Drayton discovered their engagement was nothing but a ruse and married Charlotte himself. And she stared up at him with an adoring smile.

He thrust the mangled bed linens from his body and sat on the edge of the bed, rubbing his eyes. Not even in his dreams was he free of her.

His hands paused and his brows furrowed at a strange sound.

What was it?

It came from Charlotte's bedchamber. Perhaps she too was having unpleasant dreams—but more than likely, the unpleasantness in hers would take the shape of being forced to marry Anthony after all.

He reached for the ceramic jug beside his bed and poured himself a glass of water, drinking the entire thing within seconds. Setting the glass down, he ran a hand through his hair and glanced at the door to Charlotte's bedchamber. The distinct sound of chair legs grating against the floorboards met his ears.

What in heaven's name was she doing at this hour of night?

More importantly, though, why did he care?

He lay back on the bed, staring up at the ceiling with wide, thoroughly alert eyes that were not even considering sleep at this point.

There was a muffled clatter in Charlotte's room, followed swiftly by a muted exclamation.

Anthony scrambled out of bed, snatched his dressing gown from where he had slung it over a chair, and shrugged his arms into it.

He knocked on the adjoining door as firmly and quietly as he could, then cocked an ear to better hear the chaos within. The door opened a bare inch, and Charlotte's eyes stared back at him. A disheveled braid hung over her shoulder. Behind her, the room was lit with four candles, all concentrated around the escritoire.

"Did I wake you?" she asked, apology in her eyes.

He shook his head, and his eyes narrowed. He reached a hand toward her face, his heartbeat racing. "Is that blood?"

Her hand beat his to her cheek. "Heavens, no. It is only paint. I was clumsy enough to knock it over."

"That explains the clatter."

They stared at each other another moment.

"I shall endeavor to be silent now," she promised.

"Not on my account, I hope. I cannot for the life of me convince myself to sleep." His gaze returned to the small portion of the escritoire visible to him over the top of Charlotte's head. "Are you painting Higgins's caricature?"

She nodded.

"At this hour?"

"I must send it with the post in the morning, or Mr. Digby will—" She stopped.

Anthony's brows drew together. "Will what?"

"Be disappointed."

But that was not what she had been on the verge of saying.

"In any case," she continued, "I shall be awake at least another hour, for now I must clean up before continuing on. Thankfully, we have no engagements tomorrow, so I may claim a headache and rest half of the day if I wish."

"Ring the bell," Anthony said. "A servant can clean the paint."

She shook her head. "How would I explain why I am painting at this hour? Besides, I have no wish to rouse any of the servants. They need sleep as much as we do. More, I suspect."

Anthony searched her face. He had thought her so intractable and disagreeable at first, but here she was, determined to clean the paint she had spilled because she was too concerned for the welfare of the servants.

"Wait until morning, then," he suggested.

"It will be dry and a horror to clean, speaking from unfortunate experience. I shall simply do it now."

"Let me help you, then," he said.

"Oh, no." She closed the door another fraction of an inch, as though she feared he might slip through the miniscule space. "That is unnecessary."

"I will not be sleeping either way, which means I will be sitting here uselessly while you toil and lose sleep."

She chewed the inside of her lip, then opened the door wider.

"Good heavens," Anthony said, taking stock of the area around the escritoire. "It looks like a rainbow was massacred at your desk—and on your nightgown."

The front of her was generously splattered with various colors of paint, which grew more sparse away from the nucleus of chaos. Still, though, a few drips and drops adorned the pale skin of her chest visible above the drawstring of her chemise.

The sleeve of it slipped over her shoulder, and she hurried to put it to rights, then strode over to where her wrapper was draped at the edge of her bed.

Anthony averted his eyes, though they fought him tooth and nail.

His gaze surveyed the part of the room that did not put him in danger of admiring Charlotte, falling upon the basin of water that sat upon the dresser beside her bed. Beside it were two folded towels.

He carried the basin and towels over to the desk and dipped the edge of one towel into the water. Charlotte followed suit with the other, and they set to wiping up the wet paint that had splattered the chair and the desk.

"I was hurrying so that I could sleep," Charlotte explained as she scrubbed at a spot on the top of the chair back. "I was too careless."

"And now your sleep is even more delayed."

"A cruel irony."

Their towels migrated down the length of the chair back, then to the legs, requiring them both to crouch. Their hands bumped as they reached for the same spot, and Charlotte drew hers away quickly. Evidently, she could touch Drayton easily enough, but even accidental contact with Anthony was something to avoid at all costs.

He suppressed a sigh, finished working on the chair, then moved to the floor, settling on his knees.

"The party begins sooner than we thought," she said. "We have but a few days to prepare."

"A great deal of our strategy will depend upon what we find when we arrive—the location of the desk, for instance, and how many people will be in attendance. The more there are, the easier it is to slip away unnoticed, but the more likely we are to encounter someone."

She glanced up at him with an amused smile.

"What?"

"This sort of scheming comes quite naturally to you, it seems. Have you thought of everything?"

"Hardly." In fact, he had spent the better part of his time trying to understand his fluctuating feelings toward Charlotte. "I have had the better part of the night to consider a few things, though." Like the way the color of her lips so perfectly matched her cheeks when she was embarrassed.

She smiled and surveyed the area. "No matter. Between the two of us, I am certain we will think of everything important. Did we clean it all?"

Anthony looked around. "It is difficult to say without more light. No doubt we will find a few spots in the morning, but we have certainly removed the bulk of it."

Charlotte pushed herself up and shifted her braid from her shoulder to her back, as Anthony too rose to his feet.

"Ah," he said. "We *have* missed a spot. The paint on your face."

Charlotte's hand flew to her face, searching for it. She rubbed haphazardly, apparently trying to cover as much area as possible to increase the likelihood of finding her target. She looked at him for confirmation she had rid herself of it.

His lip pulled up at the corner, then he dipped the dry edge of his towel in the basin on the desk and stepped toward her. "Not quite."

He wiped gently at the red spot on her forehead, then moved to the one on her cheek. His eyes wandered to her lips, sending a jolt of heat into his veins, captivating him with the desire to hold her as he had that day when he had found her crying in this room. But this time, he wanted more. He wanted her to close her eyes as he pressed his lips to her perfectly pink ones and showed her what he would do if they were truly engaged.

His gaze moved to hers.

Her eyes were alert and watchful. Or were they wary?

He pulled his hand away and stepped back, ignoring the disappointment in his chest. "There." At the edges of his vision, he could see the splatters of paint on her chest, but even if the light in her eyes hadn't warned him against any further contact, Anthony knew his limits, and they would not survive long if he tested them in such a way.

"I will leave you to your painting," he said.

She nodded. "And I shall attempt to finish without further mishap."

He offered a small smile, then made his way to the door, stopping just shy of it and turning to her. "Thank you, Charlotte."

Her brows drew together. "For what?"

"For what you did this evening. I had my doubts that you would find success, but I should have known better."

"You should have indeed," she said with a soft, teasing smile.

He chuckled, remembering with a lump in his throat how it had helped to hold her hand as he spoke with Drayton, to know that it was not his burden and his alone anymore to help Silas. "You have no obligation at all to help me, Charlotte. But I am grateful you are willing to."

She lifted her shoulders. "What is a spurious engagement for if not to help one another? Besides, now that I have spent more time with Lord Drayton, I would be tempted to pursue his ruin on my own even if you decided against it." Her eyes twinkled merrily, even in the dim light.

"I believe you would. Good night, Charlotte."

"Good night, Anthony."

He stepped through the door to his bedchamber, closed the door behind him, then let out a long breath as he stared ahead.

He was falling in love with Charlotte Mandeville, and he hadn't the slightest idea how to stop.

21

CHARLOTTE

Charlotte turned over and clenched her eyes shut more tightly, grasping at precious sleep. Even with her eyes closed, she could feel the heaviness of her lids. It had been nigh on two o'clock when she had finally felt satisfied with the painting and tumbled into bed.

Her eyes popped open as memories from the night returned—spilling the paint, Anthony knocking on her door, then helping clean the mess.

She shot up, awareness of the amount of light filtering into the bedchamber at the edges of the curtains making her wonder what the hour must be. She needed to send off the caricature without delay to ensure it arrived in time.

She reached for the cord beside the bed and gave it a tug, then threw off the bedcovers and grabbed her wrapper, sliding her arms through the sleeves. A glance in the mirror on the dressing table made her eyes widen. Half of her hair had come out of her plait. Had that happened during her sleep, or had it been that chaotic when Anthony had come to help her?

Bracing her hands on the edge of the table, she leaned

even closer to the mirror, inspecting her face. She stroked her cheek where the faintest bit of red was still visible. She closed her eyes, and her heartbeat thrummed in her ears as she thought on Anthony's gentle attempts to wipe it away. She could have sworn he had almost kissed her in that moment.

Just as importantly, she had wanted him to. It had terrified her to no end—the way she was beginning to feel for this man she had so despised, and the fear that a kiss would not hold the significance for him that it would for her.

What might it have felt like to have his lips on hers? To pretend for just a moment that they truly did mean to marry, to share the bed, the home, the life everyone thought they would?

Heat flooded her, and her eyes flew open as she fixed her gaze upon herself in the mirror.

"Enough, Charlotte," she said severely.

Her gaze dropped to the skin on her chest and the half-dozen small drops of colorful paint there. Had Anthony not noticed them? Would he have wiped them if he had?

Her cheeks grew even warmer, and she jumped at the knock on the door.

She fanned her face for a moment. "Come in."

A maid entered holding a large tray. "Good morning, miss."

"Good morning. What is that?"

"Breakfast, miss. Mr. Anthony asked that it be sent up when you rang the bell."

Charlotte was silent. Was he *trying* to make her fall in love with him? What had happened to the unbearable and ill-humored man she had met at The Crown and Castle? This would all be far easier if she could see more of that man instead of the thoughtful, loyal Anthony she was engaged to.

Having set the tray on the bedside table, the maid turned

toward Charlotte and clasped her hands in front of her, waiting to be instructed.

"I need this letter to be posted without delay," Charlotte said, taking it from the escritoire and handing it to her.

"Right away, miss. Shall I help you dress after I see it posted?"

Charlotte hesitated, feeling her lids fight being kept open. "No. I shall rest a bit more, I think. I will ring the bell when I am ready."

"Very good, miss." She curtsied and left the room.

Charlotte ate the breakfast on her tray, directing her mind toward the approaching party rather than allowing it to explore last night's occurrences. That was a dangerous road to travel.

When she set the tray aside and climbed under her covers again, however, she found sleep refused to return. Anthony gladly danced into her thoughts again and again within minutes of her banishing him.

Curse him.

"Did you manage to finish the caricature and send it off?" Anthony asked as he and Charlotte walked two dozen feet behind Mama, Lillian, and Tabitha. The sky was a patchwork of interchanging blue sky and clouds as they took the path in the park that led toward Kensington Palace.

"I did," Charlotte said. "Without further mishap, even."

"Admirable," Anthony replied.

Letting her gaze wander over the multitude of trees that dotted the wide lawns, Charlotte sighed. "And now I must set my mind to the next caricature."

"Which, I take it, does *not* bring you pleasure?"

She glanced at him. "Not as it first did, no."

"How did you come to begin creating them?"

Charlotte took a moment before responding, but there was little point to hiding anything from Anthony. She couldn't even pretend she didn't want to tell him at this point. He knew more than anyone about her secrets, and it felt strangely . . . normal. "It was mere happenstance, really. I have always enjoyed sketching and painting—far more than Lillian and Tabitha do —but I had seen one of Rowlandson's caricatures. Someone had brought it to The Crown and Castle, and I was struck by how playful yet skillful it was, and how it satirized its subject. My grief over Papa's death was still fresh at the time. Fresh enough that I was full of anger toward the world, eager to place blame wherever I could. So"—she shrugged—"I made one of my own."

They followed the others into an arched tunnel, every inch covered in greenery.

"Who was the subject?" Anthony asked.

"No one in particular. It was a table of enormous, wealthy men eating a lavish dinner together, while men of less consequence poured money into the wealthy's purses. It was hardly my best work, but it caught people's attention despite that."

"And what of Digby?" Anthony asked. "How does he come into the story?"

Charlotte's brows knit. That day had changed everything. "I was proud of my work and eager to vent my anger at the world. So I placed the caricature where I knew it would be seen by the people it targeted: at the inn. But, unbeknownst to me, I was seen by one of the maids. When Mr. Digby saw the paper, he questioned the servants, and Mary confessed she had seen me place it there. The paper was already drawing attention, and when Mr. Digby tried to remove it, there was protest. The inn had its most lucrative night in some time, as everyone was eager to discuss the caricature. Apparently, that sparked the idea in his mind, and when I next saw him, he proposed that I continue making caricatures in return for money. We so desperately needed money, and I had enjoyed the process so much, I eagerly accepted."

Lillian and Tabitha took a seat on one of the benches ahead beneath the long archway, and Anthony and Charlotte stopped. They retraced their steps until they reached another bench, which was littered with leaves and a few small sticks.

"But you do not enjoy it as much now?" Anthony used a handkerchief to brush off the debris, then helped Charlotte to take a seat.

She shook her head.

"Then why not stop?" He took a seat on the other edge of the bench, angling his body toward her and resting his arm along the back of the bench so that his fingers were just an inch from her shoulder.

She sent him a grimacing smile, aware of the impulse to reach up and take his nearby hand. "It is not quite so simple as that."

"Because you need the money?"

"That and—other things."

"Charlotte . . ."

She pressed her lips together, trying to decide how to explain. "Mr. Digby has become . . . attached to our arrangement."

Anthony's gaze fixed on her. "To the arrangement? Or to you?"

"No, no," she reassured him, seeing how intently he waited for her response. "To the arrangement. If it was the latter . . ." She shuddered.

Anthony relaxed slightly, but there was still an edge to the way he watched her. "You mean he refuses to let you end the arrangement."

"He has made it clear that as long as it continues, my secret is safe."

"Meaning that if you end it, he will reveal your identity." His jaw hardened, and he turned his head to the side, obscuring his face from view. "He is every bit the despicable lowlife I had thought."

"I cannot argue with that," she replied. "He was agreeable enough at first, though. The threats did not come until recently. Which reminds me . . . when I paid him a visit before we left for London, I might have been obliged to make some threats of my own." She cleared her throat. "On your behalf." She clenched her teeth.

Anthony's mouth pulled up at the edge. "I am glad to hear that. Surely, though, you had no need of me when you have such sharp claws." He reached for her gloved hand, and her heart rushed up to her throat.

"I should have thought to use them," she said, keeping still for fear he would let go of her hand if she made too swift a movement. "But Mr. Digby responded more readily to the mention of your name than he would have to anything else, I think. Enough so, in fact, that I felt emboldened to insist he begin paying me more."

Anthony's eyes lit up as he looked at her with an admiration that made her feel warm. "Bravo, little kitten." His smile faded slowly as he regarded her. "But you should be able to stop if you wish to, Charlotte."

She nodded. "And I will. Someday. It seemed the wrong time, however, when he was so suspicious of our engagement. I tried to satisfy his skepticism, and I daresay I managed it— thanks to your threats."

"Vicarious threats," he amended.

"Precisely. For now, though, the money is still too welcome for me to wish to put an end to the arrangement. I must look toward the future, for there is no telling how my family will be regarded once our engagement ends."

"Charlotte," Anthony said, the deep furrow of his brow returning. He took a pause that felt like an eternity. "Perhaps we should reconsider—"

"Please don't," she said.

He stared at her, his eyes questioning.

She didn't know that she could bear to hear him suggest marrying her out of pity. She forced a smile and spoke in a cheery tone, pulling her hand away. "We will come about. I am certain of it."

He watched her in silence for a moment.

"It looks as though we are pressing on." Charlotte indicated her family rising from their bench. She stood, and after a moment, Anthony joined her.

She turned the conversation to safer and less painful avenues, recounting Tabitha's crushing disappointment upon learning that Lord Drayton had not included her or, indeed, anyone but Charlotte and Anthony in his invitation.

"And when Mama insisted that, if you and I were to leave London, the three of them should return to Bellevue House, I feared Tabitha would burst into tears. Thankfully, your aunt insisted even *more* firmly that they remain with her. I think she and Mama have become genuine friends."

"I have noticed the same thing," he replied, but she could tell his mind was far away.

Unfortunately for Charlotte, her own mind insisted on settling firmly on the man beside her, with whom she was fast falling in love.

Two days after their walk in Kensington Gardens, Charlotte was reading in the library with her sisters when the door opened. The footman appeared with a silver tray balancing on one hand.

"A letter for you, Miss Charlotte," he said, bringing it to her and bending for her to take it.

Charlotte frowned but thanked him, and he soon disappeared.

"Do not tell me you and Anthony are writing letters to one another in the same house," Tabitha said.

Charlotte ignored her, breaking the wafer and unfolding it. Her gaze dropped to the signature at the bottom, and she immediately refolded it, unease filling her.

"Well?" Tabitha asked. "Who is it from?"

Heart thudding against her chest, Charlotte sent her sister an enigmatic smile, rose from her chair, and walked toward the door.

"Where are you going?" Tabitha asked.

"To enjoy my letter in peace," she replied.

"It *is* from Anthony," Tabitha said as Charlotte closed the door behind her.

Her smile evaporated, and she hurried up the stairs and to her bedchamber, resting her back against the door once she was inside and opening the letter.

Dear Miss Mandeville,
I trust this letter finds you well. It was with great relief that I received your letter yesterday, as you promised. It is some of your best work, which requires not just skill but a deep understanding of people and their secret lives. Everyone has secrets, after all.

You better than most understand how easily reputations can be marred by the slightest whisper or the faintest hint of scandal. It is a delicate balance we all maintain, is it not?

Allow me to provide a small but striking example: what might result if it were to become known that an engagement had been entered into, not as a matter of the heart as so widely believed, but rather for the sake of saving an already fragile reputation?

Fascinating how such arrangements can be quite delicate if not handled with the utmost care and discretion. Do you not agree? Given your personal experience on the subject, I am certain you do.

In light of such matters, I feel our own business arrangement merits further reconsideration—specifically previous assurances of my continued discretion. Maintaining such secrets comes at a cost, one that I am sure you can appreciate.

I propose, therefore, a simple financial arrangement to ensure continued silence on my part—nothing more than the reasonable sum of fifty pounds. A small price for the peace of mind it will afford you, and easily sent with your next caricature.

I trust you will find this proposal acceptable and act accordingly. Failure to comply, I fear, may lead to unforeseen complications that could upset the balance we both strive to maintain.

I eagerly await your prompt and favorable response.

Yours sincerely,

Mr. Josiah Digby

Charlotte's heart thudded against her chest.

He knew.

But how? When not even her own family was aware that the engagement was a sham.

There was only one explanation: Mary.

Mr. Digby must have realized she knew more and pressed her for information. And Charlotte knew Mary well enough to know that her loyalty would have kept her lips sealed until the risk to her own family became too great.

How Mr. Digby had come to know mattered little, though. What did matter was what would happen if Charlotte failed to give him the money he demanded.

Fifty pounds!

And yet, what would be forfeit otherwise? It would drag her, her sister, her mother, and the Yorkes into scandal. Charlotte could never forgive herself for that—not when they were making such progress in Society.

But every part of her revolted at the thought of giving him that money. It would be to surrender, to let him win.

And yet, either way, Charlotte and her family would lose.

Curse the day she had said yes to doing business with Mr. Digby.

Dashing a tear from her eye, she crumpled up the paper and threw it with all her strength at the empty grate, where it tumbled and settled amongst the ashes.

22

ANTHONY

"Have you decided on a date for the wedding yet?" William asked as he poured from the decanter in Aunt Eugenia's drawing room.

Anthony considered saying a date a few weeks in the future —he was sick to death of the question—but he was learning that each lie required more lies, and he was *also* sick to death of lying. "Not yet."

"Why ever not?" William handed him a glass, then took a seat in the chair beside him. "I can see no reason for delaying the inevitable."

"The family lost their father, William. It makes settlements a great deal more complicated, for everything is being held in trust until they can identify the heir." There. That was true enough, wasn't it?

Of course, the thing that made the wedding and settlements *most* complicated was the fact that there would *be* neither. If Anthony had Aunt Eugenia's fortune, he would be tempted to gift some of it to the Mandevilles. He hated thinking of their uncertain future. Where would they go when the heir to the estate inevitably came to claim Bellevue?

"She has improved you, you know," William said, his gaze on Anthony. "You have been so miserable and irritable since . . ." His brows drew together, and his gaze shifted to the drink he held. "The point is, you are more like yourself again now."

"Only imagine how marriage might improve *you*," Anthony quipped. "Why are *you* avoiding it? I can see no reason for delaying the inevitable."

The corner of William's mouth drew up at the edge for a moment before his expression shifted to something more pensive. He swirled the last bit of brandy in his cup. "I have yet to find a woman who feels right for the role."

Anthony scoffed lightly. William took his role as heir and firstborn all too seriously. "And if you *do*, she will likely want nothing to do with you," Anthony teased.

William chuckled, then tossed off the last of the brandy and rose to his feet.

"Leaving already?" Anthony asked. William had been there less than a quarter of an hour.

"I have business nearby. When do you leave for Barrington?"

"In two days," Anthony said. He and Charlotte had spoken more than once about how to handle their time there, but Anthony still felt unprepared and unsettled. They were entering the belly of the beast, and he was simply grateful he did not have to do so alone.

Which was a problem all its own. He was far too comfortable spending an inordinate amount of time with Charlotte. His mind was capable, he had discovered, of finding excuse after feeble excuse to seek her out.

"Then I shall see you afterward." William cocked a brow.

"And I expect to be informed of the wedding date when I do." He shrugged into his tailcoat, then turned and left.

Anthony remained in his chair for another few minutes, staring at nothing in particular.

Absentmindedly, he thumbed the post in his hand. It had been delivered with the day's post just before William had joined him in the drawing room. Anthony had also noted a letter addressed to Charlotte. The penmanship had been decidedly male—and just as decidedly messy. Given that Charlotte had sent off the caricature recently, Anthony suspected the letter was from Digby.

Though, what reason would that villainous man have to write her? What could not wait to be said upon her return home? If he knew what was good for him, the letter would be one of gratitude—or a plea for forgiveness. But Anthony had no real hope that such was the case. He went in search of Charlotte, looking in the morning room where her sisters and mother were, then the library. But it was not until he glanced through the windows that looked onto the garden that he saw her sitting alone on the bench.

He hesitated, then opened the door and joined her.

She smiled at him as he approached, a fact which would have made him marvel for the contrast to how she *used* to regard him, except that the smile clearly required effort.

She moved to afford more space for him on the bench, and he stole a glance at her as he sat.

Gads, she was beautiful. Beautiful and distracted.

"Something is amiss," he said after a few seconds of silence had passed. He hesitated. "Is it Digby?"

Charlotte's gaze flicked to his in surprise.

"I saw a letter addressed to you with the post and wondered."

"Yes," she said, looking ahead again. "It was from Digby."

"And what did he have to say for himself?"

"Nothing of import." Her nostrils flared slightly, belying her words.

Anthony kept silent, watching her as she stared forward. He wouldn't force her confidence. He might have attempted to do so before, but things were different now. He wished it to be given freely.

Evidently, she was not willing to offer that, a realization that tasted bitter on his tongue. Bitter but not unexpected. What had he allowed his mind and heart to make of this ruse they had concocted? He had certainly not anticipated falling in love with the woman he had so recently despised.

Charlotte blinked and shifted in her seat, as though coming out of a reverie of sorts, then forced a smile. "Shall we speak more of Lord Drayton's party? I have been wondering whether it makes most sense to take the diary early on or nearer the end."

It was as they conversed on that subject that Anthony noticed the way a few of her lashes clung together, as though she had recently been crying. Devil take Digby.

When they parted ways so that Charlotte could join her mother and sisters for a quick shopping expedition before dinner, Anthony waved them off from the front door with a smile. When they disappeared from view, the smile faded.

He made his way up two sets of stairs, down the corridor, and into his own bedchamber. He strode to the door that connected his room to Charlotte's, paused for a moment, then opened it.

He stood on the threshold, his gaze flicking to the escritoire. There was nothing there, though. His eyes traveled around the room—over the bed, to the trunk at the foot of it, then to the dressing table.

But there was no sign of the letter. Perhaps she had put it in a drawer.

That was when he saw it—the bit of crumpled paper hidden amongst the ashes in the grate.

He strode over and picked it up, ignoring the black powder that had lodged in its myriad creases.

His gaze consumed the message like flames would tinder, and with each line, his grip on the paper tightened. He stared at the signature at the bottom for a few seconds, then crushed the paper in one fist, threw it back into the grate, and stormed from the room.

Anthony put a foot in the stirrup and swung a leg over the saddle of his chestnut gelding. The groom released the bridle and stepped off the street and onto the pavement. Anthony gave him a curt nod, then nudged the horse forward with his heels.

He had gone no more than a hundred feet when he came upon the Mandevilles.

"Anthony," Charlotte said in surprise.

His brows drew together. "Back so soon?" They had only left for shopping a quarter of an hour ago.

"Not even begun, in fact," she said ruefully. "I forgot my reticule, which has the money in it."

"Ah, I see." The mere mention of money made something flicker in her expression. No doubt she was thinking of Digby.

"Cloaks might be wise, as well," Lillian remarked, glancing up at the sky with misgiving.

"Where are you going?" Charlotte asked Anthony.

"I have some urgent business to attend to," he said. "I shall return as soon as possible, but I shan't be in time for dinner."

Was he imagining it, or did Charlotte look disappointed? He didn't particularly wish to miss dinner, but the journey was nigh on twelve miles, which meant it would be more than three hours before he returned, and likely nearer to four.

"Travel safely," Charlotte said.

His eyes fixed on her. Was she truly worried for his safety? In many ways, her life would be made easier if he *did* come to some accident on the road. No one would blame a woman whose engagement had ended in tragedy.

"Yes, we wish you a safe journey and a quick return," Mrs. Mandeville said with a warm smile.

Anthony thanked them, then waited for them to pass before continuing on his way, wondering what Charlotte would say if she knew his destination.

Soaked to the bone and temper in tatters, Anthony thrust open the door of The Crown and Castle Inn. Water droplets cascaded from the shoulders of his greatcoat, wetting the walls of the entry way and falling to the wood planks of the floor.

A young boy peeked his head around the back of the staircase that stood in front of the door. His eyes widened at the sight of Anthony, and he took refuge out of sight.

"Boy!" Anthony called out.

The boy's head slowly reappeared until just one, terrified eye was visible.

Anthony took a deep breath. His anger was getting the best of him. He wasn't there to scare innocent young children.

He pulled a coin from his pocket and showed it to the boy, along with the most reassuring smile he could manage given the tenseness in his muscles and temper.

The boy's eye widened, but he made no move to approach.

Anthony crouched down and held the coin out further, then nodded to signal he was safe to come.

Slowly, the boy's body appeared, and he walked toward Anthony like a mouse approaching a cat offering cheese.

"Where is your master?" Anthony asked, setting the coin in the palm of the boy's hand.

"In the back, sir," he replied, turning the coin every which way to inspect it. He put it between his back teeth and bit down.

Anthony couldn't stop a smile, even in his ill humor. "How old are you?"

"Five, sir," said the boy, shooting a wary glance over his shoulder, then slipping the coin in his coat pocket.

"And what do you do here?" Anthony supposed he shouldn't be surprised to know Digby employed children barely breeched.

"Whatever Master Digby says, sir," he replied. "And if I does a good job and gets him coin from the guests, he gives me tuppence at the end of the week."

"How obliging of him," Anthony said drily. He took the boy by the shoulders and looked him in eye firmly. "That coin I gave you is for *you*, not Digby. Do you understand?"

The boy nodded, a sense of awe in the shape of his lips.

"Will you see to it that my horse is fed and watered?" Anthony asked.

"Aye, sir."

Anthony ruffled the hair on his head, then stood, and went out the way he had come. He followed the walls around to the back, where he paused and watched Digby. He was attempting to push one of the horses into the small gated area abutting the side of the stables. The ground all around the fence was a bog of mud and water from the rain, with deep holes where Digby and the horse had stepped. The horse was resisting Digby's efforts, and Digby pulled back just long enough to throw his shoulder into its breast.

The horse was forced back, but the suction of the mud on its hooves prevented it from moving, and it stumbled and fell on its hindquarters as Digby mumbled curses against its stupidity.

Anthony's teeth ground together. The man used and took advantage of children, extorted and threatened young ladies, had made his inn a hotbed for *ton* gossip, and here he was abusing animals—animals that likely did not even belong to him.

And he had made the most formidable and capable woman of Anthony's acquaintance cry.

"Digby," Anthony called out, striding toward him.

Digby whipped around, his eyes rounding at the sight of Anthony. "Mr. Yorke," he said, infusing his voice with a tone of pleasant surprise, even as his eyes watched his approach warily. He brushed at his dirty clothing, ignoring the horse as it struggled to find its footing behind him.

Anthony strode to the horse and took hold of the halter, helping pull it out of the mud. His own boots were already caked until they looked like giant mud stockings.

Once the horse was standing and stable, Anthony faced Digby.

"Really, sir," Digby said as Anthony came close enough that he was obliged to lean back to meet his eyes. "That was very kind but unnecessary. The brute is a clumsy oaf."

"Not as clumsy or brutish as the oaf who pushed him *into* the mud."

"I slipped right into him," he lied with what was no doubt meant to be an embarrassed smile. "But tell me what I can do for you, sir."

"You can stop threatening my betrothed."

Digby laughed nervously, and took a step backward. The mud made a slurping noise as it released his boot, only to engulf it anew when he set it down a few inches behind. "I'm sure I haven't any notion what you are referring to."

"Do you not?" Anthony took a step toward him.

"Miss Mandeville and I have an arrangement, as you know. One that is mutually beneficial. That is all."

"I saw the letter you sent her, Digby, and let me assure you of one thing." He grasped the fabric at Digby's chest and yanked him closer. "Your arrangement with Miss Mandeville is at an end. If you so much as whisper her name in the presence of another person, I will see that this inn becomes a ruin of its former self, and you an outcast. Where footsteps once sounded, only ghosts will walk. Not a soul amongst London's elite will set foot between those walls. Everyone will know that *you* commissioned those caricatures, and you will be sued for libel by every peer or gentleman who has appeared in that dingy window of yours. Do you understand me?"

Digby nodded quickly, his jowls shaking under his wide eyes. "Yes, sir."

Anthony held his gaze another moment, then retreated enough for Digby to stand straight. "And if I ever hear Charlotte's name associated with those caricatures—"

"But, sir," Digby said plaintively.

"What?"

Digby hesitated. "Is this reaction not a bit excessive?"

"After all you've put Charlotte through, this is barely satisfactory."

"I only mean that, well, you and Miss Mandeville are not . . . truly engaged, are you?" He rushed on. "Which, I own, is a relief to me, for it cannot but sit ill to hear of a distinguished Yorke stooping to the level of a—"

Anthony thrust his fist into Digby's jaw, throttling the last words. Digby tumbled back into the mud, while Anthony fell sideways, thrown off balance by the way his boots insisted on sticking in the mud. His brow made contact with the splintering wood of the fence, sending a shock of pain through his skull.

He pulled himself up with one of the posts, brushing at his brow with the back of his wet sleeve while Digby nursed his jaw.

"Never," Anthony said breathlessly, "so much as speak of the Mandevilles again. *Do I make myself clear?*"

Digby's head nodded frantically. "I swear, sir!"

Trudging through the mud, Anthony strode toward the stables.

"Mr. Yorke!"

Anthony turned to see the maid, Mary, hurrying toward him, a look of distress on her face.

"Where is Miss Charlotte?" she asked.

"In London," Anthony said tersely, his brow throbbing.

Mary looked over her shoulder to where Digby was still struggling in the mud. "Did he threaten her, sir?" She wrung her hands, anguish in her eyes. "I shall never forgive myself, for I swore to her I would not tell him what I knew, but he threatened to dismiss me and tell everyone I had stolen. I didn't know what to do, sir, and my mother is—"

"Mary," Anthony said as the rain began to patter on the inn roof again. "I am the last person to whom you should feel the need to explain Digby's depravity."

She nodded, her chin trembling. "But Miss Charlotte—"

"Would never blame you for doing what was necessary to protect your family." That was something she understood as well as anyone.

Mary's shoulders shook, and she covered her mouth with a hand. "Please tell her I am sorry, sir."

He nodded, his eyes flitting to where Digby had finally managed to stand on his two feet. His jaw clenched. He had better go before he *and* Silas were accused of murder. "If you ever wish for other employment, I will find it for you. I must go now."

He strode to the stables, tossed the boy another coin, and swung back onto his horse.

23

CHARLOTTE

Charlotte stared ahead at nothing, her face a blank while her mind hummed with the incessant chatter of competing thoughts. Across from her, Mama sat in a chair, sewing the new ribbon they had just bought to Tabitha's bonnet. The curls framing her face had all but disappeared, a result of the downpour they had encountered on their way home.

On the sofa, Lillian repaired a hole in a stocking while Tabitha embroidered the hem of a sleeve to wear to Almack's that evening.

A lump settled in Charlotte's throat as she looked at the three of them. How she loved them!

Ever since receiving Digby's letter, her stomach had been an ocean of nausea. No matter what she did, she could not bear the consequences. To buy Mr. Digby's silence was an affront to her pride, to the very justice she had been seeking—however twisted had been the means. She sensed, too, that this would only be his first demand. In a few months, he would raise another threat, and then, he would have every reason to expect her to comply, for she would no longer have her association with the Yorkes to protect her. It went against everything in her to submit to intimidation, though.

But to *not* buy his silence . . . well, that option held all its own dangers. It would put a number of reputations at risk— her own, her family's, Anthony's.

But how long could Charlotte keep this secret? How long could she lie, even if her intentions were good? She had ached watching Anthony carry the burden of his secrets, declining to relieve some of the weight onto the capable shoulders of his family. Why, then, was she so insistent on doing precisely the same thing as him? Her excuse had been her great love for her family. But they also loved her greatly.

"Anthony and I are not getting married." The confession spilled from her lips in a cascade of words she was sure Mama and her sisters would not understand. All three of them looked up from their work to stare at her.

Charlotte swallowed. There was a measure of relief in the blurted confession, but the difficult parts of the conversation remained.

"My dear," Mama said, "whatever do you mean?"

"I mean," Charlotte said more slowly, "that Anthony and I shall not be getting married." To her chagrin, tears burned her eyes.

Mama set the bonnet aside and rushed over to kneel before her. She took both of Charlotte's hands and looked up at her with her characteristic warmth and sympathy. "Did something happen? A lover's quarrel, perhaps?"

Charlotte's smile trembled, and she dropped her gaze, unable to meet Mama's. "A hundred quarrels, but never one that could be called a lover's quarrel." Why, oh why, did she wish that were not the case?

"Charlotte," Tabitha said, her embroidery forgotten, "what are you talking about?"

Charlotte shut her eyes and took in a slow breath. Lifting her chin, she met her family's gazes, one by one. "If I am to explain, I must begin some months ago. Mama, you had better take a seat again."

Mama nodded, watching Charlotte with uncertainty and a degree of fear that made Charlotte's heart ache.

She told them of her first caricature, of Mr. Digby and his increasing demands upon her, of the journal and of meeting Anthony. She told them of their subsequent encounters and the night of the engagement, all the way until Mr. Digby's most recent letter.

The only thing she did not tell them was about Silas, for that was not her secret to divulge. She kept Anthony's reasons for wanting the diary vague, trusting her family would be too concerned with all the other information to press her about that part.

When she quieted at the end, the silence was deafening, and Charlotte hung her head, not bothering to wipe her wet cheeks.

It was Mama who finally spoke. "What of Mrs. Ashby? Does she know?"

Charlotte shook her head.

"Shall you tell her?" Tabitha asked.

"It is not my place. That is for Anthony to decide."

Silence fell amongst them again.

"She will be devastated," Lillian said softly.

"Or furious," Tabitha said with a significant look. She placed a hand over Charlotte's. "At Anthony, of course, not at you."

Charlotte swallowed. That hardly made her feel better. She hated to think how betrayed Mrs. Ashby would feel. Would she blame it all upon Anthony? It was not his fault, much as Charlotte had tried to convince herself of that in the beginning.

"I have made the most terrible bungle of it all," she said, shaking her head. "I have betrayed your trust and put our family's name in peril. And whatever money I managed to save must now be used to buy Mr. Digby's silence, for I am certain he will threaten me again when it serves him to do so."

"No, Charlotte," Tabitha said firmly. "You cannot surrender to that snake. Let him do his worst! We will survive it. Together."

Charlotte's chin trembled as she met her sister's obstinate gaze, which turned wondering after a moment.

"I can hardly credit that it has been *you* making the caricatures all this time," Tabitha said. "How did you keep it from us so long?"

"With little enough pleasure, I assure you."

Mama's eyes regarded Charlotte with a bit of wonder. "You are the reason we have been receiving more money from the trustees than expected. And that is why you offered to be the one to handle correspondence with them."

Charlotte grimaced. "I did not know how else to make the money available to us while keeping its source hidden. I am sorry for being dishonest, Mama. And for putting the Mandeville name at risk."

Mama grimaced, but there was sympathy in her eyes. "It is not what I would have wished for you, Charlotte, but I understand why you have been doing it—for us. And, if I am being entirely honest, I am quite proud of your talent."

"While *I* rue the day I ever put pencil to paper," Charlotte said.

Tabitha looked at Lillian through narrowed eyes. "Did you not once disparage the caricatures?"

"It was Charlotte who did so," Lillian countered swiftly.

"And you agreed with her."

Lillian's lips flattened with displeasure. "I was merely disapproving of the furor they produced amongst the village and those passing through."

"If you say so," Tabitha said mischievously.

Mama reached over and squeezed her hand. "As you have assured us so many times: all will be well. We shall come about."

Charlotte gave a trembling smile. How she loved her family! If only she had told them sooner, she might have spared herself a great deal of anguish. She would *not* pay Mr. Digby. She wished she could abandon him entirely. But they would need the money more than ever once the engagement with Anthony came to an end.

As Mama said, though, they would survive it together. She needed to tell Anthony, though, for his name would be associated with whatever scandal might result. She needed to inform him, too, that she had told her family the truth. He could decide whether to do the same with his brothers and aunt. She hoped he would be forthcoming with them. For his own sake.

She waited, perched on the edge of her bed until she finally heard the sounds of movement in his bedchamber. She shot up, both nervous and eager to see him. She had seen the flash of anger in his eyes when she had told him of Digby's first threat; what would he do now that those threats had intensified?

Heart beating erratically, she walked over to the door that separated their rooms. Her fist hung in the air for a moment before she knocked softly.

"Come in," said Anthony.

She turned the knob and urged the door open.

Anthony was seated on his bed with his boots, generously caked in mud, sitting on the floor nearby. Charlotte had assumed his business was in Town, but the state of the boots and of the greatcoat that hung over the chairback said differently.

"Good heavens," she said.

He looked up at her, and her eyes widened.

She rushed over and crouched in front of him, looking up at the crimson gash near his brow. "Anthony, what happened?"

He shook his head. "It is only paint. A mere accident." He attempted a smile.

"There is nothing *mere* about it. Wait a moment, and I shall tend to it." Without pausing for a reply, she strode to the water basin and dipped a towel in it.

"Really, Charlotte," he said, "there is no need."

She took a seat beside him on the bed. "Stop being stubborn and turn your head this way so I may clean the wound."

With a sigh, he obeyed, and she touched the wet end of the towel to the gash softly.

He winced almost imperceptibly.

"Forgive me," she said, tending to it more gently. "How will you frown properly with such an injury? You will be unrecognizable."

The corner of his mouth turned up at the edge, though the amusement did not extend to his eyes.

"Do you truly mean not to tell me what happened?"

The smile faded. He took a moment before responding. "I paid a visit to Digby."

Charlotte's hand went still, and she met his gaze. Their eyes held for a moment.

"You have nothing to worry about from him anymore," he said, "and no need to continue the caricatures."

Charlotte's mouth hung open, but no words would come.

Anthony searched her face, his frown still intact. "I saw the letter he wrote you, Charlotte. The threats he made." The muscle in his jaw jumped.

She lowered her hand, staring at him. "You . . . you read my personal correspondence?"

"When I found you in the garden and realized you had been crying, I was almost certain Digby was the reason. I assure you I would not have read the letter had I not suspected his hurting you. But I didn't realize the depths of his villainy until I read it myself." He shook his head, his brows furrowing even more deeply as he stared forward.

Charlotte couldn't explain the emotion filling her chest— some strange mixture of relief and betrayal and anger. "And, having gone behind my back in that, you thought you might as well pay him a visit without my knowledge?"

Anthony's head whipped toward her. "Yes, Charlotte. You are welcome."

"Welcome? You violate my privacy and meddle in my affairs, then expect my thanks? Did you think me incapable of handling things on my own?" She held his gaze, and when he said nothing, she stood and began pacing. He had ended the arrangement without even speaking to her. What would she do now to support her family?

"I *thought*," Anthony said clearly, "that it was time I made good on the threats *you* made to him in my name." He stood. "Do you think you can bandy about my name and make threats on my behalf and I shall stand by while my betrothed is threatened? I am well-aware you think little of me, but good heavens, Charlotte."

She paced the long rug that ran the length of the bedchamber, from the head of Anthony's bed to the wall opposite. Why *was* she so angry? There was nothing but relief in knowing she would not be obliged to defy Mr. Digby, in knowing she was no longer under his power. There was gratitude—tenderness, even—in knowing Anthony had gone to such lengths to protect her.

She stopped mid-stride. That was it. She was coming to rely upon Anthony more and more . . . and it terrified her. He had stopped her only means of providing for her family, and—as horrid as the employment and employer were—her family desperately needed that money. By taking that away, Charlotte needed Anthony more than ever.

Yet, he would not stay. He would not be there to pick up the pieces that would inevitably shatter when their engagement ended. He would not be there to face the future and decide what to do next.

She shut her eyes, for the thought made her sick, and not only out of fear. How would she bear to lose him?

"I can take care of myself." She said it as much to convince herself as she did for his benefit.

"I don't doubt it," he replied.

She turned toward him. "Then why? Why would you do such a thing? Why not simply ask me about the letter if you assumed it was from Mr. Digby?"

"I did, Charlotte." He rose to his feet and approached her. "I asked you, and you said it had contained nothing of import. But I knew that was not true. I had *hoped*, fool that I was, that you would confide in me of your own volition, just as I confided in you about Silas. We are engaged, Charlotte."

"We are *not*!" she cried out. "Can you not see that your insistence on trying to get me out of scrapes is precisely the reason we find ourselves in this unbearable situation in the first place?"

The room went silent, and they stared at one another from inches apart.

Anthony swallowed and dropped his gaze. "True enough," he said softly.

Charlotte's chest rose and fell, and she fought the aggravating desire to cry. Her gaze went to the wound on his brow, and her throat thickened. "Did he strike you?"

Anthony shook his head and returned to sit on the bed. He took the damp towel in his hand and pressed it to the gash. "I slipped in the mud when I struck him. Hit my head on the fence."

Charlotte cringed at the image his words conjured. The only reason he had this injury was because of her. She had brought nothing but trouble to him since their first meeting, and she hated knowing that.

She hated how her heart throbbed looking at him nursing the injury, hated how much she wanted to hate him as she had once done. But she did not hate him. She loved him. Fiercely.

Guilt pricked her conscience, and she let out a sigh, joining him on the bed. She reached for the towel in his hand, but he resisted. She waited, meeting his gaze, her fingers firm around his until he finally released the cloth, and their hands broke apart.

"So, you struck Mr. Digby," she repeated.

"Something I have wished to do since the first time I met him."

"And you have me to thank for giving you the opportunity." Charlotte stole a furtive glance at him, hoping he would take the olive branch she was extending.

His gaze met hers, a subtle twinkle in his eye. "You were merely my excuse."

"You are insufferable," she said, using her free hand to move the hair that had fallen near the wound.

"And you unbearable."

They smiled slightly at one another, and Charlotte felt that increasingly familiar nudge that teased with questions of what it would be like to kiss Anthony. Would it be so very bad to try?

She cleared her throat and pulled her hand away. Yes, it would be so very bad. As she had just said, they were not truly engaged or in love at all. She could not allow herself to fall any further.

"There. That is better. Perhaps your aunt's cook can make up a poultice in the morning." Standing, she took the towel back and placed it beside the porcelain basin. "I told my family the truth, Anthony."

He looked at her, a question in his eyes.

"Not about Silas," she clarified. "But about . . . us. And the caricatures."

"And what did they have to say?"

"They were crushingly kind and understanding," she said ruefully. "Far better to me than I deserve."

"Hardly. They simply recognize the sacrifices you have made on their behalf, and they love you all the better for it. How could they not?"

Charlotte's eyes flicked to his. His expression was impassible, however, giving her no clue as to whether he loved her all the better for what he saw in her. After his standing up to Digby, she couldn't doubt that he cared for her, at least as a friend. But did he feel the love she felt?

"I was thinking," she said, "that perhaps it would be wise to take the diary you already have to Barrington."

Anthony's brow furrowed, only to relax again as comprehension dawned in his eyes. "To replace the one there with. Yes. A capital idea."

She walked to the door that led to her room, then stopped with her hand on the knob and shot him a smile. "I am not so incompetent as you think me."

"I think you a number of things, but incompetent is certainly not one."

Charlotte's breath stuttered, and she forced a wavering smile. She desperately wished to know what he thought of her, but she dared not ask.

Instead, she wished him goodnight and returned to her bed, no nearer to sleep than she had been two hours ago.

24

ANTHONY

Anthony stared at his aunt, entirely bemused. "What do you mean *you knew*?"

She shuffled through the handful of correspondence that had come with the morning post. "Well, I suppose I did not *know*, but I surmised as much." Her mouth turned down in disgust. "Does Lady Sarah honestly think I would accept an invitation to her soirée after her appalling behavior at church on Sunday?"

Anthony blinked, still trying to comprehend. He had been certain his aunt would be livid when he revealed to her that he and Charlotte were not truly engaged. "And since when have you surmised this?"

She shrugged, setting the pile down to open the topmost letter. "The night you announced the engagement. It was obvious something was afoot."

"But you were so thrilled . . ."

She laughed. "Of course I was! My nephew Anthony, engaged? What did I care how it had come about?" She cocked a brow at him. "When I offered that five-hundred pounds, I admit, I hadn't expected you to act quite so quickly."

"I did not do it for the money," Anthony said, annoyed.

She surveyed him with a shrewd gaze. "I am glad to hear that. I admit I thought so at first—suspected perhaps you had agreed to the marriage because you were both in need of the money. But I stopped thinking so some time ago, for it is obvious you are head over heels in love with the girl."

"Aunt," he said, looking away.

She picked up the correspondence again. "Very well. I shan't tease you about it, but neither shall I pretend it isn't precisely what I had hoped for. She is a rare and precious jewel, Anthony. I have been observing her closely, and she is passionate, loyal, and kind. And beautiful, of course."

"I know," he said softly, staring at his clasped hands.

There was a knock on the door, and Saunders informed Aunt Eugenia she had a caller.

She strode to the door, handing the correspondence to Saunders, then turning to Anthony. "Exert yourself, my dear," she said. "Capture her heart before some fool at this house party does the job for you."

Before he could respond, she turned and left.

He frowned and stared at the door. *Capture her heart.* Aunt Eugenia made it sound so easy. His conversation with Charlotte last night only went to show how far he was from succeeding. He had hoped she was coming to feel differently about him, to view their engagement as less of an encumbrance. But she was eager as ever to be free of it—to be free of his meddling.

The clock chimed, jarring him from his thoughts, and he hurried to his feet, for there were a number of preparations yet to be made before they could leave to Barrington Hall tomorrow, the first of which was a meeting with Harris.

Their meeting resulted in discovering even more preparations needed to cover the theft of the diary, and before he knew it, he was away all day.

Anthony had hoped to find a way to use the diary's contents to extract some sort of agreement from Drayton. Perhaps Drayton could use his influence to clear Silas's name, without having to take the fall for his own crime—which of course Drayton would never do. But what the man *could* do, in good conscience, is offer up false witness to the courts for how Langdon died, therefore exonerating both himself and Silas.

Upon reflection, however, he decided against that route. In part because he had no confidence in the word of Drayton. But mostly because although Drayton could do such a thing in good conscience, Anthony wasn't sure he wanted to. Both Silas and poor Langdon deserved justice, and that meant publicizing the diary's contents.

He and Charlotte would have to push the diary into the public eye as soon as they returned from Barrington, or Drayton would notice the theft before they had the chance. There was no doubt he would suspect Anthony or that he would use his significant powers to take the journal back before any damage could be done.

After Charlotte had left his bedchamber last night, it had occurred to Anthony that, while replacing one diary with the other would help delay Drayton's realization of the theft, it was hardly ideal to put more *ton* secrets in the hands of a man who had no qualms about using them for his own ulterior motives.

For that reason, Anthony spent nearly two hours tracking down a blank diary of near enough likeness to pass for the one they would take from Drayton. It was not perfect, but it would suffice. He hoped.

The following morning, the carriage was brought around

to the front of the London house and loaded with their belongings. When Charlotte emerged, her family and Aunt Eugenia following behind, Anthony watched her carefully. Their interaction last night had been strange. Confusing. Painful, even.

This unbearable situation. That was how she had referred to their engagement. In fact, she had not even conceded that they *were* engaged. It should not have hurt him to hear her deny it, for he knew as well as she how it had all started. And yet, her reaction to his visit to Digby, her passionate response to his mentioning that they were engaged and should confide in one another . . . they had been unwelcome reminders that the engagement was not something Charlotte wanted. She found his desire to protect her aggravating. If that wasn't evidence that she felt differently for him than he did for her, he didn't know what was.

Perhaps he had been too impulsive when he had entered her room to find the letter from Digby. But what if he had not done so? It was not that he doubted her ability to manage her own difficulties; it was that he could do so with far less risk.

But she had not appreciated it.

Charlotte embraced her sisters one by one while Aunt Eugenia opened her arms for Anthony to step into. He obliged, but rather than releasing him immediately, she kept him close with an unyielding grip on both elbows.

"What have you done?" Aunt Eugenia hissed in his ear. "Why is she behaving so strangely toward you?"

"It is hardly something I can explain at the moment," he muttered with annoyance.

Her grip tightened. "If you lose her," she said, her voice ominous, "that gash on your brow will feel like a pat on the cheek compared to what I will do to you. Do you understand me, boy?"

Anthony could only nod. He had not been called *boy* in a great many years.

She released him and pulled back, smiling genially, as though she had not just threatened his life.

Perhaps it was merely the stark contrast it provided to his aunt's embrace, but when Mrs. Mandeville pulled him into her arms, Anthony found his throat becoming thick.

"I needn't ask you to take care of my Charlotte," she said, "for you have done so from the beginning. I shall always be grateful to you, Anthony, even if you shan't be my son."

Anthony could not even manage a reply, so he merely tightened his embrace before stepping back.

Charlotte finished her goodbyes with Aunt Eugenia and smiled at their farewell party, then turned toward the carriage.

Aunt Eugenia's pleasant expression transformed as soon as her gaze met Anthony's, becoming severe again. She shot him a significant glance, a clear indication that he should be handing Charlotte into the carriage. Little did she know how fiercely Charlotte defended her independence.

But he obeyed his aunt despite that.

Soon, they were waving through the carriage windows and traveling down the busy London streets.

"I am still angry with you, you know," Charlotte said as she removed a glove.

Anthony retreated into the squabs, his wary gaze on her bare hand. "Is that why you are removing those?"

"What? To scratch you with?" She smiled and laid the glove on her lap. "Hardly. I have an itch. How is your wound?"

"Better," he said curtly. He had lain awake for some time last night, imagining what life would be like if he had Charlotte to tend to his every hurt and to be by his side through every difficulty.

The bleak truth, however, was that Charlotte was shaping

up to *be* his greatest hurt. He could hardly concentrate on Silas's predicament for thinking of her and wondering what he would do when things came to an end between them.

But that was what they had agreed upon, and it was not as though he wished to force her to marry him.

"Perhaps we should discuss what will happen after the house party," Anthony said.

Charlotte paused, glancing up from the work of putting her glove back on, her gaze intent on his. There was just enough uncertainty there that he felt obliged to expound.

"You had mentioned your desire to make use of some *ton* scandal to—"

"Ah, yes," she let out a shaky laugh. "To distract from our breaking off the engagement. Of course. Go on. Forgive my stupidity. It is only that I am a bit nervous about all of this."

He scooted to the edge of his seat, frowning. "Charlotte, you needn't take any part in stealing the diary. I myself feel uncomforta—"

She closed her hands around his. "That is not at all what I meant. I am utterly determined to steal that diary. You could not persuade me against it at this point. It is the party itself that makes me nervous. I am not in the habit of attending such events, and I do not wish to embarrass you or my family."

Anthony's eyes roved over her face. Of course she was not afraid of one of the most powerful men in England; her fear was all on account of others. She was always concerned with others, never with herself. He had never met anyone like Charlotte Mandeville, and it weighed heavily on him knowing that he never again would.

She was everything he wanted and more. But she was not his.

She released his hands and sat back. "Now, what is it you

were saying? About a scandal to help with ending the engagement."

He cleared his throat. "It was only that, well, it had occurred to me that revealing Drayton's crimes might be the perfect opportunity for that."

She held his gaze for a moment. "And you mean to reveal that directly?"

He nodded. "As soon as can be managed. I cannot risk Drayton coming after the diary. I have engaged the services of a man who will copy the relevant portion of the diary to ensure the only evidence cannot be destroyed."

"Very wise." Her gaze turned to the window, her expression becoming pensive and frowning.

It was silent for a moment, and Anthony would have given anything to know what was in her mind as she stared through the window.

"Perhaps it is *not* the most ideal bit of scandal, though, for it involves your family too closely, and your part will be heavily discussed. Ending the engagement would only increase that, would it not?"

"I suppose that is true," Anthony replied.

"Though, if you are anxious to put an end to things, of cou—"

"No." The response came from him unwittingly, drawing an intent stare from Charlotte. "That is," he said in a more measured tone, "it is not an urgent matter in my view. Is it in yours?"

"No," she agreed quickly enough that Anthony had to persuade his heart not to read anything into it.

"Shall we leave that decision until later, then?" he asked.

"Yes, if you please."

He *did* please. He would postpone the discussion indefinitely if she would let him.

No, that was not true. An eternal engagement to Charlotte without an actual marriage on the horizon would be an unparalleled form of torture.

"Then consider it postponed. There are other things we should discuss before we arrive at Drayton's, and we have less than an hour."

They set about going over their strategy for the party. They agreed that they should wait to take the diary until the final evening of the party. That would give them time to put Drayton entirely at his ease with them. It would also mean they could quickly put distance between them and Drayton rather than risking his realizing the absence of the diary while they were still at Barrington Hall.

When the carriage crested the hill that led toward Drayton's estate, Charlotte grimaced sympathetically. "Spending so much time with Lord Drayton will not be easy."

"No," Anthony said. "It will not." But he was every bit as worried about the time he would be spending with Charlotte, pretending they were on the cusp of marrying. After everything that had happened with Miss Baxter, Anthony had been so certain he would never allow himself to care for a woman again. And then Charlotte had come along, and now he worried he would never care for anything at all if he couldn't have her.

Barrington Hall was a grand, Palladian estate of warm stone and dozens of windows. It was less than ten years old and, according to Anthony, built expressly to allow Drayton to escape Town without being obliged to drive all the way to his estate in Staffordshire.

Anthony and Charlotte were greeted by the butler upon arrival, then guided across the checkered marble floors of the echoing entry hall to the drawing room. As the butler reached the door, Anthony took in a slow, deep breath, trying to prepare himself for what lay ahead.

Charlotte's hand stole through his arm, and she smiled up at him encouragingly. He looked into her warm, brown eyes, and his confidence grew.

The door opened, revealing a number of people within, sitting on plush furniture and standing upon neat rugs. Pale blue walls with cream plasterwork molding surrounded the room, with tall, curtained windows lining one side.

Drayton came over to them with a warm smile. "Here you are! What a pleasure to have you." He gave a shallow bow, and the two of them returned their own greetings.

Drayton turned to the rest of the guests. "Friends, friends. Allow me to introduce you to our newest guests." He invited them to step forward so they stood even with him. "Many of you undoubtedly already know Mr. Anthony Yorke, and if you do not, do refrain, if you please, from judging him based on . . . *other* members of his family." Drayton winked, and Anthony's hand instinctively grasped Charlotte's, his fingers curling around hers. If ever he needed her, it was now.

She returned the pressure of his hand, and he forced a smile and a chuckle for the many eyes which were on him.

"But," Drayton continued, "you may not yet be acquainted with the handsome woman adorning his arm."

The pressure of Charlotte's hand grew tighter. She took issue, Anthony guessed, with Drayton talking of her as an ornament. She, too, smiled graciously, however.

"Miss Charlotte Mandeville," Drayton announced.

Anthony waited in vain for him to add that they were engaged. Perhaps it was because it was implied by their presence at the party. Or perhaps it was because he had hopes of his own with Charlotte. Anthony doubted they were principled hopes.

It would be a miracle if Anthony survived the next week without knocking Drayton down as he had done to Digby.

The guests came to greet Charlotte and Anthony, and Anthony began to relax more. But when Drayton drew attention to the injury on his brow and expressed a teasing hope that a tendency toward violence did not run in the family, he was obliged to squeeze Charlotte's hand every bit as hard as she had ever squeezed his.

"Your claws begin to rival mine," she said as she rubbed at her hand once they had a moment of privacy, obtaining drinks from the sideboard.

"Forgive me," Anthony said, trying to relax again. He stared at the liquid in his glass, every muscle tight. "I don't know if I can do it, Charlotte. I have strangled the man a dozen times in my mind already."

"That makes two dozen times between the two of us, then," she said. "How can he smile while saying such vile things?"

Their conversation was cut short by Drayton himself, who suggested, now that the entire party had arrived and was refreshed, that they take a tour of the house, led by the eminently knowledgeable butler, Wetherby.

They were shown through the dining room, the music room, and out into the gardens. Anthony tried to appear interested when all he could think about was the library.

Charlotte ooh'd and aah'd over the sculpture garden, asking questions about each and every piece of art so that they were significantly delayed in moving back to the house. Anthony's temper, already stretched thin, teetered precariously.

When they finally returned inside, Anthony leaned his head closer to Charlotte's. "What in heaven's name was that about?"

"It was necessary, I assure you," she muttered in response.

"I told Lord Drayton how eager I was to see the famed sculpture garden. I did not wish him to ask the butler about my reaction to it and grow suspicious when I showed nothing but a passing interest."

"*Are* you a devotee of sculpture?" Anthony asked, feeling he should perhaps know this about his betrothed, be she counterfeit or otherwise.

"Heavens, no," she replied. "Once you have seen one, you have seen them all."

Anthony chuckled as they took the stairs up to the portrait gallery and various sitting rooms. Just when he had begun to despair, Wetherby began to speak of the vastness of his lordship's library as they made their way back down the stairs.

Charlotte glanced up at Anthony, the same hopeful spark in her eyes that he felt in his chest. Every chance they had to see the library would help them.

Anthony tried to look mildly attentive in the library, making his eyes sweep over the shelves, though his focus was squarely on the desk there.

Charlotte released his arm and walked about the room, marveling at the tall shelves lined with gilt-lettered spines. Slowly, as Wetherby droned on about the rarity of various books contained within the room, she made her way nearer the desk.

Anthony watched her with amusement and admiration, then made his way over to join her on the pretense of showing her a particularly large book of maps of the Orient, facing her so he had a view of the desk drawers.

The butler brought his dull monologue to an end just then, however, and they were obliged to follow the guests out. No matter. They would have time enough to visit the library over the next few days.

By the time they all separated to dress for dinner, however, there had been no fewer than four references to Silas by those present, and Anthony's muscles ached from their tenseness.

Both he and Charlotte let out long breaths as they separated from the rest of the guests.

Charlotte grimaced sympathetically. "It is as though they are all *trying* to drive you mad."

Anthony shut his eyes. "I cannot do a week of this, Charlotte. I am simply not strong enough. It has been all I can do to hold my tongue—and my fists—and it has been but four hours."

They stopped in front of the door to Charlotte's bedchamber, and she nodded swiftly, her brows knit with worry. "I understand. I have never even met Silas, and I nearly slapped Lord Buxton. But what can we do?"

He lifted his shoulders. "I hardly know. To leave early would be to risk raising suspicion. But so would planting Drayton a facer."

Charlotte couldn't help laughing. "Very true. Hmm . . ."

At the end of the corridor, voices sounded on the stairs.

"Here," Charlotte said, opening the door to her bedchamber and pulling Anthony inside. The windows were shrouded with thick curtains, making the room almost entirely dark. Anthony couldn't see Charlotte, but he could feel her hand around his arm. An impulse to close his eyes and pull her to him made his heart race and his blood warm.

It was yet another reason to cut this visit short—the longer he spent with Charlotte, the more his thoughts filled with ideas about her and the more he dreaded the future without her.

Being near her like this was becoming a special sort of torment.

He strode to the windows, forcing her hand to release him, and drew back the curtains.

"Tell me truly," Charlotte said. "Do you feel unable to bear it for the week?"

Rather than joining her again by the door, he stayed by the windows. More space meant a clearer head. "When I am with you, I can manage. It is when I am alone that I fear I may say or do something unwise."

She nodded. "And you will certainly be alone with the men after dinner."

"Not to mention the billiards tournament I heard the others mention." He ran a hand through his hair. Curse his temper.

Charlotte regarded him with sympathy. "Perhaps we should not wait. It would be a shame if . . ."

"If I threw a billiard ball at Drayton?"

She laughed softly. "Precisely."

"If we took the diary tonight, we could leave in the morning." It was desperation that made him suggest it.

She gave him an incredulous look. "That would be terribly suspicious."

"Not if everyone believes you to be ill. You could plead the headache."

"A headache?" Charlotte protested. "Again? Why must *I* always be the ailing one? I think you should take a turn. You could be plagued by . . . flatulence. Or suffer from a deranged digestion."

Anthony stared at her, unamused. And yet very much amused. "Charlotte."

"We can decide upon your ailment later," she conceded. "Do you really think we can manage it tonight?"

"I am not sure. But I think we must make the attempt at least." How had he ever thought he could bear a week here? He just wanted that diary in his hands.

"When?"

He thought for a moment. If they attempted it now, they ran the risk of someone entering the library. There would be servants running about preparing for dinner too. They needed people to be reasonably occupied. "While the men are drinking their port and the women are . . . doing whatever it is you do during that time."

"Pleading the headache."

Anthony's mouth twitched, but he continued. "We can both excuse ourselves without anyone being the wiser that we are together, and we will know everyone is occupied. Even the servants will be below-stairs, eating their dinner." Anthony's brow furrowed as he looked at her. "Though if they do find out we're together . . . no matter what the assumptions are, they won't be good ones. Charlotte, perhaps you should—"

"Do not even think it," she replied. "I am coming, Anthony. And no more trying to persuade me otherwise."

He let out a breath and nodded. He would be glad for her company. "We should dress for dinner."

With their goal that much nearer, Anthony managed to keep his temper in check for the duration of dinner, a small miracle given the way Drayton sat beside Charlotte and leaned in to make private comments with nauseating constancy.

For all Charlotte's concerns, she handled the questions and conversation directed toward her with amiability and grace, and when Anthony managed to catch a few snippets of her conversation with Drayton, she offered flowery praise of the detail on the fingernails from a particular sculpture from earlier.

Anthony smiled, and it grew wider as Drayton fashioned a polite response, then rose to his feet, inviting the men to remain and the women to follow Lady Buxton through to the drawing room.

Charlotte and Anthony locked eyes, and she rose to follow the women.

He watched as she retreated with the others, wondering how in the world he had managed to find such a capable and kind woman through such mischance—and how he would bear to lose her.

They had agreed to meet in the library ten minutes after the men and women separated, but as Anthony needed to first get the false diary from his bedchamber, he watched for when the clock showed seven minutes. Hand on his stomach, he excused himself, subtly implying he needed the privy. That would serve to support Charlotte's wish that he plead a deranged digestion tomorrow.

Within minutes, he was walking toward the library, thankful to see the corridor empty. He trusted the servants were enjoying their meal before they would be called upon to help their masters and mistresses prepare for bed.

The library was dark when he opened the door, and when he pulled the door shut softly behind him, he was engulfed in blackness. He paused on the threshold while his eyes tried to adjust.

"Anthony?" Charlotte's hushed voice asked.

"Yes," he whispered back. "Where are you?"

"Over here."

He followed the sound of her voice and finally saw her barely distinguishable silhouette just to the right of the desk.

"Do you have the decoy?" she asked.

"I do."

"Where are you?" he asked, losing sight of her again in the darkness. "I can hardly see a thing." He caught a short glimpse of her hand searching the dark just as her fingers brushed against his neck. They traced their way up until her palm reached his cheek.

His heart thudded like a drum. He was *this* close to the thing he had been working toward for months, and suddenly all he could think of was searching this darkness for Charlotte's lips.

Her fingers slid gently up his cheek and past his temple.

Anthony's blood raced through his veins, setting him afire, making him acutely aware of the intoxicating scent of violets as she drew nearer.

"Charlotte . . ." he breathed, his hand stealing around her waist as her thumb brushed against his brow, settling upon his wound. His brows pulled together at the tenderness of the spot.

"It *is* you," she said with relief.

He dropped his hand from her waist, the flame effectively doused by her words. Evidently, her delicate exploration of his face had not been what he had thought but rather an attempt to ascertain his identity. "Would you like to press a bit harder upon it to be sure? Perhaps give it a good squeeze?"

She laughed softly. "Did I hurt you? I did not mean to."

She *had* hurt him. But not in the way she thought.

He took a step back and looked around. His eyes had adjusted a bit more, but it would be difficult to see the contents in the desk drawers without more light. He set the blank diary on the desk, then strode to the curtains and slowly drew one to the side, securing it with the knotted tassels. It provided little light, but it would be enough, he hoped, for them to find the diary. And for his mind to wander to Charlotte's lips less. In the dark, he could more easily imagine her welcoming his advances.

Charlotte took up the decoy diary and opened the top left

drawer of the desk, while Anthony went to the right-hand side drawers.

Charlotte's movements suddenly halted. "Wait," she whispered urgently.

Anthony went still, and his gaze darted to hers. He heard it too: footsteps approaching.

Clenching her teeth, Charlotte carefully shut the drawer she had opened. Anthony followed suit, but his mind was a blank. What would they do? How would they explain themselves if the person chose to stop at the library?

The footsteps paused in front of the door, and Anthony's wide eyes locked with Charlotte's.

Suddenly, she stepped toward him, placing a hand on his chest to drive him backward until his shoulder hit the bookcase.

A second later, her soft lips pressed against his, and her arms draped over his shoulders, filling the air with sweet violets. His senses swam, and his eyes fluttered closed, the warmth of her mouth and body against him bringing his pulse to a perilous speed, dispelling every thought from his mind, every awareness of the world around.

Her hand threaded into his hair, and a small and involuntary groan rumbled in his chest as he pulled her flush against him, devoting himself fully and completely to the task of kissing her. Her body quivered just as the door opened.

"Oh." A man's voice interjected.

Anthony knew he should pull away, but his body protested, and he allowed himself another taste of her lips before wrenching his away and looking to the door, where Lord Drayton stood.

25

CHARLOTTE

I t took a moment for Charlotte's senses to return to enough order that she recognized the man staring at Anthony and her. Lord Drayton stood in the doorway, the light from the candlelit corridor streaming in around him and illuminating the two of them.

The kiss had been her idea—the only thing she could think of to explain their presence in the library at that moment—but she had not been prepared for the press of his lips to hers, the passion with which he had entered into the kiss, or the way it had consumed her.

"Lord Drayton," Anthony said with surprise.

Charlotte was grateful to him, for she could not have strung two words together to save their lives at that moment.

Anthony stepped away, dropping his hands from the small of her back and leaving her to wonder how she had gone her entire life without them there.

"Forgive us, my lord," Anthony said. "We were . . ." He trailed off.

"Yes, I can see that," Lord Drayton said with a hint of

amusement in his voice. "And here I had thought you meant to go to the privy, Yorke. Clever, clever!"

"We meant no disrespect," Anthony said.

Lord Drayton laughed. "None is taken, I assure you. One must give a bit of leeway to young persons in love. But come now, we are joining the women, and unless you wish to set tongues wagging, it will be best for you to join the rest of us in the drawing room."

They both nodded quickly and walked to the door. Lord Drayton held it open for them to pass through, then closed it behind them.

Charlotte still felt only half-aware of where she was, for flashes of those moments in the library intruded again and again, making her cheeks hot and her gaze steal to Anthony beside her.

His brows were pressed in a deep *v* again. Had he disliked the kiss? Did he kiss every woman in such a way? Miss Baxter, for instance.

Once they reached the drawing room, it was clear that tongues were *already* wagging, for they were the recipients of more than one knowing glance. No doubt, Charlotte's rosy cheeks were giving them away.

"Where is the false diary?" Anthony whispered once attention had moved away from them.

"I slipped it into the bookcase behind you while . . ." The words would not come.

She had done it immediately, and thank heaven for that, for if she had waited even two more seconds, she could not have told anyone her name, much less had the forethought to hide the diary.

"Good," Anthony said.

There was no opportunity for private conversation until everyone retired for the night well after one. As they walked upstairs beside Lord and Lady Buxton, though, all Charlotte could do was hope Anthony understood the look she had shot him as she had opened her door, conveying that she expected him to come see her without delay when he could manage it.

She paced her bedchamber for nearly a quarter of an hour before the knock came. She rushed to the door and opened it just enough to see who it was. Despite the fact that she had been expecting him for more than fifteen minutes, her heart skittered at the sight of Anthony.

Had those lips truly been on hers?

One of his brows quirked at her hesitation. "May I come in? Or do you need to touch the wound again to be certain it is truly me?"

She pulled the door open, and he slipped inside, bringing with him the smell of sandalwood that made her eyelids flutter.

Enough, Charlotte. She jostled her head to clear away the distraction and faced Anthony.

"Lord Buxton would not stop talking," he apologized.

"Anthony, what do we do?"

He rubbed his chin, his other hand on his hip. "I haven't any idea."

"I *think* Drayton believed us." She certainly hoped so. There had been nothing pretended about that kiss . . . at least not for her. "Should we wait until tomorrow evening to try again?"

Anthony remained quiet.

"Or perhaps we should steal it in the middle of the night?"

Anthony still said nothing. His eyes were glazed over, his brow pulled taut, his focus on nothing in particular.

"Anthony."

There was no response.

Charlotte stepped directly in front of him, her frustration and nerves reaching a peak. "Anthony," she said more loudly.

His gaze flicked to her as though he had only just noticed her there.

"What is it?" she said. "You are distracted."

His eyes roved over her face, his expression unreadable. It was as if he was still not hearing her.

Was he dwelling on the day's many tasteless comments? As frustrating as they were, Charlotte needed the man to focus. "This is important, Anthony," she hissed.

"You think I don't know that?"

She drew back at the frustration in his voice.

His dark eyes blazed bright as he stared at her. "For months and months, I have thought of nothing but clearing my brother's name, Charlotte. It has been my sole focus, the subject of all my efforts, the thing consuming me. And yet, now, when I am *this* close to succeeding, I cannot even *think* for wanting to kiss you again."

Charlotte's lungs searched for air in vain as his gaze bored into hers, devouring her until she felt faint.

"You have driven me mad from the moment I met you," he said. "Mad with disdain, then frustration, then curiosity, then love and want. And now . . ." His throat bobbed behind his cravat, and he stepped back, all the passion in his face slipping away so there was only anguish left in his eyes. When he spoke, his voice was soft and bitter. "And now I fear I shall go mad when I lose you."

Charlotte's heart struck blow after blow against her chest as her mind tried to fathom what he was saying. Could it possibly be true he, too, found himself dreading the end of an engagement that had started in enmity?

She swallowed. "Why must you lose me?"

His brows pulled tighter, his gaze searching hers. "What do you mean?"

She kept silent, willing him to take her meaning.

"You cannot abide me, Charlotte," he said, looking away. "Whatever I do, no matter how well-intended, it only serves to anger you."

She shook her head and stepped toward him, her chest full to bursting. "If I have been angry, it has been the growing realization of how I have come to need you, Anthony. It has been the dread of saying goodbye."

His eyes searched hers intently.

"Do not lose me, Anthony. Keep me." She tried to smile to counter the vulnerability of her request. "Keep me, for I am yours, as sure as I am my own."

A fire ignited in his eyes, but the step he took toward her was slow and cautious, as though he feared to scare her away.

And so, she waited.

For the feel of his fingers stealing around her waist. For his eyes to rove over her face until they settled on her lips. For the warmth of his breath as his mouth drew near hers.

She waited until she could bear it no longer, a need rising to a crescendo within her. She lifted her chin, and her bottom lip touched his.

There was a pause, then his lip swept over hers, sending a torrent of chills tumbling across her skin and down her back.

Using his finger, he urged her chin up and their lips together. He kissed her with excruciating tenderness, until Charlotte's knees went weak and the entire world narrowed to each point of contact between them.

He kissed her as a man kisses his betrothed—his true betrothed—knowing her lips will touch his and only his.

"Anthony," she finally said, grasping at her rapidly disappearing sense of reality. "Silas."

Anthony pressed his forehead against hers and nodded. "Yes. Silas."

They drew back and looked at one another. The sight of

him after minutes of feeling and tasting him made her breath catch. Could this man truly want her? Want her as a man wanted a wife? It seemed impossible. Glorious and impossible.

"Now is as good a time as any," she said, though her lips begged to be allowed to kiss him just once more. "I will stand watch while you take the diary and replace it."

Anthony nodded. "And if you are discovered?" His gaze dropped to her lips, and he stole a quick kiss.

"How am I supposed to think when you do that?" she asked. Then she stole a kiss from him. She took a step back immediately after, forcing distance between them so she could think more clearly.

Anthony smiled and took a mischievous step toward her.

"If I am discovered," she said, stepping backward, "I shall make up a story about clearing my mind or some such thing."

Anthony pursued her, matching each step of hers with one of his own.

"Heaven knows I need it," she said ruefully, stopping so that he could catch her.

He swiped an arm around her waist and brought her up against him, sending her heart into a fluster of chaotic beating. Brushing a lock of hair from her forehead, he looked into her eyes. The mischief in his eyes gave place to worry. "Are you certain?"

She used two fingers to smooth his brow, avoiding the gash. "Yes. Let us save Silas."

Charlotte's hair was plaited and her dressing gown wrapped around her chemise as she watched Anthony open the library door.

He shot her a quick smile, then disappeared with his candle

into the dark room. Her heart thrummed at the thought of the night's strange events, and she glanced down the corridor, forcing her mind to stay present.

The house was quiet, the servants all to bed hours ago. No one would be walking the corridors, but she couldn't help being nervous despite that. She had explained to Anthony where she had placed the diary, but the unease was difficult to banish.

The burden of Silas's exile weighed on Anthony so heavily, and Charlotte desperately wanted him to succeed tonight.

She tapped a fingernail against her teeth as she stared at the library door, trying to imagine what Anthony was doing at that precise moment and how long it would take him. Not above three minutes, surely.

How would they ever manage to sleep until morning once they had it? Perhaps they could depart immediately, leaving a note of explanation behind.

A sound brought her head around just as a dark figure's cold hand stole around her mouth, stifling her cry. Horror instantly filled her.

She was promptly scooped up and carried down the dark corridor.

26

ANTHONY

Anthony found the diary easily enough, slipped between two volumes of Donne's poetry. Though his mind attempted to venture to the kiss he and Charlotte had shared there, he reined it in, for he had a mission to accomplish, and the sooner he completed it, the sooner he could be with her. And the sooner Silas could come home. The thought of the woman he loved being able to meet the brother he missed so fiercely sent a flash of determination through him.

He crept over to the desk and set the candle upon it, then began opening the drawers, one by one. When he reached the one on the bottom right, he lifted the stack of papers within, and his eyes fixed upon the thing he had come for.

His heart raced, and he set the papers down, eagerly pulling the diary from the drawer. He compared it with the one he had purchased two days ago. The color of the leather was different, and of course, the true one had a much more used look to it. He set the real diary down and bent and flipped the pages of the false one.

It did little to help, but the truth was, if Drayton noticed anything amiss, his suspicions would be confirmed the moment he opened it and saw the pages were blank—if not sooner.

Anthony set the false diary down in the drawer, then replaced the papers atop it, just as a creaking made him go still. His gaze flew to the door, but it remained shut. The creaking intensified, leading his focus to the wall to his left, where a door, hidden amongst the bookshelves, was open.

"Good evening, Yorke," Drayton said from the dark doorway, his tone one of unshakeable calm.

Anthony did not respond. There was nothing he could say, no excuse he could possibly give to explain his presence at this time of night or the diary in his hand.

Drayton strode into the room casually, each step bringing him closer to Anthony. "I had wondered when you would return." His mouth curled up at the edge. "Yes, Yorke. I knew. I suspected from the moment you and Miss Mandeville approached me at that ball. But I wanted to be certain. I prefer to keep my enemies near, you see." He stopped just shy of Anthony and put out his hand for the diary.

Anthony made no move to give it to him. He couldn't. Not now. Not when he was this close.

"The diary, Yorke," Drayton said, the pleasantness in his voice slipping slightly.

"No."

Drayton chuckled and dropped his hand. "If you prefer to do this the hard way, so be it. I will leave it up to you to choose." He turned away and began walking toward the door to the corridor where Charlotte was.

"Choose what?" Anthony asked reluctantly, raising his voice so that Charlotte would hear it. *Please let her be wise enough to run.*

But he knew it was folly. Charlotte Mandeville did not run. She engaged directly.

And yet the door remained closed. Had she not heard them?

Drayton reached the door and turned his head, revealing his profile and the satisfied curl of his lip. "Perhaps you should follow me."

"I think not," Anthony replied, his words belied by the hammering of his heart. It would be better to keep Drayton in the library than to involve Charlotte. Anthony cursed himself for ever allowing her to implicate herself. Not that he could have easily stopped her.

Drayton grasped the door handle. "Then let us hope your kiss with Miss Mandeville this evening was sufficient enough farewell."

Every muscle in Anthony's body went taut as the icy fingers of fear gripped his heart.

But Drayton was already passing through the door. It closed behind him, and Anthony ran to it, yanking it open. He looked one way down the empty corridor, then turned his head in time to see Drayton turning the nearest corner.

Anthony hurried after him. "Where is she?"

"Patience, Yorke," he said calmly, leading the way through the large front door. "Patience."

Patience was precisely what Anthony did not have. He had nothing but rage. Rage and, beneath it, a simmering fear. Drayton would not harm her, would he?

But all Anthony could think of was Langdon.

The stars in the inky sky outside made their path clear enough. Drayton walked, still eerily calm, toward a grove of trees.

"Have you hurt her?" Anthony asked.

"Not yet." Drayton replied as though Anthony had asked

whether he had been to the latest exhibition at the British Museum. "Whether I do so will be entirely up to you."

Anthony's hand curled more tightly around the diary. There *had* to be a way for him to ensure Charlotte's safety without sacrificing the diary. He merely needed to think.

Perhaps he could incapacitate Drayton. Drayton was taller, but he was also older and weaker. But until Anthony knew where Charlotte was, he couldn't risk anything. But the moment he saw her face . . .

"Ah," Drayton said. "One thing, Yorke, in case you had any . . . thoughts." Without bothering to turn around, he reached into his coat and pulled out a pistol. It glinted in the last bit of moonlight, then became bathed in shadow by the canopy of leaves that signaled the beginning of the forest.

Anthony cursed under his breath. Drayton would have no compunction shooting Anthony. Or, heaven forbid, Charlotte. And there was no doubt he would come up with some story everyone would swallow as easily as they had swallowed the one about Silas.

Anthony's jaw worked frantically as they followed the path for another two hundred feet until the trees began to thin. A flickering light appeared through the trunks ahead, and he strained his eyes for any sight of Charlotte.

"You see?" Drayton said with a smile as they came to the clearing. "She is perfectly well. With a fire, even, for her comfort."

Mouth bound with a cloth, Charlotte was seated upon a large log, her arms behind her. Tied, surely.

He rushed toward her, but Drayton's arm came up to stop him, his fingers curled around the butt of the pistol.

"She tried to escape, sir," said Wetherby, who stood beside Charlotte, a pistol in hand. "Kicked me as hard as she could."

Anthony was torn between admiration and wanting to

scold her for being so careless with her own safety. What if the butler had shot her? Gaze on her, Anthony stepped back, and Drayton dropped his arm.

"So," Drayton said. "Now that the choice is clearer, what will it be, Yorke? Save the diary? Or save the girl? You can only take one with you."

Anthony's mind raced, trying to decide what he could do to salvage things, to save the woman *and* the brother he loved. But he was outnumbered, and his mind refused to focus on anything but the way the gag pulled on Charlotte's mouth— the mouth that had kissed him so tenderly but half an hour ago.

"And what assurance do I have that you will let us leave if I do give you the diary?" Anthony asked, never taking his focus from Charlotte.

There was no fear in her eyes. Only anger and frustration.

"You have my word," Drayton said.

Anthony spat in his direction, and the man beside Charlotte raised his pistol, pointing it at Anthony.

"Thank you, Wetherby," Drayton said, directing him to lower his pistol. "The truth is, Yorke, that I have no interest in harming you or Miss Mandeville. So, what will it be? Some pieces of paper? Or Miss Mandeville?"

Anthony's jaw worked as he stared at Drayton, the bitterness of unadulterated hatred filling his chest. He would give the diary back to Drayton. How could he not? But he would not stop until he had it in his hands again, until Drayton's reputation was utterly destroyed.

He extended the diary toward Drayton, who smiled.

"Good boy," he said, taking it. He looked to the butler and nodded. "Untie her."

Wetherby slipped the barrel of his pistol into his

pantaloons and set to untying the gag around Charlotte's mouth, then the cord around her hands.

The moment her hands were free, Charlotte shoved him, and Drayton's pistol came out, pointing directly at her.

Anthony put both hands out, one toward Drayton, the other toward Charlotte.

"Take a moment, Miss Mandeville, to consider your actions," Drayton said coolly. "If either of you attempt to harm either one of *us*, I will not hesitate to shoot you."

Charlotte's nostrils flared.

"Charlotte," Anthony begged, seeing the stubborn flame in her eyes. There was nothing either of them could do at this point. They would have to find a way to get the diary, but now was not the time to concern themselves with it. Anthony couldn't bear to think how close they had been to saving Silas. And all for nothing. But it wasn't worth their lives.

"Let us go in peace," Anthony said.

Drayton's gaze remained fixed on Charlotte for another moment before he nodded. "Go."

Anthony ran to Charlotte and wrapped his arms around her, burying his face in the hollow of her shoulder. What if he had lost her after only truly having her for such a short, impossibly joyful evening? He had bartered her safety for Silas's.

"I am sorry," she whispered.

Anthony shook his head. "You are safe. That is what matters." He pulled back and, taking her by the hand, shot one last glance at Drayton before leading her around the dancing flames and toward Barrington Hall.

"Yorke."

Anthony paused but didn't look back, and Charlotte followed suit, holding his hand more tightly.

"I have found a great deal of enlightenment within these

pages," Drayton said, "and I am admittedly loath to part with it..."

Anthony turned enough to see Drayton looking at the diary thoughtfully.

"But," he continued, "I would hate for you to waste your time coming to look for it again, so—"

"No!" Anthony cried out, reaching in vain as Drayton tossed the book into the flames.

"Have a pleasant journey back to London."

Anthony's stomach swam, his throat thick with bitter grief as Charlotte pressed his hand and pulled him into the woods.

27

CHARLOTTE

Charlotte stayed ahead of Anthony as they hurried toward the house, for she couldn't bear to look at him. Her throat was thick and her eyes stung, making it even more difficult to see in the dark of the night.

"Are you hurt?" Anthony asked.

She shook her head and swallowed, forcing her voice to remain even as they emerged from the trees and onto the open lawn that led to Barrington Hall. "Shall I tell the servants to have the carriage prepared?"

"I will do it. You will have more to do to pack away your things."

She nodded, unable to speak more, and silence fell between them again, the only sound their quick footsteps on the soft grass. Charlotte glanced over her shoulder for any sign of Lord Drayton. She prayed fervently they would not be obliged to interact with him before they managed to leave for London.

When they reached the door, Anthony opened and shut it warily, avoiding any creaking or whining of the hinges. They hurried toward the staircase, up the stairs, and finally slowed in front of Charlotte's bedchamber.

Reluctantly, she turned to Anthony for the first time since the forest, trying to keep control of her fraying emotions.

"Is a quarter of an hour enough?" he asked in an urgent whisper. There was no sign of anger or frustration in his face, and it made Charlotte feel sick. He was trying to seem unaffected, but Charlotte knew better. The blow this all was . . . there was no doubt in her mind it was crushing him inside.

She nodded, not trusting her voice.

He held her gaze a moment longer, as if he might say something. He brought her hand to his lips, pausing as her fingers trembled in his, then pressed a kiss there before turning toward his own bedchamber.

Charlotte slipped into her room and shut the door. Her left hand clasped her right where Anthony had kissed it. She hardly dared hope his precious feelings for her had survived the last hour, but that small gesture gave her hope. Though tonight, hope felt like a cruel thing.

She tugged the bellpull beside the bed and began accumulating her belongings—unpacked just hours ago—on the bed, her fingers still trembling. She so desperately wanted to leave this miserable place.

Within minutes, the door opened, revealing a maid, whose cap covered hastily pinned hair. Her eyes were tired and heavy.

"I must leave immediately," Charlotte said. "Will you help me pack my things?"

The maid's gaze widened, but she nodded and went straight to work.

It was just over a quarter of an hour since Charlotte and Anthony had parted when she arrived in the entry hall. There was no sign of Anthony there, but a glance outside the window revealed him near the carriage.

The maid opened the door, and Charlotte stepped outside, trusting she would never have to set foot within those walls again.

Anthony turned at the sound of their arrival, then hurried to assist the maid with the various items needing to be loaded onto the carriage. His movements were quick, with frequent glances at the house. He was as eager to be gone as Charlotte was.

Her throat thickened as she watched him. Even if his feelings for her, his desire for her was still intact, how would he ever be able to forgive her for the night's events? She had pushed him to pursue the diary, convinced him they could manage the tall order of gaining Lord Drayton's trust and his invitation. And they had failed. Because of her.

The sky was beginning to lighten on the horizon when everything was finally tied down and the carriage ready for departure. Anthony put out his hand to Charlotte. She did not truly need it for assistance up the carriage steps, but she took it despite that, as though the mere touch of his hand might be enough to reassure her about their future. If future they had.

She took her seat and watched with misgiving as Anthony took the one across from rather than beside her. He hit his fist on the ceiling and blew out a breath as the carriage pulled forward, letting his head drop back against the squabs, his brows pulled together.

Charlotte stared at him, wishing she could turn back time to their moments in her bedchamber—those perfect minutes when she had learned of his feelings for her.

Did he wish he could go back too?

Perhaps he wished to go back much farther in time, to the moments before he had even met her.

"Anthony." Her voice sounded strange through her emotion.

His eyes opened, focusing on her.

She tried to swallow the lump in her throat. "I am . . . so sorry."

"I am too," he said softly.

"Can you ever forgive me?"

"Forgive you?" The way he frowned stung, and she looked away.

"For ruining everything," she said. "You said it yourself. From the moment I met you, I have made your life more difficult. I kept the diary from you, then forced you into an engagement you never wanted, and tonight . . ." She clenched her eyes shut. "Were it not for my presence, you would not have had to make a choice between saving Silas or me." Her voice became too unsteady to continue.

Anthony sat forward and scooped her hands into his. "Charlotte, I gave up on the diary the moment I knew Drayton had it in his possession. *You* were the one who inspired me to hope there was still a chance. *You* are the reason I had the courage to come here at all."

"Precisely," she said. "Only look what happened."

"Of course I am disappointed at the turn of events, but more than that, I am angry with myself."

She stared at him, uncomprehending.

"I am the one needing forgiveness from *you*," he said. "I have threatened you, turned your life upside down, and put you in danger." His thumb grazed her wrist, where the skin bruised by the ties was covered by her glove. He shut his eyes and dropped his head, hiding his face from view. When he spoke, his voice was soft, tortured. "You might have been gravely wounded or even killed tonight, Charlotte. And for what?"

"For Silas," she said. "For justice."

Anthony shook his head. "Silas is safe, Charlotte. He is

strong. I shall write to him and explain what happened, and we will find a new path forward. We *will* bring him home. I am certain of it. Whether that is tomorrow or in two years, I know not. What I *do* know"—he scooted closer so that his knees came up against hers, and he stared into her eyes with a fervency that sent her heart into a flurry—"is that you have given me a hope I had long since lost. You have shared my burdens and given me courage to do things I would never have done on my own. You have taken the crushing loneliness of my life before, the haunting prospect of the solitary future I thought I deserved, and you have turned it all to a joy I cannot stand to lose. With you by my side, I feel I can do anything."

His eyes searched hers, and he tried to scoot closer, but their knees prevented it.

Keeping her hands in his, he moved to the place beside her. "There were moments tonight when I thought I might lose you *and* Silas. I could not have borne—" His voice broke, and he shut his eyes. Taking a breath, he continued. "I will forever regret that I put you in danger, and I swear to protect you as you deserve to be protected. If you will let me."

She pulled one of her hands from his and set it on his cheek. He shut his eyes and leaned into it. "Do you know when I began to fall in love with you?" she asked.

He smiled wryly. "The moment you met me?"

She chuckled, then stroked his cheek with her thumb, looking into his eyes. She had thought them dark before, but now, she saw the darkness for what it truly was: depth and strength. "I think my heart was lost the moment I realized that all your supposed selfishness and disagreeability was, in fact, devotion to your brother and to justice, that there is nothing you would not do for those you love."

He covered her hand with his.

"I do not want to be protected, Anthony. I simply want *you.*

And if there is danger to be faced, I would face it together." Her mouth crept up at the edge, and she touched a finger to the wound on his brow. "And I would not have you hit Digby when I am not there to applaud you afterward."

She caught a glimpse of his smile before their lips met, and all the disappointments and pains of the night slipped away, crowded out by the joy of being kissed by Anthony Yorke slowly, passionately, and thoroughly.

Their kisses finally slowed and their lips parted, the world around them coming back into focus.

Charlotte sat back against the squabs, letting her body find its way into the spot under his arm that seemed tailored to her. She rested her head on his shoulder and took his free hand in one of hers, threading their fingers together.

"I mean to speak with my brothers," he said softly into her hair, his fingers stroking the sleeve of her traveling dress. "About tonight. I mean to try again to convince them about Silas."

She looked up at him, searching his face. "You do?"

"They deserve to know—deserve a chance to be trusted. I have a feeling that bringing him home will require their help."

She smiled softly, feeling a warmth inside that was not entirely due to being in his arms. It gave her joy to know Anthony would no longer be obliged to carry his family's burden alone.

He rested his head on hers, and by the time they reached Mrs. Ashby's townhouse, she had fallen asleep in the cocoon of his arm.

The carriage came to a halt, however, stirring her from a short slumber. The Town was already bustling with carts and early morning activity amongst merchants and post carriages and urchins.

Anthony smiled down at Charlotte sleepily, then kissed her temple. "I shall be but a moment."

"Where are we?" They were not, as she had expected, stopped in front of Mrs. Ashby's townhouse.

"William's," Anthony answered.

Charlotte raised her brows, and Anthony chuckled ruefully.

"Amidst moments admiring your beautiful sleeping face, it occurred to me that our arrival at my aunt's is likely to cause quite a stir. She will hound us with questions."

"Oh, yes," Charlotte said, blinking. "I had not got so far as to think of that. What will we tell her? Or my family?"

"The truth," Anthony replied simply. "But I cannot in good conscience do such a thing without telling William and Frederick as well. I will tell him to come with Frederick to Aunt Eugenia's." He kissed her forehead again, then left through the carriage door.

Charlotte looked through the window, watching the light begin to change as dawn arrived. She could hardly credit all that had happened in the last twenty-four hours. Bliss, determination and hope, fear and guilt, danger and disappointment. And now . . .

She closed her eyes and let her head fall back on the squabs, her heart full in spite of it all. Just as Anthony said, she could face anything with him by her side.

He was back within a matter of minutes, and as he came down the short steps and toward the carriage, Charlotte couldn't help but admire him. He was taking the disappointment of losing the diary far better than she had anticipated. She had been certain he would retreat behind walls impossible for her to scale. But instead, he was taking such a terrible thing in stride.

"A messenger has been sent to Frederick," Anthony said as he climbed in, "heaven help him. I would not wish rousing

Frederick earlier than ten o'clock upon anyone. We should see them at Aunt Eugenia's within the hour."

It was less than ten minutes to reach his aunt's from there, and after a few minutes of waiting, Mrs. Ashby's butler answered the door, looking far from pleased at the early callers. When he saw who it was, however, his expression turned to one of concern, and he ushered them in quickly.

"You needn't disturb my aunt," Anthony said as a disheveled footman appeared to help unload the carriage. "I can speak with her when—"

"Is that you, Anthony?" Mrs. Ashby's voice reached them from the top of the stairs, followed by the sound of her descending footsteps. "What in heaven's name are you doing here?"

28

ANTHONY

Anthony glanced at Charlotte, who looked at him with laughing eyes as Aunt Eugenia's capped head and vibrant blue dressing gown appeared in the doorway of the entry hall.

"Good morning, aunt," Anthony said. "How are you?"

"Don't *how are you* me, boy. Tell me what this is about. Are you well? And our dear Charlotte?"

"Yes, aunt."

"Then what—"

"Perhaps we can discuss that in a more fitting place and when Charlotte has had some refreshment." He put a hand on Charlotte's back.

Aunt Eugenia's eyes followed the movement, her brows rising until they disappeared under her cap. "Saunders," she said, her eyes never leaving Anthony's hand placement. "Refreshment. Breakfast parlor. Immediately."

Anthony's mouth twitched. "Saunders, please see that plenty of refreshment is brought. William and Frederick will be here shortly."

Aunt Eugenia's eyes widened to the size of dinner plates.

"You have time to dress for the day if you wish, aunt," Anthony said.

"Is that meant to be an insult to this dressing gown?"

"Not at all. Merely a statement about how long Frederick takes to deem himself presentable."

Charlotte and Anthony had taken seats in the small breakfast parlor, and Aunt Eugenia was pouring tea when Tabitha's hastily coiffed head of hair appeared in the doorway of the breakfast room. Charlotte's mother and Lillian were just behind, their eyes full of worry at the news of Charlotte and Anthony's unexpected and premature return.

Aunt Eugenia motioned for them to come in. She had never poured tea so quickly nor been so efficient seeing to the comfort of her guests, Anthony was certain. The moment the final cup had been filled, she set down the pot. "Now, if you please . . ."

"We must wait for William and Frederick," Anthony said.

Aunt Eugenia let out a huff and took her seat, fingers tapping on the arm rest of her chair just as the door opened, and the brothers appeared.

Normally the most jovial of the bunch, Frederick wore a sour expression and William one of long-suffering that struck Anthony with a jolt of affection. Perhaps things could be different between them going forward—more like the relationship between the Mandeville sisters. If only they would believe the truth.

"Finally," Aunt Eugenia said, hurrying up to pour them tea. "Now we can begin to understand this highly unusual turn of events." She directed a pointed gaze at Anthony, then Charlotte.

"I must warn you that the explanation will not be brief"— Anthony ignored the sound of annoyance from Frederick—

"and that it requires me to broach a subject you, Frederick, and William dislike."

Aunt Eugenia's gaze became wary. "A subject we dislike . . ."

Anthony nodded.

Aunt Eugenia studied him. "Silas."

He nodded again.

"Well, get on with it, then," she snapped.

Anthony took a deep breath, then embarked on the story of his and Silas's experience doing business with Drayton, Silas's suspicions against Langdon, the meeting with Drayton and Langdon's murder, and Silas's escape to France.

Anthony paused there, giving the information a chance to settle before he proceeded with the rest of the story.

"We have heard this all before from you, brother," William said, his intense gaze boring into Anthony. "But Drayton's testimony directly contradicts this. Besides, why would he undercut his own company?"

"Because he had grander plans, William," Anthony replied in frustration. "He jumped at the opportunity Silas and Langdon's well-known animosity presented, killing Langdon and blaming Silas. And now Drayton all but owns the competitor he was colluding with." William was far too quick to believe the best of those with prestigious titles—a result of the way their father had raised him to value tradition.

"But how can you be certain?" Frederick asked. "You were not there."

"Because I know Silas!" The words came out angry and condemning, and Charlotte's hand sought his under the table, her fingers squeezing his. He took a deep breath and spoke in a more measured tone. "If you have doubts on the matter, rest assured they will flee as you hear the rest of the story."

"Let us hear it, then," Aunt Eugenia said.

With Charlotte's hand still in his, Anthony continued, telling of the first diary and his meeting with Charlotte, the particulars that led to their engagement, and the discovery of the second diary. When he reached the bit about Charlotte being taken and bound, her mother's and both sisters' hands flew to their mouths.

Charlotte shot them a reassuring smile and nodded for Anthony to continue. He finished with Drayton's threats, the choice he had been obliged to make, and the burning of the diary.

When he finished, the room was utterly silent.

"Good heavens," Aunt Eugenia whispered, her eyes staring blankly ahead.

"As you say." Frederick, too, was unblinking as he processed the information.

William's brow was furrowed, his mouth covered with a hand as he leaned an elbow on his knee.

"I assume I needn't mention," Anthony said, "that everything I have just told you must be kept in the strictest confidence. For Silas's sake, as well as for Charlotte's."

There were nods all around the table.

He directed his attention to the Mandeville women. "Perhaps you are wondering why I have even brought you into such confidence."

Mrs. Mandeville gave a guilty smile. "I confess to asking myself that precise question, though I am certainly grateful for your trust."

Anthony glanced at Charlotte beside him, and she shot him the veriest hint of a smile that made his heartbeat skip and stutter. "I tell you," he said, keeping his eyes on her, "because we are to be family."

More silence followed, accompanied this time by confused

glances. Aunt Eugenia was the only exception, and her eyes danced as a grin stretched across her face.

"Good boy, Anthony," she said.

"Hold on now," Frederick said, one hand up. "You've only just told us that you became engaged to protect her reputation and that you both had every intention of ending it when the opportunity presented itself."

"Which was the truth," Charlotte said. "Until it wasn't."

"Are you blind, Frederick?" Aunt Eugenia asked, her smile sapping the insult of its power. "Their little ruse has turned into real romance."

Anthony pulled their clasped hands from under the table, offering them as a testament to the claims. Charlotte brought them to her mouth and placed a kiss upon his knuckles.

Face wreathed in smiles and eyes full to the brim, Mrs. Mandeville rose from her chair and came to embrace them, and the others soon followed.

Aunt Eugenia set her hands on Anthony's shoulders and surveyed him with twinkling eyes. "You had me worried, you know."

"I am well aware," he replied.

"But you are far too intelligent to let a woman like that slip through your fingers." She pulled him in, wrapping her arms around him and holding him tightly. Her tone hushed, she added, "But, just to be sure, you shan't have the five-hundred pounds until your names are signed in that registry."

Anthony chuckled and pulled away. "Fair enough."

William was waiting behind Aunt Eugenia. "Congratulations, brother," he said, pulling Anthony into his arms.

"Thank you," Anthony said, his throat thick. It had been some time since he and William had been on the sort of terms that would allow for an embrace.

William's smile had faded by the time they pulled apart,

however, and his brows were knit. "I have been a fool, Anthony. I see that now, and I am ashamed of it."

Anthony gripped his arm bracingly.

"You have my full support now," William said. "We will find a way to bring him home."

Anthony swallowed the emotion in his throat. He should not have given up so easily on persuading them of Silas's innocence. Silas had feared the danger it would be to them, but what was danger when compared to bringing justice to one's own family?

"I must write him," Anthony said. "He should know what has happened, though I wish I had better news to offer."

"But you do," William said, nodding at Charlotte, who was laughing with Aunt Eugenia.

Anthony couldn't stop a smile at the sight. "True enough."

"What of the wedding date?" William asked.

"I have no date for you," he replied. "But I mean to marry her as soon as I can manage it." He strode to Charlotte and slipped his arm around her waist. "May I steal you away for a moment?"

Aunt Eugenia flattened her lips, but there was a twitch at the corner. "If you must."

"I decidedly must." Without a backward glance, he led Charlotte away out of the room.

"Where are we going?" Charlotte asked as they walked down the corridor and into the dining room.

"Away from everyone," he said, pulling her through the room and onto the balcony.

"You were the one who insisted your brothers come," she said as he shut the doors behind them.

"And yet I have tired of them already." He whirled toward her, scooped an arm around her waist, and pulled her flush against him, delighting at the sound of her breath catching.

"Somehow, when I met you, I could not stand to be near you for seconds, even. And now ..." He brushed her lips with his. "I cannot stand anyone *but* you."

"How unsociable of you," she said, her voice breathless. "Anthony ..."

"Hm?" he asked, teasing her as he swept his lips lightly across hers again.

"Is this not where ...?"

"It is, my love," he replied. "The very same place."

"You nearly ruined my reputation on this balcony."

"I have no regrets," he said through a smile.

"*I* do."

Anthony drew back just enough to look into her eyes. "What regret?"

There was a hint of mischief in her eyes. "Well, if you were going to ruin my reputation, you ought to have been thorough about it and at least kissed me."

He chuckled softly, relaxing. "And, what, have my eyes clawed out?"

She had no retort for that.

"I will gladly kiss you here," he said. "As long and as thoroughly as you could ever wish for. But there is something I must do first."

Her eyebrows hitched up. "Something more important than kissing your betrothed?"

"Shocking, is it not?"

She laughed softly, but her eyes held a curious light in them.

He lifted her hand, pressed their palms together, and threaded his fingers through hers. "I cannot kiss my betrothed until she has first agreed to *be* my betrothed. I never had the chance to ask you that question. But I would like to now."

She took in a shaky breath, her hand squeezing his.

"Will you marry me, Charlotte?" he asked softly. "*Truly* marry me? Not for reputation, not because Society demands it, and not because Aunt Eugenia will have my head if you do not."

She laughed nervously, and it delighted him to see her cheeks turning pink.

"Marry me," he continued, "because you love me as deeply and recklessly as I love you, because now that you have tasted life with me, you cannot bear to think of it without me, as I cannot bear to think of mine without you." His eyes searched hers. "Will you?"

She gave a quick and fervent nod, her mouth stretched in a smile as full of joy as he could ever wish to see—a smile he promised himself to elicit as often as he possibly could. He pressed a kiss to the back of her hand, still intertwined with his.

"And now," he said, locking his eyes on her lips and sliding a hand around her waist. "About that reputation of yours . . ."

EPILOGUE
CHARLOTTE

C harlotte went up on the tiptoes of her silver slippers to see over the full hedges that surrounded the parish church of Stoneleigh. The road beyond, however, was empty as far as it was visible.

"Do not fret," Tabitha said. "He will be here."

"He had better," Mrs. Ashby said, "or we will have a real, dyed-in-the-wool murder in this family."

"If you could please refrain from murdering Anthony on our wedding day," Charlotte said, "I would greatly appreciate it, Aunt."

"Then stop fussing," Tabitha said. "You are making us all nervous."

"Can a woman not await the arrival of her betrothed in peace?" Charlotte asked, adjusting the crown of flowers in her hair.

"Here, miss," said Mary, rushing over to tuck a stray stem into place.

"Thank you," Charlotte said warmly. As of five days ago, Mary was no longer employed at The Crown and Castle. Today, she would begin her employment in Anthony and Charlotte's household.

Anthony had arranged it all without Charlotte's knowledge, including ensuring that Patrick was sent to school rather than working for tuppence a week at the inn.

Frederick and William joined the group, both looking tidy in their best tailcoats.

"If Anthony fails to arrive," Frederick said, "do I get the five-hundred pounds by default, Aunt Eugenia?"

She used her reticule to smack his arm. "Hush. And no. Not unless you marry Charlotte instead."

Charlotte laughed, but she couldn't help stealing another glance down the lane. It wasn't that she feared Anthony would fail to make an appearance at their wedding but because she worried he had perhaps met with an accident on his way from London.

He had readily agreed to being married at Stoneleigh's parish church. He understood that Charlotte's family might not call it theirs much longer. She lifted her eyes to the tall spire of the stone edifice. It was surrounded on all sides by tall oaks that swayed gently in the summer breeze.

Part of Charlotte hoped they would simply never find the heir to Bellevue, so that Mama, Tabitha, and Lillian could live there as long as they wished. For now, there was no impending departure required of them, for Mama had received a letter just last week informing her that the quest continued, requiring an in-depth search of various parish registries scattered across the country, undertaken by more than one solicitor. Even when a removal elsewhere was required, Charlotte slept content knowing her family would not be homeless. Anthony would take them in gladly. But Charlotte still had hopes that Tabitha and Lillian would make their own happy matches. Her own joy would be well and truly full then.

"There he is!" Tabitha cried, pointing at the road.

Everyone rose to their tallest height to personally verify that the carriage drew nearer.

Charlotte's heart skipped as Anthony came nearer and nearer. While everyone was busy watching and waving to him, she slipped away through the trees and to the back of the church, holding the reticule that hung on her wrist steady with the other hand.

Resting her back against the cool stone of the church wall as she waited, she smoothed her lilac skirts. She smiled at the sight of the small flowers in the grass that matched almost perfectly. Reaching down, Charlotte plucked one from its place and twirled it in her fingers, wondering what she had done to deserve the happiness she felt today.

Joyous shouts erupted from the front of the church as the rolling of the carriage wheels came to a final stop. The same joy was bottled up inside her and about ready to burst. Today was as perfect as the small petals of the flower she held.

Two hands stole around her waist, taking her breath as she found herself pressed up against Anthony.

"Did you despair of me?" he asked.

"Never," she said, grinning shamelessly now that he was here. "But you are terribly late to our rendezvous." They had promised to meet one another behind the church before the ceremony to enjoy their last few moments as an engaged couple.

"I am," he acknowledged. "But not without good reason." He released her and reached into his blue tailcoat. He pulled from it a folded paper, his eyes alight as he watched her take it.

"What is it?" she asked.

"Oh, just something I noticed in the windows of various print shops in Town."

Her eyes widened at his unapologetically delighted smile.

She hurried to unfold the paper, and one of her hands stole to her chest at the sight before her: her last and final caricature. Not wishing to give it to Mr. Digby, she had sent it to Rowlandson himself—the king of caricatures.

In the center of the drawing, hidden behind a curtain except for his eyes, was Lord Drayton, while his hand manipulated the strings of various puppets, shaped like men and women. At the side of the stage were various, discarded puppets.

"Did you say print shops? As in, more than one?"

Anthony nodded. "Evidently, Rowlandson felt it worth his while to copy and reproduce. And, based on the crowds I had to fight, he was correct."

Charlotte could hardly believe her eyes. Her own work had been hung up all over Town. And not only that . . . Lord Drayton's cunning could now be seen by the public as a result.

"Whispers about Drayton abound there now," Anthony said.

"Do you think it will make a difference?" she asked.

"I know it will. People will watch him more closely, and men like him are bound to slip up when they are being observed."

She smiled and nodded. She was sure he was right.

"Harris is still at work too," Anthony said.

"I wish Silas could be here," Charlotte said, folding the caricature and uncinching the strings of her reticule.

"So do I," Anthony said. "But he will be soon enough. Is that . . . ?"

"It is indeed." She held the reticule in her palm for him to see.

He rubbed the fabric with a finger and smiled. "God bless this little bag."

"Look inside," she said.

Narrowing his eyes at her in a question, he obeyed.

"Not that one," she said. "That is the one you just gave me."

He pulled out another folded paper. "I thought you said you were done with caricatures."

"This one is different," she said. "It is only for you."

He cocked an eyebrow at her as he opened it. She watched him intently as his eyes took in the drawing: a man nursing a woman on the side of the road while a kitten sat nearby. The man and woman regarded one another adoringly, the fingers of their hands entwined.

"My little kitten." The corners of Anthony's lips pulled into a smile. "A day that will live in infamy."

"And in your lively imagination alone," she shot back, pleased to see he liked it.

"Would you rather we had met this way?" he asked, looking up at her thoughtfully.

She took the caricature and surveyed it again, her eyes drawn where they always were: to Anthony. He was handsome in the caricature, but she hadn't the skill to ever capture him quite right. There was a perfection in the real Anthony that was driven as much by his strengths as it was by his flaws.

She folded the paper and set it back in the reticule, then met his gaze. "We might have met a thousand different ways, Anthony, and I would love you in every one of them."

Anthony pressed his lips to hers, his kiss fierce in its tenderness, the press of his hands on her waist firm and insistent. His lips left hers, brushed across her cheek and down to her neck, leaving chills and a streak of heat in their wake.

"Marry me, Charlotte," he pleaded, pressing kisses to the hollow beneath her ear. "Marry me now before I go mad."

She fanned her face. "I might need a moment."

His lips smiled against her skin, and he pressed another kiss there.

"Anthony," she chastised, closing her eyes to revel in the feeling. "Everyone is waiting. Besides, I thought you said you wished to marry me *now*."

"I do," he said, pulling back enough to look at her with eyes that smoldered. "But only if we can come back here immediately after."

"And where, precisely, would we tell everyone we were going?" She tried to sound severe, but instead, she was breathless and smiling.

"I could hardly care less," he said. "Tell them I have a deranged digestion. Or a case of persistent flatulence. I will claim it all if only I can have more of these moments with you."

Charlotte broke into laughter and grabbed hold of his hand. "Come *on*."

Grinning, he allowed her to pull him around the church. Everyone was waiting within, including the vicar, who raised a brow at the bride and groom.

The next twenty minutes passed in a blur, Charlotte's and Anthony's eyes never leaving one another until the vicar made the final pronouncement, declaring her officially Charlotte Yorke.

Frederick gave a cheer that brought a frown to the face of the vicar, who guided them to the registry book while the family filed outside to prepare for Charlotte and Anthony to make their exit as husband and wife.

Rice sprayed in the air as they came through the door, accompanied by cheers and embraces and applause. Charlotte embraced each one of their family members heartily, overcome with joy to have so many she loved here to enjoy this day.

Her embrace with William was cut short when a young man arrived on horseback and called to him.

"Who is that?" Anthony asked.

But no one had an answer.

William stepped away to speak with him just as Aunt Eugenia grabbed hold of Anthony from her place at the end of the line. With a poorly suppressed smile, she handed him a fistful of banknotes. "As promised. It had better tide you over for another two decades. I have no intention of sticking my spoon in the wall until then."

"Keep your spoon for better things, Aunt," Anthony said. "Charlotte and I would rather have you."

Charlotte nodded her agreement, while Aunt Eugenia looked at them through suspicious eyes, though her mouth twitched.

The others had left the line and were gathered around William.

"What is it?" Anthony asked as he and Charlotte made their way over. "William?"

William didn't respond immediately, his eyes fixed on the paper recently delivered. When he looked up, his face was pale, his expression blank.

Charlotte waited, holding tightly to Anthony's hand.

When William spoke, it was in a colorless tone. "I am"— his cravat bobbed—"the new Duke of Rockwood."

THE END

OTHER TITLES BY MARTHA KEYES

Wyndcross (Book 1)

Isabel (Book 2)

Cecilia (Book 3)

Hazelhurst (Book 4)

Romance Retold Series

Redeeming Miss Marcotte (Book 1)

A Conspiratorial Courting (Book 2)

A Matchmaking Mismatch (Book 3)

Standalone Titles

A Suitable Arrangement (Castles & Courtship Series)

Goodwill for the Gentleman (Belles of Christmas Book 2)

The Christmas Foundling (Belles of Christmas: Frost Fair Book 5)

The Highwayman's Letter (Sons of Somerset Book 5)

Of Lands High and Low

Mishaps and Memories (Timeless Regency Collection)

The Road through Rushbury (Seasons of Change Book 1)

Eleanor: A Regency Romance

AUTHOR NOTE

I have done my best to be true to the time period and particulars of the day, so I apologize if I got anything wrong. I continue learning and researching while trying to craft stories that will be enjoyable to readers like you.

The character and diary of Marlowe were inspired by the real-life Joseph Farington. Farington was a well-connected Englishman who kept a daily diary from 1793 until his death in 1821. The sixteen volumes are full of information about current events, the internal workings of the Royal Academy, and whatever anecdotes he personally found interesting.

ABOUT THE AUTHOR

 Whitney Award-winning Martha Keyes was born, raised, and educated in Utah—a home she loves dearly but also loves to leave for stints of world travel. She received a BA in French Studies and a Master of Public Health from Brigham Young University.

Her route to becoming an author was full of twists and turns, but she's finally settled into something she loves. Research, daydreaming, and snacking have become full-time jobs, and she couldn't be happier about it. When she isn't writing, she is honing her photography skills, looking for travel deals, and spending time with her family.

ACKNOWLEDGMENTS

Little did my husband know when he married me how much of his time would be taken up talking through imaginary stories with his wife. He's so patient and makes sure I have the time and resources to keep going. I love him dearly for it!

Thank you to my critique partners and dear friends, Kasey, Deborah, and Jess. Couldn't do this gig without you, and I wouldn't want to.

Thank you to my beta readers: Brooke, Emily, Heidi, and Kelsy. All your feedback was instrumental with getting this story into shipshape!

Thank you to my editors, Jacque and Molly, for helping make sure this book was fit to see the light of day.

Thank you to Nancy Mayer for always being willing to share her abundant knowledge of the Regency Era.

Thank you to all my readers who make it possible for me to continue writing stories. I will forever be grateful to you for spending your precious hours on my books!

Made in the USA
Coppell, TX
17 April 2024

31408828R00203